FORBIDDEN OBSESSION

Club Genesis - Dallas, Book 1

USA Today Bestselling Author

Jenna Jacob

FORBIDDEN
OBSESSION

USA Today Bestselling Author
JENNA JACOB

Forbidden Obsession

Club Genesis - Dallas, Book

by Jenna Jacob

Published by Jenna Jacob

Copyright @ 2023 Dream Words, LLC

Edited by: Raw Book Editing - http://www.rawbookediting.com

ePub ISBN: 978-1-952111-32-7

Print ISBN: 978-1-952111-33-4

This is a work of fiction. Names, places, characters and incidents are the product of the author's imagination and are fictitious. Any resemblance to actual persons, living or dead, events or establishments is solely coincidental.

NOTE FROM AUTHOR

I can't tell you how excited I am about this new series or how good it feels to be back in the dungeon again. It's like coming home.

When I finished the Club Genesis: Chicago series, I knew I wanted more. Because seriously...what's not to love about a whole new family of decadent Doms and sassy subs begging for their command? What I didn't know was how intense and sizzling Grant and Emma's chemistry was going to be or how they utterly stole my heart.

I hope they capture yours as well.

Huge Hugs,
Jenna

She's beautiful, alluring…and lying.

Grant

After serving years as Master Chief of an elite SEAL team, extracting targets from hostile foreign lands, I'm no stranger to danger. But I'm wholly unprepared for the fallout after rescuing a devastatingly gorgeous woman from a violent twister. The tall, curvy blonde with big hazel eyes and plump lips—made for sin—ignites my libido with a passion that sears my blood. I'm already planning ways to lure her to Club Genesis and show her the ropes. There's just one problem…

The compelling beauty is masquerading as my dead sister.

Emma

When I discover my billionaire fiancé is embroiled in an illegal bribery scheme, I methodically establish a new identity, then run… straight into a tornado, and the rugged arms of a blue-eyed savior with a commanding presence who sets my soul on fire. Desperate to put out the flames, I surrender to the blistering attraction between us. Drowning me in unimaginable bliss, he introduces me to a world of utter freedom. There's just one problem…

He's discovered my true identity.

Forced to come clean, I spill my secrets. But instead of turning me away, he vows to protect me. And he does—until the past catches up to me. Can Grant save me again, or will he merely become a memory of my...*Forbidden Obsession*?

Prologue

Emma
Saturday, July 8th

"Oh, Emma, darling. You look simply stunning," my mother gushed as she peered over my shoulder and stared at my reflection in the gilded mirror positioned in the center of my bedroom.

The unprecedented warmth and approval in her voice had me inwardly gaping. I peeled my gaze off the obscenely over-priced, but gorgeous, white tulle and hand-beaded Chantilly lace designer wedding gown hugging my body and blinked.

"The first time I held you in my arms," she continued. "I dreamed of this day. I knew then you'd make a beautiful bride. And here you are." A genuine smile—another rare anomaly—tugged her lips as she pretended to wipe a tear from her eye.

Was that when you began arranging my marriage to Wesley—the weasel—Fairchild? The question seared the tip of my tongue, but I swallowed it down. I couldn't afford to bait my mother into an ugly fight. No way would I risk the weeks of planning and preparing I'd done to escape this farce of a wedding.

"I'm glad I'm able to make your dreams come true, Mother," I replied, forcing a placid smile.

"Don't screw this up, Emma," she warned in her usual superior, arctic tone. "Our future hinges on this Bishop-Fairchild union." She paused and glanced at her watch. "In less than an hour, we'll all be filthy rich."

I didn't bother reminding her the Bishops and Fairchilds were already filthy rich. Instead, I simply nodded and forced another smile. "I know what's at stake, Mother."

My sanity. My future. And likely, my life, if Wesley ever discovers I know about his illegal activities.

"Make sure you don't forget," she bit out, snatching her Louis Vuitton Pochette off the dresser. "I'm going to give your maid of honor a script to read during the toast at the reception and check in on the other bridesmaids."

"Who's the lucky maid of honor?" The question rolled off my tongue before I could stop it.

I didn't have many friends. The ones I had my mother loathed because they were all co-workers at my father's company. Like our maids and cooks, they were nothing but hired help in her eyes because they didn't come from the right families…rich ones.

The twenty girls—total strangers to me—down the hall primping in several guest rooms had been hand-picked by my mother. They were all daughters of her friends from the country club.

Any normal twenty-eight-year-old woman would have told her controlling parents to take a flying fuck over a decade ago. But I'd spent my entire life unknowingly being indoctrinated…blinded and shielded by their rules and expectations. Even when I went away to college, I didn't realize the depth of their brainwashing. It wasn't until four weeks ago that my eyes were finally opened, and the veil of subterfuge lifted when I'd accidentally overheard Wesley on the phone. That was the same day I began plotting my way to freedom.

The dress, bridesmaids, caterers, food, and flowers, along with the multitude of guests now gathering in the garden, didn't matter. The only things that did were getting off the estate, unseen, staying alive, and starting a new life far, far away.

"Her name's Tina or Gina, something like that. It's not important," my mother said, absently waving her hand. "She's Constance Willingham's daughter, the model."

Because Lord knows we can't have any average-looking bridesmaids...not with the dozens of news crews Father and Ted Fairchild demanded cover the "Wedding of The Century".

As my mother reached for the doorknob, she paused and peered over her shoulder. "Your father will be here in forty minutes to escort you to the garden for the ceremony. Be ready when he arrives. I will not have our guests waiting due to your tardiness."

The instant the door closed behind her, I hurried over and turned the lock. Then I kicked off my heels, peeled off the twenty-five thousand dollar designer wedding dress, and tossed it on the bed. Heart hammering, I raced to my closet and slid on the black dress pants and white button-down shirt I'd specifically purchased for this very moment. After tucking the tails of the shirt into my pants, I slid on a pair of black tennis shoes and hurried to the ensuite.

I quickly yanked out the hair pins from my perfectly coiffed wheat-colored curls, then dragged a brush through my hair. Cinching the strands in a hair tie, I retrieved the short, black wig I'd hidden beneath the sink. Wrapping the ponytail in a tight circle, I tugged on the wig and tucked my cell phone in my bra.

Breathless and trembling like a leaf, I hurried to the door and cautiously pulled it open. Though the hallway was blessedly empty, I tucked my chin and hurried toward the stairs. As I bounded off the bottom step, I lifted my head and started toward the kitchen before freezing in my tracks. Beyond the floor to ceiling windows on the living room in front of me, a massive tent—draped in white silk—stood in the garden. Rows and rows of white wooden chairs were lined up in the shade beneath it. Arbors and awnings, draped in a sea of billowing peach silk, dotted the expansive lawn, flanked by massive marble vases bursting with white and peach chrysanthemums, tulips, snapdragons, and roses.

Months ago, when I couldn't decide what colors I wanted for the wedding—because I didn't give a shit—Mother announced *she* would take over the planning of my *special day* since I was too inept. I wanted to hate it, but I couldn't. It was beautiful…breathtaking, like something out of a fairy tale.

But this stunning, lavish wedding wasn't for me, for love, or some imaginary happily ever after. It was contrived of pure, old-fashioned greed.

Shaking away the depressing fact I was nothing more than a convenient pawn, I watched as dozens of caterers, dressed in the same black slacks and white button-down shirts as me strolled through the crowd, carrying silver trays teeming with flutes of champagne and finger foods.

Afraid a guest might peer inside the house and recognize me, I lowered my chin again, and strode straight into the kitchen. I'd no more taken two steps into the room when a surly faced man with a big, round belly, and a chef's hat on his head, shoved a tray of bacon wrapped scallops adorned with white ribbon-tipped toothpicks in my hand.

"Take these out and pass them around before they get cold," he barked.

Frozen in place, panic pulsed through my veins. The air seized in my lungs.

"What are you waiting for?" he snarled. "Get your ass moving."

Spinning on my heel, I swallowed tightly and retraced my steps. No way in hell was I going to stroll around the garden chocked full of people who knew me. Darting a wild glance around the living room, I was just about to put the tray on the coffee table and run when a young man—carrying an empty platter—hurried into the room.

"Here," I said, extending the tray of scallops. "I'll refill yours and meet you outside."

"Thanks," he murmured before hurrying away.

Determined not to let the bossy bastard derail my plans, I strode into the kitchen and slid the empty platter on the counter. Then I darted across the room and through the door leading to the garage. As the knob snicked behind me, I sprinted to my silver Mercedes-Benz and climbed in behind the wheel. My purse, with several thousand in cashier's checks, was still on the passenger's seat. It was enough to tide me over until I got settled. The rest of my money—from the distribution of my trust fund when I turned twenty-five—was safely sitting in the secret account I'd opened three weeks ago. I'd stayed up until two a.m., packing my suitcases before clandestinely loading them into my car. Though confident my luggage was safely stowed in the trunk, I flipped the latch below the armrest and hopped out of the car... just to be sure. Relieved to find all four bags exactly where I'd left them, I closed the lid and quickly climbed back inside the vehicle. Sucking in a deep breath, I started the engine, then pressed the garage door opener.

While the wide door slowly lifted, my heart drummed against my ribs. And as sunlight spilled into the darkened garage, it took all the willpower I possessed not to push the accelerator to the floor and peel out of there in a cloud of smoke and squealing tires.

Chapter One

"What the fuck is this son of a bitch made of...cement?" I grumbled as I eased the heavy St. Andrew's cross off my back, and propped it against the frame of the wooden porch.

Tugging the rag from my back pocket, I wiped the sweat from my face. It was hotter than a cast-iron skillet in hell, and twice as muggy, but that was normal for Texas in July.

Even though I was sweating my balls off, I didn't mind hauling the remaining dungeon equipment from the abandoned BDSM club in Denton to Club Genesis in Dallas. I'd happily volunteered when Dalton Barnes—the new club manager of Genesis—asked for help. Not only was the man fair, honest, and an exemplary Dominant, he'd grown to be a trusted friend in a short amount of time.

Eyeing the heavy cross, I shook my head. "Since you're not gonna load yourself in the back of my truck...come on, you heavy bastard."

As I reached for the glossy wooden beast, my cell phone rang. Abandoning my task, I dragged the device from my jeans and checked the caller ID.

"Hey, Dalton."

"Hey, Grant."

"What's up?"

"Just wanted to let you know there's a hell of a storm heading your way. Keep an eye on it and take cover if needed."

"Thanks, man. I appreciate the heads up," I replied, biting back a chuckle.

It wasn't his fault, but Dalton knew nothing about pop-up summer storms in Texas. He and his fiancé/slave Blair had moved from Chicago a few months ago to manage Club Genesis for the new owner, Mika LaBrache. The couple was looking forward to a winter without blinding blizzards and lake effect snows.

"I'll be fine," I assured as fat drops of rain began falling from the sky. "Heat storms are a normal part of summer around here."

"This isn't a normal storm, man," he continued as the wind suddenly kicked up and the temperature instantly dropped.

Like a kick to the balls, fear slammed through me. Spinning on the heel of my boot, I glanced over my shoulder. A dark, ominous, mile-wide cyclone swirled across the open fields, spewing dust, tractors, cattle, and other debris from its core as it headed straight toward me.

"It's a tor—"

"Tornado!" I yelled. "And the motherfucker is heading this way."

When Dalton didn't say a word, I yanked the phone from my ear and checked the signal.

"No bars, fuck!" I barked.

As the beastly roar of the twister grew louder, I turned to take cover in the storage room—a repurposed meat locker—deep inside the club. But before I could lift my boot off the ground, a car horn sliced through the thundering howl of the tornado. Jerking my head toward the sound, I watched a black Audi A5 Sportback speed into the parking lot, and skid to a stop.

Behind the wheel, a woman—whose eyes were wide—darted her panicked glance between me and the encroaching swirl of death.

"Come on. Come on," I yelled, waving my hand for her to join me.

Instead of doing as I'd directed, she leaned over the passenger's seat.

"No! No, lady. You're gonna die if you stay in the car," I barked.

Realizing she probably couldn't hear me, I started off the porch to fetch her, but paused when she suddenly sat up. After shoving the driver's side door open, she launched from the vehicle.

"Hurry," I yelled, frantically waving her my way again.

Clutching her purse to her chest, she raced toward me. Rain pelted her body, and her long, wheat-blonde hair whipped across her face as dirt and broken tree limbs sailed through the air. When I darted a glance at the roaring beast swirling toward us, my heart rate spiked and fear rolled through me.

Though the woman ran like an Olympic sprinter, the tornado was moving faster. I worried we wouldn't make it to the storage room in time.

"Move it, lady," I bellowed.

Right as the words left my lips, a thick piece of wood, jettisoning through the air, clipped the back of her knees…sending her sprawling across the gravel with a frightened scream.

Bolting off the porch, I raced to her and scooped her into my arms.

"Hold on tight," I yelled above the howling winds as I turned and hauled ass toward the club.

She didn't hesitate this time. Wrapping her willowy arms around my neck, she buried her face in my chest. The touch of her fingers cupping my nape sent a jolt of electricity sizzling through me. It didn't matter the Grim Reaper was fixin' to eat us for lunch; I couldn't ignore how perfect she felt nestled in my arms.

As I stepped onto the porch, the heavy cross lifted off the ground and disappeared above my head. An ominous chill skipped down my spine. Darting into the club, I ran as if the hounds of hell were nipping at my heels. The entire building shook. The sounds of snapping wood and shattering glass thundered in my ears as pieces of ceiling tile and drywall rained down on me.

I tossed a glance over my shoulder and bit out a curse as the roof peeled back, granting a gut-churning view of the violent twister. I squinted my eyes to shield them from the swirling debris. A deafening roar vibrated through me as the front of the building tore apart before being sucked away.

"We're gonna die," the woman wailed in terror.

"Not today, darlin'," I yelled above the cacophony of destruction as I yanked the thick, metal door of the former meat locker open and darted inside...slamming it shut behind me.

Though plunged in total darkness, I didn't need any light. Having spent all day hauling dungeon furniture from the fifteen-by-fifteen-foot room, I knew exactly where we needed to go. Striding toward the far-left corner of the room, I gently eased the woman onto a padded bondage table. There were plenty of items, sealed in big plastic totes, we could use to ride out the twister.

Not the floggers, whips, or handcuffs, but candles, blankets, and a first aid kit.

Tugging out my cell phone, I tapped the flashlight app. As light flooded the room, I finally got a good look at her, and my heart nearly stopped. My mouth went dry.

She was the most beautiful woman I'd ever seen.

Though a concerning trickle of blood seeped from her forehead—melding with the tears staining her delicate cheeks—and her wet-clumped hair hung lifelessly over her slender shoulders, her big, hazel eyes, and plump, pink lips awakened something primal inside me I'd never felt before.

"Thank you. That's much better," she whispered with a ghost of a smile before glancing around the room. "What is this place?"

"It used to be a club...a private club," I replied, purposely omitting the topic of BDSM.

I could tell by her confused expression, she wasn't in the lifestyle. I didn't want to explain the kinds of things that had been done here and freak her out. She was already scared enough.

When she lifted a bloodied hand toward her face, I gently cupped her wrist. Struggling to ignore the tingles of electricity sputtering through me again, I guided her flesh-torn hand back to her lap.

"You're bleeding," I said, nodding toward her knuckles.

She glanced down and scowled. "Oh, I hadn't even noticed."

"Give me a second I know there's a first aid kit in here somewhere."

Just as I stepped toward the plastic tubs stacked against the other wall, a deafening crash sounded above us. The woman yelped and covered her head as I aimed the light toward the metal roof.

"It's all right," I assured. "I think the roof's been welded in place."

"Does that mean it's not going to fly off like the other one did?"

The fear in her voice cut through me like a knife.

"I don't know. But I'll take the fact it hasn't as a good sign." I winked, hoping to reassure her.

While the wind continued howling and pelting the metal roof with debris, I tore open the plastic totes and started gathering the things we needed. The woman nervously watched as I quickly spread several after-care blankets beneath the bondage table.

"What do you say we get under the table, where it's safe, before I clean your wounds?"

"I say yes." She nodded, anxiously eyeing the roof still being pummeled by hail and debris.

After scooting off the padded leather, she sucked in a hiss of pain, then bent and grabbed her ankle.

"Is it broken?" I asked.

"I don't think so. I think I just twisted it."

With a nod, I scooped her into my arms again. Savoring the current of energy humming through me I squatted, and carefully eased her onto the blankets.

"Sit back and relax as best you can. I'll join you in a second."

As if connected by some strange invisible thread, I felt her eyes on me while I lit several candles and placed them on the cement floor near the table. Clutching the first aid kit, I crawled in and joined her.

Starting with the cut on her head, I gently wiped away the blood. Thankfully, the gash was small and didn't need stitches.

"I didn't know I'd been rescued by a Boy Scout." She softly chuckled.

"Trust me. I'm no Boy Scout," I replied without expounding on all the reasons why.

Not only was she scared enough from narrowly escaping a certain death by Mother Nature's wrath, but she was also huddled under a table in a former meat locker with a man she didn't know.

"Thank you, by the way," she softly said as I placed a small adhesive bandage over the cut on her forehead. "I'd be dead if you hadn't carried me in here."

"No need to thank me. I wasn't about to leave you lying in that parking lot, darlin'," I confessed, lifting her hand before softly cupping her palm in mine.

Heat rolled up my arm and down my spine. I knew then, if I ever got lucky enough to get the stunning beauty naked and under me, she'd sear the flesh off my bones.

"I really tore them up, didn't I?" She grimaced, staring at her bloodied, tattered knuckles.

"Well, my momma always said, if you're gonna do a job...do it right," I drawled with a smirk.

"She sounds like a smart woman."

"She was." I nodded.

"Oh, I'm sorry. I didn't mean to—"

"No. You're fine. She's been gone a long time." Four years really wasn't a long time, it just felt like it. As I clutched a bottle of peroxide, I peered into the woman's pretty hazel eyes. "This is gonna sting."

"I'd rather deal with the sting than an ugly infection." She shrugged. "At least it's not alcohol."

"Yeah, I wouldn't do that to you."

A tiny noise of discomfort rattled the back of her throat as I doused first her left hand, then the other, with peroxide.

Though we'd only been inside the shelter a matter of minutes, it seemed hours before the tornado moved on and the winds died down.

The rain continued pelting the metal roof as I bandaged her hands before moving on to her bloodied knees.

The craggy gravel had left holes in her jeans. Unfortunately, they weren't big enough for me to tell how much damage had been done to her skin, let alone give me enough room to properly clean her wounds. I bit back the demand she take them off and dug the pocketknife from my jeans.

"I need to cut your jeans a little bit so I can clean your knees," I said apologetically.

"It's okay. They're ruined anyway. I have more in my suit—" she stopped mid-sentence, and winced. "What are the chances my car's still outside?"

I pursed my lips. "I'd say slim to none. It's probably mangled in a field somewhere between here and Tyler…right alongside my truck."

"Great," she groaned.

"That's why God made insurance," I drawled. "You *do* have insurance on it, right?"

"Thankfully, I added it when I rented the car. I just hate that all my clothes, shoes, and makeup I had packed in my suitcases are gone."

"I know you're a long way from New York, but we have lots of malls here in Texas," I teased, as she bristled.

"Who says I'm from New York?"

Though her words were wrapped around a chuckle, the hint of defensiveness in her tone piqued my curiosity. I sliced the denim, then peeled it back from her knee and glanced up at her. "Ahh, the license plates on your rental car."

"Really? I never noticed that. I just got in and drove it off the lot," she said, darting her eyes everywhere but on mine. "So, the car's from New York, huh?"

"Yep." I nodded as my bullshit meter pegged red.

Another man might have believed her, but I knew she was lying. Not because I was a cynical son of a bitch—which I am—but because I'd been trained to spot deception during interrogations. My former SEAL skills came in handy in my new line of work as a bounty hunter.

Jenna Jacob

But I didn't need to use them on the ball-churning beauty before me. The woman was a terrible liar.

Five seconds ago, I didn't give a fuck if she was from New York or Mars.

But now that my SEAL senses were on high alert, I wanted to slice her open, like a ripe peach, and uncover every secret she kept.

Chapter Two

Emma

As the lie rolled off my tongue, I looked everywhere but at the intense, piercing blue eyes of the drop-dead gorgeous stranger who'd saved me.

The same stranger whose intoxicating masculine scent filled my senses and made me dizzy.

The same stranger whose wide, calloused hand, cupping the back of my thigh, sent heat and arousal rolling up and down my body.

The same stranger whose thick, capable fingers smearing antibiotic ointment over my damaged knee made my nipples ache and my girl parts throb.

Confined to the safe, small space—beneath the strange, bed-like table—with the rugged man had my hormones swirling faster than the tornado that had nearly killed us. Everything about him, from his thick, sandy-blond hair, sculpted, sun-bronzed face, tempting full lips, sharp defined jawline dusted in prickly scuff, and mesmerizing blue eyes, to the dark tee hugging his chiseled body like a second skin called to all the neglected, feminine cells in my body.

I'd never been the aggressor in any relationship—not that I'd had that many—or in bed. One, because no man had ever ignited my libido like the sexy stranger. And two, because according to my mother, a proper woman lets her man do his business in the bedroom. If he wants a shameless woman to get wild with, he hires a hooker.

But the longer I spent with my arousing savior, the more I wanted to strip him bare and ride him like a rodeo cowgirl.

"So, where are you from?" he asked, peeling back the flap he'd just cut on my jeans

"Here. Well...Dallas, I mean," I stammered, inwardly cringing.

Though I'd spent months mentally practicing my cover story over and over, it was much different than saying the words out loud, even to a total stranger.

"Why'd you have a rental then?" he pressed, bandaging my knee.

"Mine's in the shop. It's got a little transmission trouble."

"Ahh, I see." He nodded, inching backward. "Let me take a look at your ankle."

When he lifted my leg, removed my tennis shoe, and cradled my foot on his thigh, sparks of electricity splintered through me.

"It's okay. It's just a minor sprain," I assured, forcing the words past the ball of lust lodged in my throat.

"Major or minor, doesn't matter. I still need to wrap it."

"Why?"

"If our vehicles were blown away, we're gonna have to walk out of here to find help."

"We've got cell phones," I said, digging mine from my purse. "Why don't we just call an Uber?"

"Because the cell towers are down. I was on a call right before the twister hit, and I lost service. Hold on to yours. When we get outside, keep checking to see if you get a signal."

"Okay. How far is the next town?"

When he raised his head and pinned me with a dubious stare, I

16

knew I'd just screwed up. If I really lived in Dallas, I would know the answer.

"Denton…it's about twelve miles from here."

"Denton, right." I nodded. "I-I knew that. I guess I hit my head harder than I thought."

Shut up, Emma. Just shut the hell up, screamed a voice inside me.

With a noncommittal grunt, he finished wrapping the wide, elastic bandage tightly around my ankle, then glanced at the door.

"Sit tight. I'm gonna take a look and see what's left."

"I'll go with you," I blurted. For some reason I couldn't put my finger on, I didn't want to be left alone in the strange room. He opened his mouth, likely to argue, but I cut him off. "If we've got to walk out of here, we might as well start now."

"It's still raining."

"So? We're already wet."

"Good point." He softly chuckled. "All right. Give me a minute, and we'll head out."

When he crawled from under the table, and rose to his feet, like a beautiful Roman Gladiator, the breath caught in my lungs. I'd been so scared of the tornado I hadn't paid attention to how brutally big he was or how his bulging muscles strained beneath his sun-kissed skin. I was definitely paying attention now. In fact, I couldn't peel my eyes off his tight ass as he bent and picked up a candle, then strode around the room, blowing the others out.

Bending, he peered at me with those gorgeous piercing blue eyes and extended his hand. "Ready?"

"Yes," I replied in an unintentionally sultry whisper.

Cheeks burning from embarrassment, I dipped my head, slung the strap of my purse over my head, then placed my fingers in his palm. A tingling heat slid up my arm as he helped me to my feet and cupped my elbow.

"Take a step to make sure you can walk on that ankle."

The intensity of his stare nearly burned a hole right through me as I lowered my foot to the floor and gingerly shifted some of my weight. Pain streaked up my leg, but I clenched my jaw and bit back a hiss.

17

"You good?" he asked.

"Yeah." I nodded, hobbling beside him.

Still gripping my elbow in one hand, he handed me the candle in his other before pushing his palm against a round metal disk protruding from the door. I suddenly realized the room we'd taken refuge in was some kind of industrial cooler or meat locker.

He tried to shove the metal door open, but it only budged an inch.

"Something's lodged against it." He scowled, releasing my elbow. "Hang tight. I'll get us out of here."

Balancing on my good foot, I watched him rear back, then slam his boot against the door with a brutal kick. The screech of metal and a heavy thud vibrated in the air as the portal burst open, revealing nothing but tree limbs and flattened fields.

Everything was gone…the building, our vehicles, and all signs of life.

"Holy fuck," he muttered.

We both gaped at the void for several long seconds before he turned and scooped me into his arms again.

"What are you doing? Put me down," I demanded. "I *can* walk."

"Not without pain, you can't." The veiled growl in his voice sent goosebumps peppering my skin and a rush of warm liquid spilling into my panties. "Don't ever lie to me again."

"I-I didn't lie."

"Oh, yes, you did. When I asked if you were good, you said, yeah. *That* was a lie," he said, pinning me with a scowl. "*Don't* do it again. Understood?"

Like a second cyclone, guilt, defiance, and lust swirled through me.

"Okay, I won't. But you can't possibly carry me twelve whole miles."

"Watch me." He smirked as if I'd tossed some kind of gauntlet to the ground.

"Fine. It's your back."

A low chuckle rumbled from his chest as he stepped through the doorway. Thankfully, the rain had basically stopped. Only a few light sprinkles remained falling from the still darkened sky.

"Don't worry about my back, darlin'," he said, striding toward the road. "I bale hay way heavier than you."

"You're a rancher?"

"Among other things."

"What were you doing at that...club?"

"Moving furniture for a friend."

Something in his tone made me wonder if he was moving it or stealing it.

A part of me wanted to ask, but I was afraid of tarnishing the glowing portrait of chivalry I'd already painted of my gallant savior in my mind. Yes, it was foolish of me to put the rugged cowboy on a pedestal, but he'd proven—in less than an hour—to be more trustworthy than Wesley had in the twenty-eight years I'd known him.

I never understood how or why his father and mine—competing media moguls—had become best friends in the first place. Had they started arranging the wedding between Wesley and me the minute I was born so they could merge their companies and corner the broadcasting market? Why wait? Why arrange our marriage? Why not just do it? It would have been a whole lot easier.

"Any service on your phone yet?" the cowboy asked, dragging me from my thoughts.

I tapped the screen and shook my head. "No."

"Are you all right? You're not in too much pain, are you?"

"No. Why?"

"You got quiet on me," he said, glancing up as the sun began breaking through the clouds.

"Oh, sorry. I was making a mental list of things I need to do," I lied.

"Like what?"

"Contacting the car rental company. I'm sure there'll be a mountain of paperwork and all kinds of hoops I'll have to jump through."

"Probably," he said sympathetically. "So, what part of Dallas do you live in?"

"North."

"North, like Frisco, Addison, or Highland Park?"

"Richardson."

"Richardson, huh? Did you grow up there?"

"Yeah."

"What a coincidence, I did too."

A wave of panic rolled through me. My heart sputtered, and my mouth went dry. I didn't know the odds of the first person I'd meet in Texas being from the same town as Aubrey—my former college roommate—but they had to be astronomical.

I'm so screwed.

"Small world," I said, forcing a smile.

"Sure is."

"Do you still live there?"

Please say no. Please say no.

"No. A few years back, I bought a ranch a little farther north…just inside the Dallas County line."

Relief chased my fears away. He'd unwittingly given me an opening. I jumped all over it, like a kid on a trampoline.

"How big is your ranch?"

"A hair over a hundred and fifty acres."

"That's a lot of land." Or so I hoped. My parent's summer house in the Hamptons sat on three acres. The mansion and the grounds always seemed enormous to me, but I was in Texas, and there was a whole lot of open land here. "What do you do with a hundred and fifty acres?"

"Raise cattle…Angus cattle. I've got about seventy head."

"Oh, wow. I've never been to a cattle ranch before. What's it like?" I asked, determined to keep the topic of conversation on him instead of me.

"Once we get back to civilization, and get you checked out at the hospital, I'd be happy to give you a tour before I drive you home."

"You have another truck?"

He chuckled. "Darlin', I've got two more trucks, and half-a-dozen cars."

"Why so many?"

"In my line of work, it's not wise to use the same vehicle twice."

Confusion crowded my brain.

"I thought you were a rancher."

"I am." He nodded. "But I'm also a bounty hunter."

Bounty hunter. Bounty hunter. The words thundered through my brain.

My stomach pitched as a whole new wave of panic crawled up my body, turning every muscle to stone. I wasn't stupid or naïve. I knew my parents had started looking for me the second they discovered me missing. Not because they were concerned about my physical or mental well-being, but because they were at risk of losing billions of dollars.

My stomach continued tumbling, like a barrel over Niagara Falls, and saliva pooled in my mouth.

I was going to be sick.

"Put me down! Put me down!" I demanded, bucking and squirming in the man's arms.

"What's wrong?" he barked, easing me onto my feet.

"I-I'm gonna throw up," I wailed, shoving my cell phone in his hand.

Hobbling toward the shoulder of the road, I ignored the pain screaming from my ankle. Bending at the waist over the tall weeds in the ditch, I barfed up my heels.

"Easy, darlin'," the man murmured, quickly gathering my hair in his fist and holding it back.

Normally, I would have been mortified puking in front of a stranger, but at the moment, I was too scared and distraught. All I cared about was putting as much distance between me and my bounty hunter savior as possible. Sadly, I knew that wouldn't be happening anytime soon.

Unlike the man now stroking my back in moral support, I didn't believe in coincidences.

In my mind, everything happened for a reason.

It wasn't coincidence, the Universe had put me, a violent tornado, and a bounty hunter from Richardson—of all places—on the same path. It was a warning shot over my bow. A warning that the man beside me possessed the power and know-how to destroy my well-planned future. A signal for me to re-think my plan or shore it up tighter.

A foreboding chill raced up my spine, stealing every ounce of the foolish confidence I'd clung to.

Slowly standing upright, I wiped my mouth with the back of my hand as he released my hair.

"What the hell just happened?" he asked, lifting my cell phone from his breast pocket and placing it in my trembling hand.

"I-I don't know," I lied, dropping the device back inside my purse. "I think all that jostling around in your arms hit me like seasickness."

"Shit. I'm sorry." His voice was thick with remorse.

"No. Don't be. It's not your fault. If I hadn't twisted my ankle—"

The blare of a car horn cut me off mid-sentence. Together, we turned toward the sound as a big black Escalade sped toward us.

"Son of a bitch." A panty-melting smile speared the man's lips as he gently cupped my elbow again. "We're done walking, darlin'. Help has arrived."

Chapter Three

Grant

The relief spilling through me when Dalton skidded to a stop, bounded out of his SUV, and nearly cracked my ribs with a fierce bro hug was immeasurable.

"What are you doing here?" I asked as he released me and blew out a huge sigh. "Don't get me wrong. I'm damn glad you are, but…why?"

"What do you mean, *why*?" the big, tattooed Dom countered incredulously. "Damn, Blade, the last thing I heard you yell before the line went dead was…*tornado*. I tried to call you back, but it wouldn't go through. That freaked me out so bad, I jumped in my car and flew out here. Damn glad I found you alive. You, and…?" He glanced at the woman beside me and arched an expectant brow my way.

For the first time in a long time, I felt like a fucking idiot. The whole time we were in the storage room, I'd never even asked her name.

"Aubrey." The woman smiled, extending her hand to Dalton. "Aubrey Holden."

What. The. Actual. Fuck?

While my head screamed, *no fucking way does she have the same name as my sister*, my heart slammed to the pit of my stomach, and the earth began crumbling under my feet. Gaping in disbelief, I studied the woman as she explained to Dalton how she'd spotted the funnel cloud, then me, and zoomed into the parking lot. She didn't look or sound a thing like my sister—not that I suddenly expected her to. She wasn't Aubrey, or her ghost. She was a totally different person…*pretending to be my sister.*

Why?

I knew for a fact, my sister—whose body had been interred, four and a half years ago, at Laurel Oaks Cemetery—was the only Aubrey Holden who'd ever lived in Richardson the twenty-eight years she'd been alive.

What the fuck was going on?

Why was the woman I'd saved lying? Why was she using my sister's identity? How did she know Aubrey had grown up in Richardson? Was the hazel-eyed beauty trying to set me up? Had one of the dirtbags I'd tracked down and hauled to jail sent her to find me?

Suspicion, anger, and betrayal gnawed deep, ripping at the still open, weeping wounds Aubrey's senseless death had left on my soul.

Like a knife, memories sliced through me, spilling open in gut-churning detail.

After completing an intense, butt-puckering mission that had FUBAR written all over it, my team had been extracted without a scratch. We were still riding high when we finally set boots back on US soil. But less than five minutes later, the thrill of victory was cut short when I was summoned to my Lieutenant Commander's office. There, along with Chaplain Miller at his side, my LC informed me that my little sister had died. As he relayed the horrific details of her death, shock and denial melded into soul-crushing pain. I stumbled back, landing on the chair in front of his desk, and shamelessly sobbed like a newborn baby. While he continued telling me about the gut-churning torture Aubrey had endured, my agony was replaced with raw, unadulterated rage. Twenty minutes later, I boarded an Air Force

Special Operations U-28 from San Diego, California to Rockaway Naval Air station in New York. Once we landed, I went directly to the morgue—a task I refused to let my mother endure—and identified what was left of my little sister's body before I flew her back home to Texas.

"If it hadn't been for…*Blade*," the woman said pensively—yanking me back to the present as tears stung my eyes. "I would have died."

"That explains why you're all banged up, and Captain America here, doesn't have a scratch." Dalton grinned.

"Very funny," I drawled dryly. "If the previous owner hadn't turned that meat locker into a storage room, neither of us would be here. It was the only thing left standing."

Dalton sobered. "That sounds scary as fuck."

"I'll admit, it was a little intense."

"Little?" the phony Aubrey scoffed. "It was terrifying."

"It would have been for me, too," Dalton commiserated. "I'm from Chicago. We don't get tornados, we get blizzards."

"Blizzards are definitely better." Aubrey chuckled, then blanched. "Or so I've been told."

It was all I could do not to laugh. She wasn't a horrible liar, she totally sucked at it. My gut told me it wouldn't be long before she said something she couldn't cover with another lie. When she did, I would unleash every interrogation tactic in my arsenal on her sexy ass, without mercy. I'd drill deep inside her mind, even if it broke her, until I discovered what the fuck she was hiding.

"You all right, Blade?" Dalton asked, studying me intently.

"Yeah, I am now that you're here." I forced a smile.

"Good. I vote we get out of here then."

"Hold up," I called as Dalton started toward his SUV. "Help me get her inside. She twisted her ankle and got sick when I was carrying her."

"Oh, shit." Dalton blanched. "You need to go to the hospital?"

"No," she barked, pinning me with a scowl. "I can walk."

"You can, but you're not going to," I countered.

"You're awful bossy, you know that?" she groused.

"Yes, I do." I smirked as Dalton chuckled.

We each banded an arm around her waist, then lifted the pretty little liar off the ground and helped her into the backseat. While she raised her leg and rested her injured ankle on top of the padded leather, I closed the door.

"You sure she doesn't need a hospital?" Dalton murmured.

"Probably," I replied in an equally hushed tone. "But I doubt she'd go. Aside from her ankle, her other wounds are superficial. I doctored them up the best I could, but I need to clean them out properly at the ranch."

"Is that where you want me to take you two…back to your place?"

"For now, yeah. I'll drive her home later. We've wasted enough of your time."

"Dude, you're not wasting my time. In fact, if you're not in a hurry, I'd like to see what's left of the club."

"I'm in no rush, but there's not much left. Though I would like to find my truck."

"What about Aubrey's car? You want to look for that, too, right?"

"Sure."

Dalton narrowed his eyes. "Is something going on between you two? Did you guys have a near-death sex marathon in the storage room during the storm?"

"No. Hell no," I bit out.

"Then you're an idiot. She's fucking beautiful."

"I know," I muttered, glancing at the cunning little vixen in the backseat peering up at me.

"Based on the way she looks at you, I'd say Aubrey's got a bad case of hero worship going on."

"Yeah, well…she'll just have to get over it."

"Why?"

"It's too involved. I'll explain later. Let's go."

Curiosity lined Dalton's face as he silently climbed in behind the wheel.

Once I slid onto the passenger's seat and closed the door, we headed back to the demolished club.

"Holy shit," Dalton barked, gaping at the flattened remains as he pulled into the parking lot. "You weren't shittin'. There's nothing left but the meat locker. You two are damn lucky to be alive."

"I know." Now that I wasn't focused on getting help, seeing the level of devastation made my stomach knot. We *were* lucky to be alive. If it hadn't been for the meat locker... I quickly shoved the gruesome thought from my mind and glanced at Dalton. "Sorry about the furniture, man. Most of it is gone."

"Don't be. It's not your fault. It would have been nice to have, but..." He shrugged. "I'll give Mika a call. He'll order what we need. It's all good."

When Dalton turned the SUV around, I glanced over my shoulder. The tornado had cut a wide gap in the field across the road.

"Hold up a sec. I want to get a picture of that," I said, digging out my cell phone.

As the other two turned to see what I was talking about, I swiveled in my seat and snapped off a couple shots. Then I paused, praying the fake Aubrey would look my way again.

I didn't have to wait long.

"Oh, my goodness," she gasped, blinking at me. "I had no idea the tornado was that wide."

Focusing on her face, I clicked several more photos, then tucked my phone away. Though I was anxious to run her image through my facial recognition app, I needed to wait until I was alone. Once I had her name, I intended to spend hours, days, or weeks—however long it took—until I'd uncovered every facet of her life. Thankfully, I had the skills, tools, and the tenacity to delve deep. I wouldn't stop until I knew everything about her, starting from the minute she was born to what she'd eaten for breakfast this morning.

"It was a monster, all right." I nodded.

"You knew it was that big?"

"Yeah." *But it wasn't as big as the lies you've been telling, darlin'.* "Didn't you?"

"No. I only caught a glimpse of it before the road curved. If I'd known it was that massive, I would have had a heart attack. Thank you," she moaned in gratitude as she leaned up and cupped my shoulder. "Thank you again for saving me."

Dalton hit me with an *I told you so* smirk as he turned off the county road and onto the highway.

During the hour-long drive to my ranch, I listened closely, waiting for the woman to paint more lies or slip up and contradict the ones she'd already told. But she didn't do either. She peppered Dalton with questions about Chicago, and me, about cattle ranching. When Dalton pulled his SUV onto my gravel driveway and stopped in front of my two-story, refurbished farmhouse, she peered out the window in confusion.

"Where are we?"

"Home," I said. "Well, my home. I'll drive you to yours after I change your bandages."

"Oh. T-that's not n-necessary. T-they're fine," she nervously stammered, glancing at her hands.

"Relax, darlin'. I'm not going to hurt you. If that's what you're thinking."

"No. I-I know that."

"Good. If I'd wanted to do something to you, I'd have done it in the storage room where there weren't any witnesses...like him." I smirked, nodding to my foreman and fellow dungeon monitor, Mack Boon, wearing a look of relief as he hauled ass toward us from the barn.

"Clearly, I wasn't the only one who was worried about your sorry ass." Dalton grinned.

"That's because you sent my sorry ass out there," I teased with a mock growl.

"I did not," he barked. "You *volunteered*."

"I'm just fuckin' with you, man."

"Very funny."

"Seriously, thank you for coming to look for me. I really appreciate it."

"Yes, I do, too. Thank you so much," the woman seconded with a smile.

"Happy to help. And trust me. You don't have to worry about Blade. He's a good man. He'll get you home safe and sound from here."

"Oh, I'm not worried."

Bullshit. She was lying again. The angst rolling off her was thicker than mud. Dammit, I didn't want her to be afraid of me. I just wanted some fucking answers. When Mack yanked the passenger's side door open, I knew my interrogation would have to wait a little longer.

"Thank fuck, you're alive," Mack greeted with a heavy sigh. "When the weather radio went off in the barn with a tornado warning for Denton County, I ran to the bunkhouse, and flipped on the TV. It looked like it was heading right for you. I tried to call and warn you, but—"

"It wouldn't go through," Dalton finished for him. "Same thing happened to me."

"Did you see it? Was it close?" Mack asked excitedly.

"Yeah, I saw it." I nodded.

"Saw it, *and* felt it," the woman added. "That massive monster went right over the top of us, and took out everything but the ground."

Mack poked his head inside the SUV and peered over my shoulder before glancing back at me.

"Who's she?" he whispered.

There was no getting around saying her name this time. I drew in a deep breath, then forced the words off my tongue. "Mack Boone, this is Aubrey Holden. Aubrey Holden, this is my friend and foreman, Mack Boone."

"Pleased to meet you." She smiled innocently.

"Hold—"

"It was the craziest thing," I interrupted with a subtle shake of my head and a warning scowl. "She was driving down the road as the twister took aim at us. After she pulled into the parking lot, we hunkered down in the storage room of the old club."

"Ahh." Mack nodded, eyeing her suspiciously.

"As you can see, she got pretty banged up. I'm gonna take her inside, change her bandages, then drive her home."

"Gotcha. Well, since you're all in one piece, I guess I'll get back to work. You gonna be at the club tonight, Dalton?"

"Damn right, I am."

"Sounds good. I'll see you there." Glancing at the woman again, Mack tipped his hat. "Pleasure meeting you, Miss Aubrey."

"You too." She innocently smiled again.

Mack shot me a puzzled look, then turned and strolled back to the barn. I knew he had a million questions, just like me. Unfortunately, I had no answers…yet.

Claiming her ankle was much better—which was likely yet another lie—the woman adamantly refused to let us help her into the house. After she gingerly eased from the SUV, we waved goodbye to Dalton as he drove away. In case she was fibbing, I stayed close beside her while we slowly made our way to the front porch stairs. Though her expression remained neutral, the sweat dotting her forehead told me she was in pain.

My palm itched. And every cell in my body screamed to plop down on the stairs, drag her over my knees, and spank her sexy, obstinate ass purple. Grasping the white, wooden railing in a death grip, she cleared the first step. But when she went to take the next one, her ankle buckled. As quick as a rattlesnake, I snagged her around the waist before she face-planted on my porch and hoisted her into my arms.

"Why are you so fucking stubborn?" I growled, hauling her up the stairs while that crazy current hummed through me.

"I-I'm sorry. I'm not trying to be difficult. It's just…I don't like relying on others," she whispered while a tiny tremor quaked her body.

Fuck! I'd scared her.

I couldn't lock away my Dominant nature—it was who I was, who I'd always been—but I could try to tamp it down. The least I could do was stop growling. The woman was scared enough, as she should be. Not only was she injured, but also stranded at some strange man's house without her car, her clothes, her shoes, or her…*luggage*?

Wait a minute. Wait a hot, fucking minute. Why's she hauling her wardrobe around in suitcases if she lives here?

Because she's doesn't, dumbass. It's a lie, chided the voice in my head.

Mentally kicking myself in the ass for not putting that puzzle piece together sooner, I clenched my jaw and peered down at her. But when I locked on to the unmistakable hunger blazing in her big, hazel eyes, my anger vanished. My cock instantly turned to granite. And I nearly swallowed my tongue.

Suddenly, I wanted to do a whole lot more than take her over my knee. I wanted to strip her bare, tongue-fuck orgasms out of her for hours, then drive my cock deep inside her hot, sexy body.

Chapter Four

Emma

Blade held me with a stare so penetrating and intense, I felt him climbing inside my soul. My heart sputtered. I wanted to look away, so he didn't see the secrets I was hiding, but I couldn't. He'd cast a turbulent, tantalizing carnal spell over me, one I'd never felt before. A part of me wanted to run and hide. But a bigger part of me yearned to stay here in his arms—drinking in the heat of his rugged body, his masculine scent, and his piercing blue eyes—until the end of time. But when his gaze suddenly turned hot and hungry, the only place I ached to be was in his bed…begging him to put out the fire licking my spine.

He dipped his chin and leaned in close. So close, his wet breath spilled over my lips. Tossing my inhibitions away, I looped my arms around his neck while another rush of wet warmth slid into my panties.

"I know it's hard to rely on others," he murmured, stare fixed on my lips. "Don't worry, I'll take good care of you if you'll let me, little one."

Little one?

The knee-jerk reaction to inform him I might be little, but with one well-placed kick to the balls, I could take him to his knees blazed through me. Instead, I held my tongue. While the two words continued circling my brain, I realized his tone hadn't held an ounce of contempt, but rather...adoration.

What the hell is going on?

I didn't have a clue. I only knew the longer his stare remained locked on my lips, the more I ached to taste his.

"Okay," I whispered.

Leaning in closer to his mouth, I inwardly prayed he'd start taking care of me now and kiss me.

But he didn't. Instead, he eased back, cleared his throat, then strode across the massive, white painted wrap-around porch. Framed with white spindle railings, I drank in the thickly padded, and inviting, white porch swing.

I tamped down my disappointment as he opened the door and carried me inside, then skimmed a gaze around the room.

The outside of his house looked like a typical American farmhouse. But inside, it was subtly elegant yet warm and inviting. I had no doubt a professional designer was responsible for the modern sophistication laid out before me. Which blew my preconceived notions about the rugged cowboy clean out of the water. Nothing about the interior—except the gleaming hardwoods and a stunning oil painting of a golden wheat field hanging on the living room wall—came close to what I'd imagined awaited me inside his house.

Processing my surprise, a crushing thought hammered through my brain.

Blade didn't hire an interior designer to create all this...his wife *did.*

"Please, put me down," I demanded.

"Why?" He blanched. "You gonna throw up again?"

"No. I-I just...don't want to cause any problems."

"Problems? I'm afraid I'm not following you, darlin'."

"With your wife."

34

"My what?" he barked, eyes flashing wide. "Hold on a minute. I'm *not* married. Never have been, likely never will be."

"Oh," I mumbled as a ridiculous wave of relief sailed through me. "I'm sorry, I thought…"

"You thought what?" he asked, striding deeper into the house.

The room laid out before me was breathtaking. But the first thing that captured my attention was a huge white and gray stacked-stone fireplace with a pale wooden mantle. Along one wall, facing the floor to ceiling windows and framed with cream-colored curtains, sat a long, comfy-looking dark leather couch. Matching chairs and glossy, polished end tables and a coffee table in the same pale-colored wood as the mantle surrounded it.

"I-I just assumed a handsome man like you would be married," I confessed as he carried me past a huge kitchen with gleaming stainless steel appliances and dozens of white wooden cabinets above cashmere-colored quartz countertops. In the center of the room stood a matching quartz covered island, and at the far end, in front of another wall of windows, stood a white, rectangular wooden table with six matching chairs.

"Sorry, darlin', you assumed wrong." He smirked before he turned and began carrying me up a wide staircase.

"Where are we going?" I asked, peering up to the second floor.

"My room."

While my hormones began throwing a *we're finally gonna get laid* party, anxiety crowded my brain.

"What for?" I didn't bother masking my apprehension.

"Because the supplies I need to re-clean your wounds are in my bathroom. Of course, it would be better if you showered first to get off any dirt I might have missed, but I doubt you're comfortable doing that."

Only if you joined me. I quickly bit my tongue. No way was Blade lusting after me, like I was him.

"A shower sounds heavenly, but it sort of defeats the purpose if I have to put my dirty clothes back on."

"You don't. I'll find you a pair of shorts with a drawstring, and a T-shirt, if you want."

The idea of wearing his clothes sent a strange and baffling thrill of arousal swirling through me. I'd never felt anything like it. Then again, I'd never been stranded with a man as hot or as domineering as Blade. He was like an alpha wolf...beautiful and regal, but dangerous. Still, the longer I was with him, the more I wanted to toss all social norms aside and jump his sexy ass.

It was as if he'd awakened something primal inside me. Something I never knew existed. That, or I was suffering an adrenaline dump after my near-death experience. Either way, it didn't matter. He wasn't offering me his body, just some clean clothes.

"I'd like that." Thank you."

As he strode down a long, wide hallway, I counted three guest rooms, a large bathroom, and an office.

"As soon as we get these bandages off, I'll start the water for you," he said, stepping into his massive master bedroom.

Unlike the bright white decor of the other rooms, this one dripped with potent masculinity. The gleaming mahogany dressers, nightstands, and huge, four-poster bed, draped in a dark gray comforter—poised against another wall of windows, framed with dark, maroon drapes—was what I'd expected his entire house to look like.

Past the windows, in the distance, I saw a group of big, black cows grazing in a lush, green field.

Without a word, he carried me into a pristine, white bathroom, then eased me onto the wide, gray and white granite vanity. I set my purse beside me, and as Blade stepped back and began gathering supplies, I spied a big, jetted spa tub in the corner. I nearly drooled. There wasn't a single thing I missed about New York, except the giant soaker tub in my bathroom.

As Blade started peeling off my bandages, I felt a little guilty for not mourning the loss of anything from my former life, except the bathtub. But then again, there wasn't much else to grieve over. I certainly wasn't going to miss working to earn my parent's approval. I'd spent my entire life trying to be the perfect daughter...trying to live up to their expectations, but always failed. It was only when my father informed me I was going to marry Wesley Fairchild—no, the asshat never bothered to propose—that I finally decided to put my foot down. I told my father no. Though shocked, he said the decision was final.

He didn't care I wasn't in love with Wesley.

Didn't care a thing about my desires or wants.

Didn't care a thing about me at all.

The only thing he cared about was the windfall of money from the merger.

I tried to reason with him, but he wouldn't listen. The next day, he and Ted Fairchild put out a press release. Within minutes, news of the wedding between Emma Bishop and Wesley Fairchild was trending like wildfire.

During my trek from New York to Texas, I'd religiously scoured every television station and media outlet I could think of, but couldn't find a single word about the blushing bride skipping out on the wedding of the century. In all honesty, I hadn't expected to. Neither my father's nor Ted's egos would allow the embarrassing truth to be broadcasted to the world.

In a way, it was a relief. I didn't have to worry about my face being plastered on every television station, website, or newspaper in the country. It gave me a window of anonymity I needed before I completely changed my appearance. Still, I wasn't stupid. I knew my parents and Wesley's parents had put a silent bounty on my head. There were probably dozens of private investigators combing the world at this very moment trying to find me.

Thankfully, I'd prepared for that as well. Weeks before the wedding, I'd started talking, ad nauseam, about Paris. I droned on and on about wanting to visit the Louvre, Eiffel Tower, and spend days relaxing in Versailles. I'd mentioned it so many times, my mother finally begged Wesley to cancel the honeymoon he'd planned in the Maldives and take me to Paris...to shut me up. He refused. Instead of wailing and demanding he bow down to her wishes, she seethed in silence. I knew then, she didn't want to make any waves that might risk the precious merger. Money my family didn't need was more important than anything on the planet...including their only child.

Though I had no way of knowing, I prayed I'd planted the Paris seed deep enough the families were focusing their search there and not the US.

The tornado had put an unexpected wrinkle in my plans, but I was confident I could iron it out. All I had to do was convince Blade to drive me to a quaint Richardson suburb and wave goodbye to him. Once he drove away, I'd call an Uber to take me to a local bank and cash out one of my cashier's checks before dropping me at the nearest car rental agency. Once I had a new set of wheels, I'd find a salon to cut my hair short and dye it black. After that, I'd buy a new wardrobe and tinted contact lenses, then find a discount hotel chain, and get a room.

Eager to get my new life started, I nearly told Blade to forget about the shower. But the thought of saying goodbye to him, so soon, filled me with an unexpected emptiness that made zero sense. He was a stranger, one who'd gone above and beyond to help and protect me. That alone intrigued me, but it wasn't the only reason I wanted to spend more time with him.

I was enthralled with Blade.

I couldn't take my eyes off him.

He aroused me in ways I'd never felt before.

Yes, he was sexy as hell. But I'd met other men, equally sexy, none of which did a damn thing for me. Why did Blade? What was it about him that flipped all my switches...made me ache to feel his hot, naked body pressed against my flesh, and his hard cock drive deep inside me?

I didn't know, but I didn't want to leave until I had some answers.

"I appreciate everything you've done, and are still doing for me. You don't have to, you know?"

"I know," Blade murmured, gently lifting the gauze from my knee.

"Why are you then?"

He paused and peered up at me. "Why wouldn't I?"

"I-I don't know. I mean, I really don't know anything about you."

"I don't know anything about you either...not really."

The knowing tone in his voice made me tense. I quickly tamped down my guilt by reminding myself there was no way he could know who I was.

"We should change that, then." I forced a smile. "Tell me about you."

"I already did." He smirked. "Why don't you tell me about *you*."

My stomach flipped.

Shit! This isn't the way it's supposed to go.

I had to give the man props; he'd turned the conversation on me without batting an eye.

He wants to know more about me? Fine, I'll tell him what he needs to know.

"Okay. Let's see...my favorite color is peach. My favorite ice cream is pistachio. Favorite food...it's a tie between Chinese and Mexican. My favorite season is spring. And my favorite band is Licks of Leather. I don't like anchovies, bell peppers, rude, obnoxious people, spiders, snakes, or snow."

"Yeah, the blizzards here in Richardson are brutal...*or so I've been told.*" His eyes flared as he pinned me with a goading stare.

Dammit. I'd hoped he'd forgotten about my *snowpocalyptic* faux pas, but clearly, he hadn't.

Time to lie my way out of this one.

"I've been in a blizzard before."

"Really? Where?"

"I was visiting Maine during a Nor'easter."

"Mmm." He grunted skeptically.

"Fine, don't believe me. I don't care," I scoffed, lifting my chin.

"You never got spanked as a child, did you?"

"What?"

"Nothing." He chuckled. "What's your favorite TV show?"

"Doesn't matter, you'll only make fun of me. Let's learn about *you*. What's your favorite color?"

"Red."

"What's your favorite ice cream?"

"I don't eat ice cream unless it's with cake, pie, or cobbler."

"Okay, what's your favorite ice cream with cake, pie, and cobbler?"

"Vanilla."

I knew he was pretending to be obtuse on purpose, but I refused to give up.

"So. what are your favorite cakes, pies, and cobblers?"

"Chocolate, apple, and peach," he said as he finished unwrapping my ankle.

Blade stood and tossed the blood-stained gauze in the trash before he strode to the shower. As he adjusted the temperature, his eyes saw clear to my bones.

"Before you ask, my favorite food is fried chicken, mashed potatoes, and gravy. My favorite season is fall. I like all kinds of music, everything from Blake Shelton to Pink Floyd. My favorite TV show is the Twilight Zone Marathon. I've watched it every New Year's weekend since I was seven."

"No way," I blurted. "That's my favorite show, too, but I didn't start watching it until I was ten."

"See, you were wrong. I wouldn't have made fun of you," he said. Wrapping his wide hands around my waist, he gently lifted me off the vanity and carried me toward the shower. "We have a lot in common. I don't like anchovies, bell peppers, rude, obnoxious people, spiders, snakes, or snow. But I especially don't like *liars*."

Guilt whipped through me. My heart rate tripled.

He knows. He knows, the voice in my head screamed.

Masking my panic, I swallowed tightly and nodded.

"You need any help getting in?"

"No. I-I'll be fine."

"Okay, I'll put some clothes on the end of my bed for you. If you need anything, holler. I'll be in the office, right across the hall."

"Thanks," I whispered, clutching the edge of the open shower as he walked away, and closed the door.

Heart in my throat, I peeled off my clothes, then hobbled in beneath the steaming spray.

The water temperature was perfect. But even more perfect was the rain forest showerhead spilling over me, while a half a dozen jets pulsating from the wall teased my pebbled nipples and aching clit. After washing my hair and body, I eased onto the marble ledge jutting from the back wall. Then, I lifted my legs, spread my thighs, and rested my heels on the corners of the ledge. The jets pummeled my swollen clit like a lover's fingers. Closing my eyes, I stroked my folds and invited the restless orgasm prowling inside me to run free.

Chapter Five

Grant

Every cell in my system wanted to burst into the bathroom, strip off my clothes, and drive my swollen cock into her succulent cunt. The longer I spent with the sassy, sexy vixen, the harder I struggled to resist making the filthy fantasies crowding my brain a reality.

"Not yet, fucker. You've got lots of digging to do first," I mumbled, storming to my office.

Whipping out my phone, I uploaded one of her photos to a face recognition app. Ten seconds later, my jaw dropped open, and I sank back in my leather chair when the name Emma Tolliver Bishop appeared on the screen. Before I could even sweep the shock from my brain, the puzzle pieces started snapping into place.

Though I'd never met Emma Bishop, until today, Aubrey—who sent me hundreds of letters while I circled the globe on missions—told me all about her famous, wealthy college roommate, and best friend... Emma Bishop.

Though I had a million and one questions, I felt a sense of relief. I now knew the naked woman in my shower wasn't hired to find me by one of the dirt-bags I'd hauled to jail. No, she was my late sister's friend and daughter of multi-billionaire, media mogul, Rupert Bishop.

Why is she here, pretending to be Aubrey?

"Let's try to find out," I muttered, tapping Emma Tolliver Bishop in the search engine of my computer.

Instantly, websites and images of Emma, some with her parents, filled the screen. I knew by the multitude of pages that were still loading, it'd take days, maybe even weeks, to comb through each link and gather the information I sought.

Turning my focus to her bio, I memorized every detail.

Emma Tolliver Bishop, Communications Executive at Bishop Broadcasting Group.

Born: January 7, 1995 in New York City. (28 years old)

"New York, huh? You told me you weren't from New York," I bitterly muttered.

Parents: Rupert Marshall Bishop and Roslyn Tolliver-Bishop.

"That explains her unusual middle name," I murmured.

There was no spouse, or any siblings listed.

The shower was still running, so I clicked on the first website and began skimming the article. It was about some mega-dollar-per-plate gala to raise money for a new art center in Brooklyn. Scrolling down further, I paused on a cock-hardening photo of Emma.

She looked like she'd just stepped off the pages of a magazine. She was dressed in a sparkling, low-cut black dress that was slit up the side to mid-thigh and hugged her lush curves like a second skin. Her wheat-colored hair was meticulously piled on top of her head in big, loose curls. Thick, dark lashes framed her pretty hazel eyes shimmering in something that looked an awful lot like mischief. A ball-churning smile stretched her ripe, red lips, and a wide ribbon of glistening diamonds banded her throat like a fucking collar.

Visions of Emma on her knees, peering up at me as she worshiped my cock, exploded in my mind. I tugged at my zipper to try to make more room for my throbbing erection as a hungry groan rumbled deep in my chest.

Keep scrolling, you horny bastard, drawled the voice in my head.

Clenching my jaw, I moved past her photo, then paused to read the glowing review about her generous donation to the art center. While the article didn't give Emma's exact address, it mentioned she lived in Central Park South, New York. I clenched my jaw. It chafed that she'd lied to me about not being from New York, but I scrolled on.

Seconds later, I came across another photo of Emma—dressed in a cap and gown, and flanked by her parents—with the headline: *Rupert Bishop celebrates daughter's Master's Degree in Communications from Columbia University.*

When I looked at the date of the article, grief and anger stabbed my heart. Aubrey would have graduated alongside Emma that day if she hadn't been brutally raped and murdered. Scrubbing a hand over my face, I exhaled a heavy sigh. Aubrey had been smart. No, she'd been brilliant. She'd completed her freshman college courses while still in high school. Before she'd even finished her sophomore year at Richardson High School, colleges had contacted my parents, offering Aubrey full-ride academic scholarships. The following year, she chose Columbia University in New York for their Cellular, Molecular, and Biochemistry courses.

Had the naked nymph in my shower been offered scholarships, too, or had Daddy's money secured her a spot at Columbia so she could follow in his footsteps?

Did it matter? No. The only thing that did was finding out why Emma was passing herself off as Aubrey.

How far had she gone to achieve her unscrupulous ploy?

Had she obtained a driver's license, credit cards, and a Social Security number in Aubrey's name? I didn't know, but had to find out. I needed to find a way to look inside Emma's purse...the one she'd clung to like a lifeline all day. There was only one problem: it was in the bathroom with her.

The shower's still running, taunted the voice in my head.

It was, but if she caught me sneaking into the bathroom now, she'd think me a pervert.

You are, the voice chortled.

I couldn't argue. But being a perv and broadcasting it were entirely two different things.

Why did I care what she thought of me? Emma was a liar, a thief, an enemy combatant. If I could charge into hundreds of dangerous missions and come out unscathed—for the most part—I sure as fuck could go through her purse without getting caught.

Muttering a curse, I pushed back from the desk and stormed across the hall.

Since Emma had already been in the shower a long time, I knew I had ten...maybe fifteen seconds to sneak in, flip through her wallet, and get the fuck out.

Counting off the seconds in my head, I turned the knob and slowly opened the door.

As I tiptoed into the bathroom and peered inside the shower, I nearly swallowed my tongue.

Emma sat poised beneath the pelting water, legs spread, with her toes gripping the edge of the marble bench. Head back and eyes closed, she quickly plunged her fingers in and out of her wet, pink pussy. Her lush breasts and rosy hard nipples heaved with each whimper and panted breath spilling from her plump parted lips.

Saliva pooled in my mouth.

My heart hammered against my ribs.

My cock instantly turned to stone and lurched toward the wet and writhing ball-churning beauty so forcefully it damn near burst from my zipper.

Son of a bitch.

Tempted to strip off my clothes, climb in the shower, and drop to my knees before latching my mouth over her juicy cunt to send her over the edge, slammed me like a wrecking ball. In the back of my mind, I knew I had a mission to complete, but I was so mesmerized by the sight before me, I couldn't peel my gaze off her.

Focus, fucker. You don't have time for this.

The voice in my head was right.

Stare still locked on Emma, I blindly reached inside her purse and groped for her wallet. When I wrapped my fingers around something thick, I quickly glanced down and found a plump envelope in my hand. Lifting the flap open, I pulled out the contents and blinked. It was a fat stack of cashier's checks. Thumbing through them, I arched a brow and gaped.

No wonder she wouldn't let go of her damn purse.

Mind spinning, I stuffed the envelope where I'd found it and plucked out her wallet. Glancing over at Emma—still climbing the mountain of bliss—I quickly examined her license and credit cards. The sight of Aubrey's name on each of them made my heart sputter and my blood boil. Yet, it also piqued my curiosity. People didn't go to the trouble and expense of changing their identities unless they were hiding from someone or something. I needed to dig a whole lot deeper.

Suddenly, Emma's whimpers melded into soft, keening cries. Throwing her wallet back in her purse, I turned to see her manically scraping her fingers over her clit. The sight of the intense pleasure playing across her beautiful face quelled my anger and curiosity.

Still, I'd completed my mission. It was time to retreat to the safety of my office.

"Please...please... Oh, please," she breathlessly begged like a quintessential sub.

My jaw nearly hit the floor. I had no clue what fantasy was unfurling inside her mind, but I'd have given my left nut for a glimpse.

Gathering all the willpower I possessed, I started to turn and leave. But when Emma whimpered, arched her hips in the air, and tensed, my resolve melted.

"Yes...yes. Oh, God...yes," she mewled, muscles straining.

Gaze locked on the desperation lining her face, I knew my mission was in danger. But I didn't care. The hunger to watch and hear her come was insatiable.

As she sucked in a sharp gasp and bit her bottom lip, I stepped closer to the shower like a fool.

Her legs trembled, and a guttural groan rolled from the back of her throat as she bore down on her busy fingers and completely unraveled. Waves of her sexual energy slammed through me and sent a shiver up my spine. Stare locked on her succulent slit, clutching and milking her digits, my cock screamed and wept with envy.

But when she arched higher still and groaned *my* name, the air in my lungs seized. My heart slammed against my ribs. And my cock lurched, painfully scraping my zipper.

Quivering and quaking, Emma's fingers stilled. I knew I needed to get the fuck out, but I couldn't move. I was frozen in place, pinging with disbelief, and aching to drag a dozen more mind-blowing orgasms from her sinful body.

No time! Get the fuck out, bellowed the voice in my head.

Cock screaming in disappointment, I bit back a curse and darted from the bathroom before quietly closing the door behind me. Then I sprinted to my office, plopped down in my chair, and heaved out a heavy sigh before branding the sight of Emma shattering to memory… and to the top spot in my spank bank.

"Shit. I forgot to the clothes."

Launching from my chair, I raced back across the hall. The instant I stepped into my bedroom, the water stopped running. Trying to wrap my head around the fact Emma had been thinking of me when she climaxed, I snagged a T-shirt from my dresser. Then I frantically searched for gym shorts. I knew I had a pair, with a drawstring, but couldn't remember which drawer they were in. When I finally found them, I started toward the bed as the bathroom door opened.

Wearing nothing but a towel, Emma hobbled through the portal, then jolted to a stop as I raked a hungry stare over her near-naked body. As I locked eyes with hers, she clutched the terry cloth tucked between her milky breasts.

"Sorry. I didn't mean to startle you," I said in a thick, gravelly voice. "I forgot to lay out your clothes earlier."

"Oh. T-that's no problem," she softly stammered, extending her hand toward the clothes in my fist. "I'll just slip back inside the bathroom and—"

"Before you get dressed, hop onto the bed and let me tend to your wounds."

It made no sense for her to drag the shorts over bandaged knees, but my inner perv didn't give a shit. I enjoyed seeing her in nothing but a towel. Thankfully, Emma didn't argue. She simply nodded shyly before I handed her the clothes and helped her to the bed. As she eased onto the mattress, images of her naked and writhing beneath me before shattering all over my cock crowded my brain.

Inwardly shaking the visions away, I strode to the bathroom and gathered up the medical supplies. When I returned, I knelt in front of her, then gently cupped her heel to get a good look at her ankle. It was swollen and had already started bruising. It had to be painful as fuck.

"You really should let me take you to the ER and get this x-rayed."

"No," she blurted as a flicker of fear darted across her eyes. "It'll be fine. I just need to get home, get an ice pack on it, and keep it elevated."

My inner beast—the one who vowed to protect all women the night I'd identified Aubrey's mutilated body—ripped off its chain and roared to life.

Who...or what has you so spooked, little one? The question burned the tip of my tongue, but I swallowed it down and nodded.

"If it doesn't get better in the next couple of days, have it looked at," I said, re-wrapping the elastic bandage around her ankle while breathing in her clean, soapy scent.

"I will."

Would she? Or was it another lie, one she thought I wanted to hear?

Adding those two questions to the other million circling my brain, I tried to ignore how close her pussy was to my face. The fact she'd been fantasizing about me when she'd shattered still pinged through my system. If she'd been anyone else, I would have pulled the towel apart, pressed her back on the bed, and slid my tongue up her pretty folds to make all her dreams a reality. But Emma was a liar, and an identity thief.

Mentally reminding myself of those two important details, I gripped my resolve firmly and finished wrapping her wounds.

"Thank you, again…for everything." She softly smiled as I stood and helped her off the bed.

"No problem," I replied, handing her the clothes. "Holler when you're dressed, and I'll take you home."

Another flicker of fear skipped across her eyes as she nodded before hobbling to the bathroom.

Chapter Six

Emma

The litany of lies spilling from my lips ate a hole of guilt through me.

Blade had been nothing short of a saint. He deserved more than my deception. But I couldn't risk telling him the truth. We were from opposite worlds. He'd never understand why I ran away or why I could never go back. Aside from our mutual fondness of old Twilight Zone episodes, we had nothing in common.

"You can stop lying soon...at least to Blade," I whispered to my reflection in the mirror while combing out my hair.

After dragging a scrunchie from my purse, I piled the wet strands into a messy bun, then carefully drew the shorts over my knees. Cinching the drawstring tightly, I tugged on his T-shirt. His masculine scent surrounded me like a blanket of serenity. It was sadly ironic that in the few hours I'd spent with a total stranger, I had felt safer and more protected than the past twenty-eight years with my parents.

Pressing Blade's shirt to my face, I closed my eyes and deeply inhaled his scent...branding it to memory. It was going to suck to tell him goodbye, but I couldn't stay here forever. I had a new life to start living.

Plucking up my purse, I limped out of the bathroom. Like a sentinel, Blade stood waiting for me right outside the door.

"Ready to go?"

"Yes," I lied.

After scooping me into his arms, he carried me down the hall before descending the stairs. Well aware this was the last time I'd ever be in his arms again, I looped my hands around his wide shoulders and drank in his strength and warmth.

As he strode out the front door, I spied a big red pickup parked in front of the porch.

"Where'd that come from?"

"Mack brought it up for me," he replied.

After opening the passenger door, Blade eased me on to the buttery leather. As I reached for the seat belt, he gently pulled my hand away. Gripping the strap, he gazed into my eyes and bent over my body. As he snicked the buckle in place, his stare stalled on my lips. The temptation to lean in and kiss his tempting mouth clawed through me. But before I found my courage to taste him, he eased back and stood, then cleared his throat.

"You good?"

When I nodded, he flashed a weak smile and closed the door.

As he climbed in behind the wheel and started the engine, I took one last, long look at his picturesque house and lush green fields.

"Where am I taking you, darlin'?"

After I rattled off the address I'd memorized months ago, Blade clenched his jaw and curtly nodded. His abrupt change of demeanor confused me. Was he as unhappy about saying goodbye as I was? Foolish ribbons of hope unfurled inside me, but I quickly reeled them in. Even if he was—which I seriously doubted—I couldn't risk getting involved with Blade, or any other man.

For now, I felt safe in Richardson. But there was no guarantee I could stay here long term. My parents weren't only cold, calculating, and controlling, they were also tenacious and unrelenting when it came to achieving what they wanted. They wouldn't stop searching until they found me. While I didn't give two shit's about leaving Wesley, it would crush me if I fell in love and had to run away again.

I didn't want to sever all ties with Blade, but it was safer this way.

Less than twenty minutes later, he pulled to a stop in front of a red brick, one-story house in a quaint, middle-class neighborhood. Peering out the window, I drank in the sight of my former college roommate's home. It looked exactly how I'd imagined. My mind swirled with all the warm and happy stories she used to tell me about her family, and a bittersweet smile tugged my lips.

I knew if Aubrey was inside, she'd be at the window, watching and waiting for me. The minute I pulled up, she'd run out the door, wearing a blinding smile, and steal the air from my lungs with an enormous hug.

But my best friend wasn't there.

She was dead.

And I never had the chance to tell her goodbye.

"This the right place?" Blade asked, studying me intently.

Unsure if I could speak past the lump of emotion lodged in my throat, I nodded.

"Alrighty then. Sit tight, and I'll help you inside," he said, shoving the gearshift into park.

"No," I barked, inwardly cringing at my harsh tone as he arched his brows suspiciously. "I'm good. I need to get used to moving around on my own."

"You sure?"

"Positive." I forced a smile. "Thank you so much for everything you've done for me. If there's anything I can do to repay you…"

"No need. It was my pleasure, Aubrey."

His voice sounded cold and brittle. I wanted to ask him what was wrong, but it was time to get out of his truck and start my new life.

"Take care of yourself," I said, painting on a plastic smile.

"You, too."

I opened the door and gingerly stepped onto the street, then closed

Jenna Jacob

it behind me. As I hobbled up the driveway, I could feel Blade's eyes boring into me. Praying no one was inside, watching me, I limped up to the porch. Then I turned, flashed him a wide smile, and waved.

With a curt nod, Blade drove away.

I stood on the stoop, watching until he turned the corner, then exhaled a deep breath. As quickly as possible, I retraced my steps and paused near the curb to lean against a shady oak tree. Plucking the cell phone from my purse, I tapped the Uber app when a big, red truck came to a tire-smoking, screeching halt in front of me.

No. No! Oh shit!

Blade's angry glare singed my flesh as my heart dropped to my toes and my stomach swirled.

Keeping his furious stare locked on me, he leaned over and shoved the passenger door open.

"Get in," he snarled.

"No. You've done enough. I'll be fine."

Embarrassment and shame thundered through my veins.

"I said, get in," he barked.

"Blade, please. Just...go," I begged, shoving my phone back in my purse.

He didn't say a word, simply continued glaring at me.

Fight or flight kicked in like a ninja. Since there was no way in hell I was going to fight the man, I pushed off the tree and limped toward the sidewalk. Behind me, Blade mumbled something, but I continued my trek without looking back. I hadn't even reached the cement before he hoisted me off the ground and into his rugged arms again. A yelp of surprise pealed off my throat. But when I saw the rage blazing in his blue eyes, up close and personal, my surprise turned to fear.

"Put me down. Now," I snapped indignantly.

He shook his head and clenched his jaw, then turned and carried me to the truck. Without a word, he unceremoniously dumped me onto the soft leather seat. Before I could try to scamper out, he whipped the seat belt around me and locked it in place.

"Let me go," I demanded, fear and panic swirling wildly.

"No."

54

"What...you're kidnapping me now?"

"Call it what you want, but the fact is...you don't live here," he growled, jerking his head toward the house. "You're alone, and got no place to go."

"So?" I didn't bother lying. Somehow, he knew the truth. Well, partially.

"If you think I'm the kind of man who'll leave you on the side of the road, like a fucking stray dog, and drive away...you're sorely mistaken," he growled, slamming the door shut.

The thought had never crossed my mind. But then, him coming back to check up on me hadn't either.

"I'm not your problem," I yelled as he rounded the front of the truck.

"You are now," he sneered, sliding in behind the wheel.

"Where are you taking me?" I asked, inwardly cursing the quiver of fear in my voice.

Blade closed his eyes, gripped the steering wheel, and deeply exhaled. Long seconds later, he swiveled his head toward me and opened his eyes.

Compassion replaced every drop of anger in his dazzling blue pools.

"Back to the ranch, where I know you'll be safe," he said, scraping a knuckle down my cheek.

Fighting the urge to nuzzle against his comforting hand, I shook my head. "That's kind of you, but unnecessary. If you want to take me somewhere, take me to a bank, then a rental car company, and I'll be out of your way for good."

"You're not in my way, darlin'. If you need to stop at a bank, I'll take you."

"And the rental car?"

"We'll talk about that on the way to the bank," he said, pulling from the curb.

While the quaint, quiet neighborhood faded behind us, I tried to purge the shame and embarrassment coursing through my veins...but couldn't.

"I'm sorry I lied," I whispered.

"Which time?" he smirked.

My heart sputtered while my guilt expanded.

"Every time."

"So, why did you?"

"It's...personal."

"Oh, so you're not a pathological liar, just a compulsive one, huh?"

"I'm not a liar at all." I bristled.

"Not a good one, that's for sure."

The realization I wasn't as savvy at deception as I needed to be stung like a slap to the face.

"Please...if you'll just take me to a bank and drop me off at a car rental place, you'll never hear another lie from my lips."

"Right," he scoffed. "Tell me something, preferably the truth. Where are you going once you get a new set of wheels?"

"Shopping...for clothes," I replied.

I purposely omitted anything about the hotel or hair salon. It would only invite more questions. The less Blade knew, the better.

A sardonic chuckle rumbled up from deep in his chest. "How about *after* you're done replacing your wardrobe? Do you plan on staying in Richardson?"

"Yes."

"Where are you gonna stay?"

"A hotel."

"Why?"

"Because I heard Richardson was a nice town," I replied obtusely.

"Like you heard about blizzards?"

He was deliberately goading me.

"I already told you; I've been in a blizzard before."

"Oh, that's right," he drawled derisively. "You were in Vermont during a Nor'easter."

"Yes. I'm surprised you remembered," I haughty replied in the same condescending tone my mother loved to use.

"I'd like to say I'm surprised you didn't...but I'm not the least bit shocked," Blade countered with a snarky smile. "The hardest thing about lyin' is keeping your story straight. The devil's in the details, darlin'. You said the blizzard was in Maine…not Vermont."

Bastard!

He was playing with me, like a cat with a mouse. My anger spiked, laying waste to every shred of guilt and shame. Fuming, I turned in my seat and glared at him.

"Maine? Vermont? What difference does it make? I've been in a fucking blizzard, all right?"

"My, my. Such language," he tsk'd, unable to hold back a crooked smile.

"Bite me," I growled. "On second thought, don't. Just pull over so I can get out."

"I already told you, I can't do that."

"Then stop mocking me and take me to the damn bank."

Blade sent me a sidelong glance and arched a brow. "First, I don't take orders from anyone. I give them. Second, you're awful damn bossy for someone who needs my help."

"Did I ask for it? No. Did I climb inside your truck willingly? No. You don't like my attitude? Tough shit. *You're* the one who physically plucked me off the ground and tossed me in the seat."

"Only to keep you safe," he reminded. "Yanno, it wouldn't kill you to be a tiny bit grateful."

Biting back the urge to yell at him for coming back to spy on me and screwing up my plans, I painted on a plastic smile.

"Thank you for saving me," I bit out sarcastically.

"You're welcome, darlin'." He flashed a triumphant smile so infuriating, yet dazzlingly gorgeous, I wanted to slap him. "I *am* curious about something. Did you make up the address of that house back there, or actually know who lives there?"

"I *knew* someone who once lived there."

"Old boyfriend?"

"No."

"Old *girlfriend?*"

"I'm not a lesbian, but yes, she was my college roommate and best friend."

"Was?"

"She died. And before you ask, because I know you will, I don't want to talk about it."

"Fair enough."

The empathy etching his face took the combative wind out of me. Blade was right. Though he'd literally kidnapped me, it wouldn't kill me to pound out my dented pride, and be a little more grateful. After all, I was the one who'd lied.

"Look, I'm sorry for being so...snarky."

"It's all right. But I'd appreciate it if you didn't lie to me anymore. Deal?"

"I'll do my best, but I can't make any promises."

"Why not?"

"Because there are things I need to keep private," I explained as he pulled into a parking space in front of the bank and killed the engine.

"Fine. Then say so, but stop lying to me."

"You'll actually respect that, and not keep prying?" I asked skeptically.

"Of course."

"Why?"

"Because I haven't done anything to earn your trust...yet."

The confidence shimmering in his blue eyes told me he planned to change that. Truth be told, I ached to let him...but couldn't. My freedom was at stake. His benevolence was overwhelming. Still, it wasn't enough for me to bare my soul.

"That's not true. You not only saved me, but you also bandaged me up...twice, let me take a hot shower, gave me some clean clothes, and are now chauffeuring me all over town."

"Those are superficial things. I haven't done enough to earn the secrets you're keeping." A ghost of a smile tugged his lips as he nodded toward the bank. "Will you let me help you inside?"

Chapter Seven

Grant

When Emma pensively nodded, I masked my surprise and hopped out of the truck.

Afraid of making an embarrassing scene, she refused to let me carry her in. I knew her ankle would take longer to heal the more weight she put on it, but I relented and cupped her elbow before escorting her into the bank.

After guiding her to the nearest teller, Emma faced me with a tense smile.

"Umm, this might take a while. If you want to take a seat," she said, nodding at a pale leather couch in the middle of the lobby. "I'll take care of what I need to."

"Are you telling me to go away?"

"No, I'm asking you to," she said, dragging her teeth across her bottom lip. "I need some privacy, please."

"Say no more, darlin'."

Prying my stare off her wicked mouth, I ambled across the room and sat on the couch before locking my gaze on her pert little ass. I'd never be able to wear those shorts again without getting a massive hard on. As if confirming my suspicion, my cock stirred. Peeling my stare from her ass, I looked around the bank. I'd never been inside this one before. The branch my family and I had used for decades was a couple of miles down the road. I'd thought about taking Emma there, but I knew the second she flashed her fake driver's license, the teller—all of whom had known Aubrey well—would likely call the cops.

No one but me was going to question Emma.

After watching her come in the shower, I wanted to do a whole lot more than interrogate her. But that was just a pipe dream. Based on how angry and defensive she got when I pointed out her lies, I knew peeling back her layers of deception was going to be a slow, arduous process.

I could have been a bit more subtle when I'd confronted her about her lies, but I'd purposely been a prick to find out how thick her walls were, and how deeply she was entrenched behind them.

I definitely got an answer.

Her walls were paper thin and her lies opaque.

Using a few ruthless tactics, I could split her wide open and force her to spill all her secrets. But in doing so, I'd destroy any chance of getting her naked and beneath me because Emma would hate me by the time I was through.

Sliding my gaze back to the sexy little spitfire, two other employees were now flanking the teller. While I couldn't see Emma's face, her rigid posture sent alarms blaring in my brain. Launching to my feet, I ate up the distance between us and eased in alongside her.

"Is there a problem?" I asked, peering over her shoulder.

Jolting, she snatched up the check and slapped it face down on the marble counter. "Nothing that isn't being fixed."

"Fixed? How?"

"Our apologies, sir," a middle-aged woman with bright red lipstick and black-framed glasses began. "It's a policy issue. When we're presented with a check as large as this one, we're required to confirm funds."

"It shouldn't take much longer," Emma assured with a tight smile.

The tension rolling off her was so thick a jackhammer couldn't cut it. Based on the edgy glances the employees shared, I knew they felt it, too. I had to do something to quell the stress bouncing off all four women before someone called the cops.

Reaching over Emma's shoulder, I plucked the check off the counter. It was one of the big ones from the envelope in her purse.

"Damn you, Uncle George," I growled with a feigned scowl. "Baby, when we get back home, remind me to call him and tell him to stop sending such big checks."

Emma blinked up at me as if I'd lost my mind. Maybe I had, but at the moment, all I could think about was protecting her and keeping her out of jail.

Slinging my other arm around her waist, I pulled her in tight against my side before sending her a clandestine wink.

"That's a good idea, honey." She smiled, covertly returning my wink.

Relieved she'd caught on to my ploy, I forced a placid smile and addressed the women behind the counter.

"My Uncle George is the Fourteenth Earl of Carlisle. He's been hopelessly in love with my beautiful fiancé since the first day he met her. He insists on spoiling my Aubrey with gifts, like this," I lied, handing the check to the teller. "I know he's trying to steal her from me, but he won't succeed, will he, precious?"

"Never," Emma said, peering up at me with an adoring smile. "I'm yours forever."

Don't I wish.

Blindsided by the insane thought, panic crawled up my spine. My heart clutched, and my stomach pitched. Sure, I wanted to fuck her, but...not *forever*. Struggling to shove the absurd notion away, Emma thwarted my attempt by reaching up and cupping my cheek.

"Uncle George is sweet," she said in a sultry purr. "But he'll never be able to compete with you, my sizzling, sexy cowboy."

Blown away by her Oscar winning performance, Emma completely

Jenna Jacob

blindsided me when she lifted to her toes and boldly pressed her lips to mine.

Frozen and stunned stupid for a hot second, the lava searing my veins finally reached my brain. Biting back a moan, I pressed my palm to the small of her back and pulled her sinful body flush against mine. Then I cupped her nape and held her in place before taking full control of the kiss.

The warm, soft texture of her lips kneading beneath mine, and the shiver quivering through her supple curves meshed to my steely frame, set my soul on fire. Lost in the pure perfection of the kiss, the outside world vanished.

Like a laser, my entire focus was on the ragged puffs of breath spilling from Emma's nose.

On her pebbled nipples prodding my chest.

On the heat and arousal swirling around us.

But it wasn't enough. I couldn't end the kiss without fully tasting her.

Gliding my tongue over her succulent seam, Emma parted with a kitten-soft moan that turned my cock to stone. Without hesitation, I delved deep, slowly sweeping over every wet crevice as I branded her sweet, cotton candy flavor to memory.

Unable to stop myself, I inched my palm up her ribs, and just as my thumb stroked the base of her ripe breast, the teller cleared her throat... loudly.

Emma tensed and tore from my lips as if she'd been burned. Blinking away the smoky arousal shimmering in her eyes, her cheeks grew red.

"If you'd like to take a seat, Miss Holden, we'll have your money to you shortly." The teller smiled, nodding toward the couch.

The sexy blush was still staining Emma's cheeks as she gripped her purse and plucked it off the counter. Clearly, she was embarrassed. If I stood any chance of kissing her again—which I desperately wanted to...right fucking now—I had to chase the remorse from her system.

With her taste still singeing my tongue, I guided her to the sofa.

Looking everywhere but at me, she eased onto the cushion before I sat beside her.

"You should be in movies, darlin'. You're one hell of an actress," I whispered.

Emma bristled, but finally looked at me. "I was simply trying to make your story more convincing."

"You definitely made a believer out of me," I murmured. "I enjoyed it. I think you did, too."

Her blush darkened as she lowered her lashes—*like a sweet little sub*—and locked her gaze on the purse in her lap.

Emma had all the markings of a submissive, but they were locked deep inside her. She probably didn't even know it, but I did. I'd seen and sensed her need to please—when she wasn't lying or being pissed off at me. And every Dominant bone in my body ached to draw out her need to please and set her submission free.

Thirty minutes later, with an obscene stack of hundreds stashed in her purse, we left the bank.

"Where were you planning to shop for clothes?"

She tensed, then nonchalantly shrugged. "I hadn't really decided."

In other words, she had no idea where the malls were in town. Instead of calling her out on that fact, I merely nodded.

"Well, there's a Wally World a few blocks up ahead, or I can take you to NorthPark Center."

"A car rental company will be perfect, thanks."

"I'm sure it would be, but I'm not taking you to any of them."

"Why not?" She bristled.

"Because I've got plenty of cars you can borrow."

"That's kind of you to offer, b-but...I-I can't do that."

"Why not?"

"B-because..." She paused and swallowed tightly. I could practically hear the wheels in her brain searching for a plausible reason. "I-I'm not on your insurance policy."

"Oh, don't worry about that. They're just work vehicles. It'll be fine."

"Please, Blade. You've already done so much, I can't ask you to—"

"You didn't. I offered," I interrupted, shutting her down. "Wally World or the mall?"

"And you call *me* stubborn?" she countered before heaving a sigh. "Fine. The mall...please."

I headed south, inwardly celebrating my victory. Not only had I devised a way to get her back to the ranch, but I also planned to convince her to stay—at least until I finished gathering my intel on her.

Once inside the mall, Emma's eyes lit up like a kid on Christmas morning as she studied the directory of stores.

"This way," she said excitedly, hobbling off.

I quickly caught up to her and cupped her elbow, then escorted her to a posh, clothing store. The minute we stepped through the door, a saleswoman dragged a critical eye over Emma's gym shorts and tee and wrinkled her nose.

"Do you have an appoint—"

"No, I don't," Emma replied with a snobbish lift of her chin. "But I'm hoping you'd like to make an obscene commission and help me replace some of the clothes I lost in the tornado that hit near Denton. Or...would you like me to take my money elsewhere?"

I had no idea where her haughty demeanor had come from, but it was sexy as fuck.

The woman blinked and shook her head, then dragged an assessing gaze down Emma's body. "I'd be happy to help you, ma'am. You're a size six, correct?"

"Yes," Emma replied on a grateful sigh.

"Right this way," the woman eagerly smiled.

As Emma limped around the store, pointing to pieces of clothing while the salesclerk gathered them up, I finally caught sight of the pampered princess, born with a silver spoon. Yes, I knew her family had more money than God. But the entire time we'd been together, she'd been so...normal, the fact had honestly slipped my mind. Emma was kind and even thanked the clerk several times, but I found the aura of wealth pouring off the woman wearing my gym shorts and tee beyond fascinating.

While she did her thing, I meandered around, biding my time. As I passed a brightly lit recessed shelf, I nearly choked at the price tag on a basic, black handbag. Curiosity piqued, I continued strolling around, furtively checking prices of clothing.

After handing over nearly three-quarters of her cash, I wasn't a bit surprised when the salesclerk only handed her two shopping bags. Lifting the packages from Emma's fingers, I tucked an arm around her and guided her out of the store.

"If I remember correctly, the directory showed an elevator up here," she said, pointing ahead.

"Forgive me being a typical man, but what the hell *else* is there left for you to buy?" I grinned.

"Us dinner," she replied, pensively peering up at me.

"You hungry?"

"I'm starving."

"Why didn't you say something? I would have been happy to buy you—"

"No. I want to buy *you* dinner. Please, Blade? It's the least I can do."

"You don't owe me any—"

"I do, but it's not a debt. It's a thank you."

Her pleading smile and gratitude shimmering in her big, green eyes was like a punch to the gut. Though it went against every ounce of chivalry in my body, I refused to crush her and tell her no.

"All right." I nodded, swallowing my pride.

"Thank you." Her face lit up like the sun. "I saw a restaurant on the directory. It's up on the third floor. Should we give it a try?"

"We can, or...do you like steak?"

"I love it."

"Let me take you to the best steakhouse in Richardson then. They have a filet that literally melts in your mouth."

"Will you still let me buy you dinner?"

"If you *insist*."

"I do." Emma's smile was so mesmerizing, I didn't mind letting her foot the bill or putting my ego in time out.

Traffic was a bitch, as usual during rush hour, and moving at a snail's pace. When a police car and ambulance screamed past us on the shoulder of the highway, I knew we wouldn't make it to Richardson anytime soon.

"Sorry. We probably should have grabbed dinner at the mall."

"No." Emma shook her head. "It's fine."

"But you're starving."

"If the steaks are as good as you say, trust me. I will survive."

"You might, but I'm not too sure I will. I'm so hungry I could eat a water buffalo."

"Why didn't you say something?" She gaped.

"What…and let you think I was a wuss who couldn't handle a few hunger pangs? No way." When she rolled her eyes and shook her head, I grinned. "I haven't eaten since six this morning. I burned off breakfast hauling furniture hours before that damn tornado hit."

"Speaking of furniture. What was that padded table thing we hid under?"

Since witnessing her submissive demeanor, I'd been plotting ways to start a lifestyle conversation. I'd never expected Emma to kick that fucking door open. I had no clue if she was prepared to learn the truth about me, and ultimately herself. But I wasn't going to let this golden opportunity pass me by.

"It's called a bondage table."

"A *bondage* table? As in…tying someone to it?"

"Yes," I replied, darting her a sidelong glance.

I could tell by her expression Emma was puzzled by the concept.

"Consensually, of course," I added, trying to ease her bewilderment.

"Why would someone *want* to be tied up?"

"Lots of people have reasons for willingly giving up their control. Some feel safe being bound and confined. Some find peace. Some get off on the thrill of being helpless and unable to physically stop what someone is doing to them."

"Doing to them? Like what?"

"Spanking, tickling, fondling…forcing them to orgasm."

"What kind of private club were you working at, for heaven's sake?"

"Have you ever heard of BDSM?"

"Of course, who hasn't," she replied, then gasped as her eyes grew wide. "That place was a *kink* club?"

"Yes."

"Why were *you* there?" she asked, eyeing me warily.

"Moving furniture."

"So, you're not a member?"

"Of that club? No. It's abandoned."

"You mean there are others like it?"

The look on her face mirrored the shock in her voice. Emma hadn't been ready for this conversation, but it was too late to turn back now.

"Yes. There are BDSM clubs all over the world."

"Are *you* a member of one of them?"

"Yes, I am."

Chapter Eight

Emma

Blade's confession sent the shock, curiosity, and arousal swirling inside me soaring to a whole new level. Like New Yorkers packing the subway, questions crowded my brain.

I'd discovered the BDSM lifestyle at sixteen when all the girls were going gaga over a taboo, trending book. Not wanting to be left out, I secretly downloaded it. After devouring it multiple times, I covertly filled my e-reader with every BDSM book I could find.

I still did, well, before my car got sucked away.

Though I'd never engaged in any kind of kinky sex, or actually known anyone who did, I constantly fantasized about being commanded by a strict, unrelenting Master.

"I can tell by your silence, I've shocked you. Don't worry, I won't tie you up unless you beg me to." Blade smirked.

"I'm not shocked. Well, okay, maybe a little. But only because I've never met anyone in the lifestyle before. What's it like…I mean, what do you do?"

Jenna Jacob

"You want to know what *I* like?"

Though I hadn't meant the question to come out like it had, I nodded. I was dying to know what kind of kinky things turned Blade on.

"It depends on what the submissive needs."

"Wait, I'm confused. You're a Dominant, right?" He smiled and nodded. "So why worry what the submissive needs? You're the one in charge...the one giving all the orders. She simply has to do what you tell her to."

"Who told you that?"

"Nobody. I've just read about it."

"Okay, first...forget everything you've ever read."

"You mean it's not like in the books?"

"Not even close," he replied. "What's your definition of BDSM?"

"Kinky sex."

"That's a common misconception, but in reality, sex has nothing to do with the lifestyle."

"I know you told me to forget everything I've read, but why are all the stories full of kinky sex?"

"Because a lot of Doms and subs incorporate sex into their BDSM relationship, but it's not the basis of the lifestyle. Have any of the stories you've read mentioned the term power exchange?"

"Some, but I don't really know what it means."

"Since it looks like we're gonna be stuck in traffic a while, I'd be happy to explain it to you, if you'd like."

"I would, very much."

A flicker of something I couldn't quite put my finger on skipped across Blade's eyes. He gripped the steering wheel tightly and dragged in a deep breath.

"BDSM is an acronym for bondage and discipline, dominance and submission, and sadism and masochism. Those might seem like several different aspects, but they all fall under the umbrella of a power exchange. Take bondage and discipline, for example. Clearly, someone's getting restrained and hands over their control...submits. The other person takes that control, combines it with their own, then

70

gives it back in various ways...Dominates. That, in basic terms, is called a power exchange. Every BDSM scene or relationship involves exchanging power. It might be for an hour, or it might be twenty-four-seven. That's up to the individuals."

Quickly realizing this man was a fountain of knowledge, I opened my purse and started digging for my cell phone. It was likely buried in the bottom of my designer bag, but I was too impatient to keep searching. So, I grabbed the manilla envelope of cashier's checks, and the pen poised beside my wallet, and started frantically scribbling notes.

"There isn't gonna be a test when I'm through, darlin'," he said with a crooked grin.

Smart ass.

"I wasn't expecting one," I replied dryly. "It's just easier for me to remember things when I write them down."

"There's an easier way to learn about the lifestyle than taking notes."

"There is? How?"

"I could teach you," he said, holding me prisoner with a stare so commanding his Dominance flowed over me like warm honey.

My heart leapt to the back of my throat.

A part of me was petrified. Yet, a bigger part—ruled by my celebrating hormones—couldn't wait to get started.

"After we get to know each other better, that is," he added, ripping the excitement from my soul. "A deep level of trust must be established first."

Banking my disappointment, I nodded.

"Trust, communication, and open honesty are necessary in order to build a firm foundation in the lifestyle," he continued as the traffic jam began to lessen. "All parties, even those who casually scene at the club, have to be open, honest, and communicate their limits and expectations. It's called negotiating, and is vitally important before a submissive hands their control over, and a Dominant accepts it."

"Accepts it?" I scowled. "You mean take it?"

"No. That's not Dominance. It's abuse. A Dom never forces or

71

coerces a sub to give up their control...*unless* the sub wants a consensual/non-consensual scene. Even then, limits are fully established during negotiations prior to any play."

"What if the sub doesn't like the limits? Can she say no?"

"Yes, and she should."

"What if he says 'no, you're doing it anyway?'"

"Then the sub calls her safeword, Dungeon Monitors step in, and the Dom is more than likely escorted from the club."

"So, you're saying submissives have a choice who they give their power...control to?"

"Darlin', the submissive holds all the power. Without willingly handing over her control, the Dominant's hands are," he paused and chuckled, "for lack of a better word...tied. They're empty, leaving him nothing to work with."

"The way you explain it makes sense, but if the sub has all the power, why isn't she called a Dominant?"

"Good question." He grinned. "Because when she hands over her power, she *submits*."

I blew out a heavy sigh. "There are a lot of ins and out in this lifestyle. How does anyone keep it all straight?"

Blade chuckled. "Little by little. It's a thrilling journey, not a final destination."

"How long have you been in the lifestyle?"

"I'm not sure how old you are, but it's probably longer than you've been alive."

"I'm twenty-eight. How old are you?"

"Ancient compared to you," Blade drawled, shaking his head. "I was eighteen when I discovered BDSM. You were ten."

After a bit of tiny mental math, I blinked in shock. "You don't look thirty-six, Blade. More like twenty-three."

He tossed back his head and laughed in a tone so deep and rich goosebumps peppered my arms and a naughty chill raced up my spine.

"Flattery will get you everywhere, darlin'."

"It's not flattery, it's the truth."

"That didn't hurt too bad, did it?"

"What?"

"Telling the truth." He smirked.

Guilt slammed me like an anvil. Lowering my chin, I stared at the envelope on my lap. Out of all the words I'd written down, the only one that leapt from the page as if mocking me was *Truth*. The ache to spill my guts and tell Blade everything throbbed through me.

"Hey, look at me." His voice was soft, but so damn commanding; I couldn't help but comply. "I was teasing. Yeah, it was a bad joke. I wasn't purposely trying to insult you or make you feel bad. I'm sorry."

I'm sorry. Those two words were so foreign to my ears. I repeated them over and over in my mind. No man had *ever* told me he was sorry.

"Look, I don't know why you're here, but I do know you're not from here."

Panic and guilt sliced through me. Jerking my head up, I narrowed my eyes. "What makes you think that?"

"You mean besides the way your eyes lit up when I pulled into the mall parking lot? Or how excited you got when you saw all the stores on the marquee? Darlin,' NorthPark Center has been around since Jesus wore diapers. If you'd grown up here, you would have known every store inside the place before we left the interstate. But you didn't. You also didn't know that Denton was the next town from where the tornado hit. On top of that—"

"Enough! You've made your point." I loathed how damn observant he was, but feared how he could see through me so easily. "You're right, I'm not from here. This is the first time I've ever been to Texas. Look, I'm sorry I lied to you, but —"

"You did it for personal reasons. Yeah, I know. I also know you're not a mass murderer, an escaped prisoner, or some nut-job from an insane asylum," he said, glancing at me with a tiny smirk.

"You sure about that?" I countered, trying to resurrect our playful banter again.

"Positive." He grinned, then quickly sobered and gently cupped my hand. "I'm also positive you're in some kind of trouble. Hopefully, soon, you'll trust me enough to tell me what's going on. Until then, I'll do whatever it takes to protect you."

My heart swelled and tears stung my eyes. This man…this amazing man I'd known less than a day, had not only apologized but also just vowed to keep me safe.

I swallowed the lump of emotion lodged in my throat, then without thinking, I smiled softly and threaded my fingers through his. "Thank you."

"You're welcome."

Blade continued telling me more about the power exchange, the codes of conduct for both Dominants and submissives. He stressed the importance of anonymity and protecting the identity of others at the club. He said, what happens in the club, stays in the club. Then he took time to explain the different types of scenes that play out in the dungeon. When he offered to take me to the club, to see them for myself, a part of me wanted to jump out of his truck and run and hide. But a bigger part of me struggled to keep from dancing in my seat.

After passing the wreck that caused the time-consuming backup, it was smooth sailing to the restaurant. When Blade pulled into the parking lot, I mentally kicked myself for not changing into one of my new outfits before leaving the mall.

Once we stepped inside, my fears were confirmed. I was definitely underdressed, but no one seemed to notice. At least, not as much as they would have if I'd waltz in wearing designer wear. I'd already pressed my luck by opting to shop at the mall. Thankfully, the salesclerk hadn't recognized me. I was such a banged up hot mess, I doubted anyone in the restaurant would either.

I did grow nervous when our waiter asked if we'd met before. Though I'd assured him we hadn't, intuition told me my window of anonymity would be closing soon.

Blade hadn't been kidding about the steak. Mine was so tender and juicy it nearly *did* melt in my mouth.

Stuffed, sated, and serene, I couldn't miss the pained expression on his face when I plucked up the bill and put some cash inside the little leather folio. I'd inadvertently dented his fragile male ego.

Reaching out, I patted his hand and flashed him a playful smile. "Tell your inner Dom to chill. It's just one dinner."

"Easier said than done. It's hard-wired in me."

"Well, if we ever meet up again, I'll let you buy me dinner. How's that?"

"Meet up again? What do you mean? You're coming back to the ranch with me, right?"

"Yes, to borrow a car."

"And then what...leave?"

"Well...yeah."

Blade pursed his lips and frowned. "How can I protect you if you leave?"

His question blindsided and confused me.

"Are you asking me to...to stay with you?"

"It's the only way I can keep you safe, darlin'."

Shacking up with a panty-melting stranger wasn't anywhere on my new life path. But his offer of protection was a tempting detour I desperately wanted to take...at least, temporarily.

"For how long?"

"As long as it takes for you to tell me what kind of danger you're in, and to make sure it passes."

I didn't have the heart to tell him it might never pass. Instead, I nodded and bit my bottom lip.

His comment hung in the air for several long seconds. Finally, Blade stood and extended his hand. After helping me from my chair, he snaked a muscular arm around my waist and escorted me to his truck. My ankle was tender, but no longer throbbing. I didn't share that revelation with him. No way would I do or say anything to break the blissful bond of his hot, rugged body pressed against my side.

When Blade turned into the driveway, seeing his house again filled me with a strange sense of peace. It was crazy, but after four days on the run, I didn't feel the need to look over my shoulder. I could finally breathe.

He pulled to the front porch and turned off the engine. "Do you want to come inside or pick one of the cars?"

In other words, was I staying or leaving?

The smart thing would have been to leave. But as I peered at the house illuminated by the truck's headlights, images of the bright, welcoming decor and his masculine bedroom flashed in my brain. The idea of checking into a lackluster hotel room, alone, made my skin crawl.

"If your offer still stands, I think I'd like to go inside."

Though surrounded by darkness, his mega-watt smile was brighter than the sun.

"Of course, it docs, darlin'. Come on, we'll get you settled in one of the guest rooms," he said before bounding out of the truck and jogging toward my door.

I would have preferred he settled me into *his* room. But after everything Blade told me about the BDSM lifestyle, I knew honesty and trust were vitally important to him. I didn't *want* to lie to him anymore, but unfortunately, I'd probably have to. I hated not being honest with him. But I hated my parents more for being so insanely controlling and manipulative I had to flee in order to find a sliver of freedom.

When Blade opened the passenger door, I shoved the depressing thoughts away and gathered my purse and shopping bags. But instead of helping me from the truck, he scooped me out of my seat and kicked the door closed.

Being in his arms and nestled to his chest again, made my heart soar, but the need to be honest—when I could, even over little things—was more important.

"You don't have to carry me, Blade. I can walk. My ankle doesn't really hurt anymore."

"Good. Let's keep it that way." He smirked before carrying me inside the house and up the stairs.

When he turned into the first bedroom, farthest from his own, I banked my disappointment.

"The bathroom is right across the hall," he announced, easing me onto the mattress. "Clean towels are under the sink, and there's a new toothbrush and toothpaste in the drawer. There's some shampoo, I'm not sure what kind, in the shower. Tomorrow, I can drive you to the drug store to get whatever else you need."

"What I need is a salon, but I can drive myself."

"I'm sure you can, but I'm taking you...to keep an eye on you."

Though I'd backed myself into my own corner, like I'd done so many times with my parents, the urge to push back and fight my way free was nowhere to be found.

"All right. I'd appreciate that. Thank you."

Blade cocked a brow and bent in close. "Stop thanking me for everything. If I didn't want to help you, I wouldn't. All right?"

"Yes, Sir." The honorific I'd read a million times slid off my tongue before I could stop it.

Heat flared in his eyes, and a slow, knowing smile kicked up one corner of his mouth. Without a word, he straightened and strolled to the door.

"I'm gonna grab a shower. If you need anything in the night, holler. I'm a light sleeper."

"I will. Good night, Blade."

"Night, little one."

Chapter Nine

"Whoa, what happened to your hair?" Mack gaped at Emma as he strode into the kitchen, like always, for breakfast.

She flashed him a smile and scraped her fingertips through the dark, cropped strands behind her ear. "I got it cut and colored yesterday."

"You sure as hell did. I damn near didn't recognize you."

That's exactly why she did it.

"I wanted a change." Emma shrugged before lifting the plate of bacon from my hand and carrying it to the table. While angry scabs dotted her hands and knees, I was relieved her ankle had healed to the point she was no longer limping. "I was tired of messing with long hair."

"Well, it looks mighty pretty." Mack smiled, darting me a knowing glance.

Thursday morning, while Emma was still sleeping in the guest room, I had grabbed a cup of coffee and strolled to the barn. I told Mack who Emma was, and who she was pretending to be. He, too, was equally perplexed about her deception, but promised to guard her secret, keep an eye on her, and note any suspicious activity around the ranch while I tried to uncover Emma's secrets.

"Thank you, Mack," she preened, returning to my side at the stove. Flashing a smile, she eased the plate of pancakes from my hand. "I've got this. You two go ahead and dig in while it's hot. I'll get the coffee."

Mack bounced a glance between me and Emma, then smirked and arched a brow as I joined him at the table. Like me, he was a Dom... blinded by her submissive nature.

"You gonna do anything about that?"

"Not yet," I muttered.

"You should. She needs it, and so do you," he whispered before Emma returned and filled our mugs.

No, what I needed was to find out why she was pretending to be my sister and hiding out in Richardson. Though I'd uncovered a ton of information about Emma off the internet over the past three days, I still hadn't discovered an answer to my questions. It might have helped if I could stay focused, but I couldn't. The sight, scent, and sounds of Emma were constant distractions. It was strange, yet soothing, to have a woman living under my roof.

Not gonna lie. The first day had been awkward as hell. But after showing Emma around the ranch and letting her choose a car to drive, she started to relax and reveal more of her personality.

She was funny, snarky, and loved to banter...with both me and Mack. Her smile lit the dark, empty places inside me. Her laughter warmed me like the sun, but hammered holes in my armor—she was still the enemy. But it was her innate need to please that turned me inside out.

"So, what do you two cowboys have planned for today?" Emma asked as we loaded our plates.

"Now that summer is bearing down on us, the fields are drying out. We have to start adding minerals to the cow's feed before we fill the troughs," I explained.

Though she was a city girl, through and through, Emma hung on my every word and asked dozens of questions.

"What do you have planned?" Mack asked her.

"I think I'm going to try to bake some cookies," she replied shyly.

"Fire extinguisher is in the mud room, darlin'," I teased.

"Ha, ha," she drawled, rolling her eyes.

"No offense, but how'd you get this far in life without learning to cook?" Mack asked.

Because her parents hired people to do it for her.

Mack was well aware of that fact. So, why was he asking? Was he trying to help me crack her open? If so, he wasn't helping.

When Emma turned his way, I sent him a scowl and shook my head.

"Other things were more important to me." She shrugged.

Yeah, like stealing my sister's identity and running away.

As the cynical thought crashed through my mind, I bit back a growl. The longer I spent with Emma, the more I had to remind myself she was playing a game...playing *me*.

I don't submit to mind fucks...I give them.

Unfortunately, I wanted to do a whole lot more than fuck her mind. I wanted to fuck her body, hard and dirty. Ever since discovering Emma was posing as Aubrey, my life and emotions had been tossed into a blender. My brain and libido were at war. Tamping down the anger rising inside me, I quickly finished my breakfast.

As Mack and I headed out the back door, Emma was loading the dishwasher—like she'd done the past three mornings. I didn't have a valid reason to be angry she'd assumed the mundane task, only that I hated feeling beholden to her.

As we strode toward the barn, Mack softly chuckled beside me.

"What's so funny?"

"You." He grinned. "Aubrey's got you tied up in more knots than I use binding Aspen for a suspension scene."

"Her name's not Aubrey. It's Emma," I growled.

"The name doesn't matter. How deep she's gotten under your skin does."

"Thanks, Captain Obvious," I drawled.

"I'm not trying to be a prick, but it's not like you to *not* have a plan."

"Oh, I have one, but it'll break her. I can't find the willpower to do that to her. Beneath all the lies and deception is a gentle and kind woman."

"Then come up with another one. We both know you can. You're one of the smartest, most resourceful men I know," Mack said, clapping me on the back.

The sun was slipping toward the horizon when I finally strolled through the back door and into the kitchen. On the counter sat a plate of perfectly browned chocolate chip cookies. Curious to find out if they tasted as good as they looked, I plucked one up and took a bite. As the buttery brown sugar and chocolate melted over my tongue, I couldn't help but smile at Emma's achievement.

"Oh, you've already tasted one." She smiled, gliding into the kitchen.

"Yep, and they're delicious. Congratulations, darlin'." I grinned.

Her face lit up, and her smile widened. "Thank you."

"Oh, no, thank *you*. I'm gonna eat the whole plate for dinner."

"No, you're not." She chuckled as I shoved the entire cookie in my mouth. "You said this morning you were gonna grill the steaks in the fridge."

"Damn. You're right." I nodded. "Let me run upstairs and wash the sweat off me, then I'll start the grill."

"While you're doing that, I'll set the table."

"Deal."

As I bounded up the stairs, I mentally replayed our conversation in the kitchen. It had been encouragingly easy, yet frighteningly domestic. Though it made me feel like a complete asshole, I needed the latter to catch Emma off-guard

I'd taken Mack's advice and devised a new plan. It was unlike any tactic I'd ever used before, but I'd weighed the risks and chosen the lesser of two evils. Emma would be pissed, and I'd likely never see her again, but I wouldn't totally destroy her. By sunrise, she'd probably be gone, but I'd finally have the answers I needed.

Pushing down the strange, empty ache filling my soul, I stripped and climbed in the shower.

When dinner was done, I helped Emma clean up the kitchen, then opened a bottle of wine.

"What do you say we sit on the porch for a while?" I asked, filling her glass.

"I'd love to." She smiled.

I slipped my arm around her waist and guided her toward the door while our bare feet pattered in synchronicity over the hardwoods. After she sat on the porch swing, I eased in beside her and slung my arm around her shoulders.

Emma peered up at me with a curious expression. We'd sat together on the couch, watching movies, the past two nights, but this was the first time I'd invaded her personal space. Instead of inching away, she subtly leaned closer.

"To perfect chocolate chip cookies," I said, lifting my wine.

"And superb steak." She smiled, clinking her glass to mine.

After we each took a sip, Emma tilted her head back and stared up into the sky.

"I've never seen so many stars before. They're beautiful."

The raw innocence and pure awe on her face, reflecting in the moonlight, slammed me like a gut-punch. Instead of looking away, my focus locked on her tantalizing lips, and I caved to the demand to taste her sweet mouth again.

"They're not as beautiful as you," I murmured, skimming a knuckle down her cheek.

Emma slowly peeled her gaze from the sky, then locked her big hazel eyes on mine. "You're pretty damn handsome yourself."

Like a summer storm, the surrounding air grew electric. Placing my wine glass on the table beside me, I lifted hers from her hand, then set it next to mine.

"Remember that kiss we shared at the bank?" I asked, staring at her inviting mouth.

"Yes."

"Me, too. I think about it all the time."

"You do?"

"Don't you?"

"All the time," she whispered.

"I want to kiss you again," I murmured, cupping her nape and aligning her lips beneath mine. "If you don't want me to, tell me to stop, darlin'."

"Don't stop. Please…don't stop."

Her breathless plea went straight to my cock. Though I ached to destroy her mouth, body, and soul, I simply slid my hand in her hair and cinched the short strands in a tight fist. As she sucked in a tiny gasp, I brushed a feather-soft kiss across her soft lips. Emma clutched my shirt, then leaned up and pressed her mouth to mine. The kitten-soft moan humming against my lips made my chest tighten and my control snap.

A low growl rumbled in the back of my throat as I claimed her in a raw, hungry kiss. Emma whimpered and parted her lips. I charged inside with a greedy groan, sweeping deeply over every crevice and swell while savoring the sweet wine staining her tongue.

Mouths fused together, our whimpers and moans melded with the symphony of crickets, tree frogs, and owls hooting in the dark. Unable to break the kiss, I ate at her like a man possessed while I snaked my other arm around her and drew her closer. She swallowed my needy growl as her pebbled nipples raked my chest, then wrapped her slick tongue around mine.

Lost in the feel of her soft body writhing against me and the wet heat of her wicked mouth, my plan completely unraveled.

I didn't give a shit.

All I cared about was getting inside the sensual woman feeding the wild, primitive flames of a fire I'd never felt before.

Mack had been right. Emma did have me tied up in knots. Not because she'd somehow snuck past my defenses and climbed deep inside my skin in a few short days. Not because I wanted to fuck her, though, I desperately did. But because, like a drug, she flowed through my veins.

Though I wasn't the kind of man who was easily rattled, it scared the shit out of me.

Before Aubrey died, I'd made a conscious decision to lock up my heart. Since I never made promises I couldn't keep, the idea of falling in love was too risky. Especially when I had no way of knowing if a bullet or bomb might have had my name on it. Instead, I focused on my job. I kept my shit wired tight and my unit alive while taking out dangerous insurgents behind enemy lines. Some of our missions were a walk in the park. Others, we barely survived.

After Aubrey's death, and the brutal stroke that took my mom, I'd locked my heart in a lead box to keep myself from experiencing the life-altering misery of losing someone I loved again.

I wasn't a monk. I'd fucked a lot of women over the past four years…mostly subs. But even then, before ever getting naked, I drew a hard line in the sand. They weren't allowed inside my life or my heart. It was safer that way.

There was nothing safe about Emma.

I had no clue why I was so fucking obsessed with her. All I knew was I needed to add more lead around my heart, and watch my six… *after* I made her shatter, screaming my name.

With a nip and a tug, I grudgingly eased from Emma's mouth and lifted my heavy lids. The moonlight spilling over her beautiful face cast her in an ethereal glow. Her lips were red, swollen, and glistening. My heart clutched. She looked like a fucking angel.

Still clinging to my bicep, Emma whimpered and tossed her head back, granting me access to her milky-soft throat. Taking full advantage of the pale canvas before me, I dragged my lips, tongue, and teeth down her slender neck before flattening my tongue over the hammering pulse point at the base of her throat.

"Blade," she moaned, restlessly rocking her hips.

"What do you need, darlin'?"

"You. All of you," she breathlessly whispered, pinning me with hopeful hazel eyes.

Jenna Jacob

Heart racing, my mind swirled with all the dirty things I planned to do to her as I stood and scooped her from the swing. Emma tossed her arms around my neck as I clutched her tight to my chest. Letting my baser instincts take over, I crashed my mouth over hers, and poured all the passion roaring inside me into the kiss. Swallowing her needy, kitten-soft whimpers, I carried her inside the house and up the stairs.

Chapter Ten

Emma

Drowning me in fiery, urgent kisses, Blade's lips never left mine as he gently eased me onto his bed before following me down. Supporting his weight on his elbows, he lowered his hips...nestling his thick, hard erection between my legs. A jolt of arousal I'd never felt before surged through me. He swallowed my gasp and ground his massive cock against my aching pussy. My nipples strained and burned. Flames licked my spine. And my panties grew even wetter from the needy ache thrumming through me.

The sensations he conjured were taking over my body in ways I'd never felt before, but it wasn't enough. I needed more...needed to feel his hot, naked flesh on mine. Gripping Blade's T-shirt in both fists, I started dragging the cotton fabric up his back. He tore from my mouth with a growl and locked me with a disapproving glare.

"You're not in charge, darlin'. This is *my* bed. We play by *my* rules here. Understood?"

His stern, commanding tone sent ripples of lust quaking through me. It was as if he'd reached inside my mind and plucked out my favorite fantasy. If he did and said all the things I dreamed about while rubbing my clit in bed alone at night, I'd be putty in his hands.

"Yes, Sir," I whispered. "I'm sorry. Please...tell me what you want me to do."

Blade's muscles tensed. His nostrils flared. And fire leapt in his eyes. But when he clenched his teeth so hard his jaw ticked, I knew that was the answer he'd wanted to hear.

Or at least, I'd thought so, until he rolled off the bed and stood.

"W-what's wrong?" I stammered as panic pushed every ounce of arousal from my system.

"Not a damn thing," he replied with a dirty grin as he extended his hand.

Unsure what was happening, I slowly sat up and placed my trembling fingers in his palm.

His blue eyes narrowed as he helped me stand before gently stroking a knuckle down my cheek.

"Why'd you take my hand?" he asked, parting his legs, squaring his shoulders, and tucking his hands behind his back.

His regal posture sent tingles racing down my spine. "Because you reached out for me."

"I did." He smiled. "But that's not why you took it, little one."

Little one.

The first time he'd used the term, I'd foolishly taken offense. I now realized that from the moment we'd met, he'd tried to show me who he really was. He was showing me again. This time, I saw him crystal clear.

Not only was Blade a friendly rancher, benevolent savior, and promised protector, he was also the gloriously commanding and panty-melting Dominant...*Master Blade.*

His question's a trap. He's testing you, whispered the voice in my head.

Oh, he was. But every cell in my body was too busy drooling at the sight of his powerful posture to come up with a response. My gut told me the answer he sought was lifestyle related. Why else would he stand there looking all Dominant and shit? Determined not to keep him hanging, I quickly replayed the conversation we'd shared while sitting in traffic the day we'd met.

There's an easier way to learn about the lifestyle than taking notes.
There is? How?

I could teach you…After we get to know each other better, that is. A deep level of trust must be established first.

Sending up a silent prayer, I lifted my chin and raised my lashes. "I took it because I trust you."

He arched his brows. I didn't know if I'd impressed him, or if he thought I was insane.

"You've only known me three days, girl."

He thinks I'm insane. Great.

"True. But if you wanted to hurt me, you would have done it by now. You haven't. In fact, you've done the exact opposite. You've helped me in ways I'll never be able to repay."

"I don't want you to repay me."

"See? That's another reason I trust you."

You're a good man, Blade.

"Fair enough." He nodded thoughtfully, pursing his tempting lips. "Based on our conversation the other day, I know you're curious about the lifestyle. What I don't know is if you're simply curious, or if deep down you ache to taste it?"

My heart bounced off my ribs and my mouth went dry.

"Are y-you asking if I want to s-submit…t-to you?"

"I am," he replied in a low growl.

"Yes." The word flew off my tongue without an ounce of hesitation.

Fire flashed in his blue eyes again and his chest expanded. I had no clue what I was actually getting myself into, but it didn't stop my heart from soaring.

"Very well." Blade nodded. "We need to discuss rules, expectations, and limits. But first, I want you to strip and kneel for me."

A wrecking ball of modesty and embarrassment slammed through me. It was a hell of a lot easier reading about a sub stripping for her

Dom, than actually doing it in real life. Desperate for a fragment of courage, I closed my eyes and dragged in a ragged breath.

He's not my Dom, merely my teacher.

"Have you changed your mind?" he asked, dragging me from my thoughts.

"No. It's just…why can't we talk about rules and stuff now?"

"Because the only barrier I'll allow between us is a condom, little one."

Praying he wasn't expecting a sensual strip tease, I swallowed tightly and pinched the hem of my shirt with trembling fingers before yanking it off over my head. As it fluttered to the floor, Blade's gaze stilled on my breasts—rising and falling with each shallow breath—bulging from the cups of my new, sheer black lace bra.

Blowing out a soft breath, he raked a hungry gaze from one breast to the other. I couldn't help but notice my boobs weren't the only things bulging. The front of his jeans was too…quite impressively.

Dragging his eyes off my tits, he cleared his throat. "You bought that at the mall the other day, right?"

"Yes."

"The next time I take you shopping, I'm joining you in the dressing room, so you can model everything that touches your sexy skin for me," he growled with a lopsided grin.

His playful demeanor erased my insecurities.

"Is that so?" I countered, teasing him back.

"Most definitely." He nodded, then sobered. "Continue."

No longer hesitant or self-conscious, I peeled off my leggings. As I tossed them beside the shirt, the scent of my feminine arousal wafted in the air. Eyes locked on my matching thong—now saturated and clinging to my swollen folds—Blade prowled closer, dragging in a deep breath before licking his lips.

The sight of his wet tongue scraping his sinful mouth sent dirty fantasies dancing through my brain. If Blade wielded his tongue between my legs as magically as he did inside my mouth, he'd destroy me in seconds. Visions of coming undone all over his face singed my blood. Heat rolled up my body. My nipples grew impossibly tighter...throbbing in time with my drumming clit. Chills slid down my spine and another rush of slippery nectar spilled from my needy core.

"If you're attempting to try my patience or stalling for dramatic effect, *don't.*"

His fierce, formidable tone turned me inside out. Shaking the carnal fantasies from my mind, I released the flat, metal designer emblem clasped between my breasts. As the soft lace fluttered to the floor, he devoured my dark, beaded nipples with a hungry gaze.

A low growl of approval rumbled deep in his chest.

The bulge in his jeans grew exponentially larger.

As Blade prowled closer, lust lined his face and shimmered in his piercing blue eyes.

His taut, sinewy muscles strained as if trying to contain the beast I'd awakened within.

As I drank in the savage command rolling off his rugged body, a bold and brazen sense of empowerment filled me. Out of nowhere, Blade's words thundered through my head...

The submissive holds all the power.

I finally understood what he'd meant...understood it on a whole new level.

Blade wasn't my *Master* and never would be. Still, he was offering me a chance to live out my darkest fantasies. All he wanted...no, all he *needed* was me to trust him enough to place my control in the palm of his hands.

Though he'd told to me to forget everything I'd read about the lifestyle, I couldn't keep from skimming the pages in my mind. I knew he'd likely forgive me if I screwed up, but I didn't want to. I wanted to please him and bask in his Dominance...just once.

Sliding the thong off my hips, I branded the approval flickering in his eyes—adding it to the sound of his laughter, the thrill of his smile, the taste of his arousing kisses, and the masculine scent that clung to his skin—to memory, and tossed the sodden scrap of silk aside.

Without waiting for Blade's instruction, I dropped my chin and lowered my lashes, then knelt at his feet. Still drawing insight from fictional submissives, I spread my legs and placed the back of my hands on my thighs.

His muttered curse—teeming with approval—spilled over me. Fighting the urge to peer up at him for a sliver of validation, I willed the need away. I refused to fail my first test of submission.

Blade stepped away, taking the sight of his boots from my periphery. Thankfully, he didn't go far, simply circled me...silently inspecting me. Though I couldn't see him, I felt his commanding stare singeing my naked flesh.

"You learned this submissive pose from books?" he asked, breaking the deafening silence.

"Yes."

"I'm impressed. You look stunning, little one." The pride and smile in his voice made my heart soar. "Let's get down to rules, expectations, and limits, shall we?"

"Okay."

"Rule number one, you will address me as Sir tonight."

"Yes, Sir."

"I assume you've read about safewords?"

"Yes, Sir."

"Good. We'll come up with one for you in a minute. Rule number two is to use that safeword if you need it, without reservation or fear. Understood?"

"Yes...Sir."

"Very nice," he murmured. "Rule number three, you will communicate with me at all times. In order to protect your mental and physical well-being, I will often ask...*where are you*? If you're enjoying what I'm doing, say green. If you're not sure, but you don't want me to stop, say *yellow*. If you can't tolerate it, say *red*, or use your safeword. Think of a stop light...green, yellow, and red. Does that make sense?"

"Perfect sense, Sir," I replied without confessing I'd read about the method a hundred times.

"Repeat the colors and meanings, girl."

"Green is good. Yellow is meh...I can take a little more. And red is aww, hell no."

"Very good." He chuckled as he circled me again. "Since I have no intention of introducing you to the lifestyle with a hard scene, I won't bog you down with a ton of rules. But we do need to decide on a safeword. Do you have any suggestions?"

"What about...tornado?"

The burst of laughter rolling from the back of Blade's throat warmed me like the summer sun. "I think that's an excellent choice, little one. Tornado it is. All right, let's move on to limits. I'm going to toss out some terms. I want you to use the same color code we discussed a minute ago. Green if you're fine with it. Yellow if you're not sure. And red if it's a aww, hell no. But in addition, I want you to say yes if you've experienced it, or no, if you haven't. If you're not familiar with the term or don't know what it means, stop me. I'll explain. All right?"

Though he knew I had zero hands-on experience, confirming the fact by playing twenty questions filled me with dread.

"I'm warning you now, there will be a whole lot of nos. But yes, Sir, I understand."

"No worries. Bondage."

"Green. No."

"Spanking."

"Yellow. No."

"Blindfold."

"Green. No." I shook my head. "See? I told you."

"Stop being self-conscious, girl. I wasn't expecting to hear yes often."

His understanding warmed my heart and eased my angst.

"Sex."

"Green. Yes," I whispered as images of Blade driving the fat cock straining beneath his jeans in and out of my weeping pussy crowded my brain.

"Oral sex, both giving and receiving."

Biting back a pitiful moan, I could all but taste his thick cock pressing past my lips and filling my mouth.

"Super green, and yes," I said, trying not to squirm as my clit throbbed incessantly.

"It's a super green for me, too, little one," he confessed in a lurid whisper.

My pussy clutched at the thought of his masterful tongue swirling and stabbing my dripping core.

"Anal sex."

Suddenly, the obscene images in my brain vanished, and I tensed. "Umm…orange, and no."

"Orange?" he asked with a soft chuckle. "I assume that means you're somewhat curious about anal, but scared it will hurt, correct?"

"One hundred percent."

"What about butt plugs?"

"Orange, again, and no."

"Dildos and vibes."

"Green. Yes."

"Orgasm denial."

"Yikes. That sounds awful." The words spilled off my tongue before I could stop them.

"It's a very effective tool for punishment, little one."

"It definitely sounds like it. Umm…orange, and no."

"Hopefully, I won't have to use it tonight." He chuckled, then sobered. "What about clamps…nipple clamps?"

"Yellow. No."

Instead of tossing out another term, Blade squatted in front of me. Cupping my chin in his warm, wide palm, he tilted my head back, forcing my gaze. The pride stamping his face and shimmering in his eyes filled me with a strange sense of peace.

"I think I have enough to work with, for tonight," he announced, threading his fingers through mine before helping me stand. Blade led me to the bed and nodded for me to sit down. As I complied, he eased onto the edge of the mattress beside me. "Let's talk about expectations.

While I don't assume you'll submit perfectly, I do expect you to get out of your own head and try your best."

"I will, Sir."

"I know." A hint of a smile tugged his lips, but disappeared as his expression grew serious. "Now that I know some of your limits, I promise I won't push them tonight. Though, I don't anticipate hitting any hidden triggers, it could happen. If so, I expect to hear your safeword, loud and clear."

"Yes, Sir."

His brows furrowed in an almost painful expression. "One more thing before we go any further. I'm not your Master or your boyfriend. I'm simply giving you a taste of the submission you crave. Understood?"

In other words, he's not offering white lace and promises. Blade's nothing more than a Dom with benefits for a night, the voice in my head reminded.

"Yes, Sir. No strings. Got it." I nodded as a strange sense of disappointment echoed inside me.

The relief crawling across his face sent a million questions unfurling in my brain. I wasn't clairvoyant in any way, but I knew someone had hurt him...badly.

"What expectations do you have?" he asked.

"I-I don't really know what to expect, Sir. I'm trying to keep an open mind."

"That's exactly what I want you to do, little one." He smiled, then stood in front of the bed before me. "You may stand and undress me now, little one."

Chapter Eleven

Grant

Mentally cursing myself for not sticking to my original plan, I patiently waited for Emma to follow my first command. Confusion lined her face as she swallowed tightly and stood. When she stepped toward me, in all her luscious naked glory, I savored the sight of her creamy, white skin.

The glide of her slender legs.

The sway of her full, lush tits.

And the wet, wheat-colored curls shrouding her juicy cunt.

Though angst rolled off her in potent waves, Emma didn't hesitate. She simply gripped the hem of my tee and dragged it up over my head.

"Mercy," she murmured on a quivering sigh, skimming an indulgent stare over my chest and abs.

As she studied the numerous scars from the bullets, knives, and shrapnel of my former life, a concerned frown settled over her face. Staring at the mark on my shoulder, from a bullet I'd taken in Libya, she lightly traced her fingertip over the marred flesh. Sparks crawled

Jenna Jacob

up my spine, and the hum of arousal throbbing in my ears grew louder. When she lowered her hand to the thin line beneath my ribs, courtesy of a crazed mujahideen who tried to gut me in Afghanistan, I clenched my jaw.

Though I ached to feel her soft, slender hands on every inch of my body, I wasn't her lover. I was her teacher.

"Did I give you permission to touch me, girl?" I asked, clenching my jaw.

Emma snatched her hands back and lowered her lashes. "No, Sir. I'm sorry."

My balls drew tight and heavy.

The beast inside me, who wanted to claim every ounce of her innocent submission, roared.

My palms itched to turn her over my knee and punish her willful behavior. But deep down, I knew she didn't know better. I was simply looking for an excuse to get my hands on her lush ass.

You royally fucked up this time, asshole, chided the voice in my head.

I had. Instead of getting her drunk enough on wine to drop her defenses so I could interrogate her, I'd let my libido, and the endless ache to taste her surrender, run wild. To my surprise, Emma was far more willing to dip her toes into the dark and kinky waters than I'd imagined.

With her focus fixed on my straining erection, she freed the button of my jeans.

As Emma pinched the tab of my zipper, I gently clasped her wrist. "I go commando, girl."

She blankly nodded before her eyes widened in understanding. She swallowed tightly, then slid her hand down my pants, and protectively cupped my cock. The feel of her soft, slender fingers made my hips jerk and my dick lurch into her palm.

Emma quivered and slowly eased the zipper down her knuckles.

Yeah, I'd fucked up, but it was too late to turn back now.

There was no stopping the freight train of lust chugging through me. As she freed me from the strangling denim and lifted her hand away, I hissed as my cock sprang free. Emma's eyes grew wide as she reared back and gaped at my thick, weeping erection.

"Woah," she blurted, then swallowed tightly.

Normally, I'd punish a sub for such an outburst. But for obvious communication reasons, I hadn't instructed Emma not to speak. I'm glad I hadn't. Her reaction was a massive stroke to my ego.

Without thinking, she reached toward my throbbing cock.

"You don't have permission, little one," I reminded, forcing the words off my tongue while a double-edged sword shredded me.

I wanted to draw out the submissive hiding inside her, so Emma could finally embrace the freedom and glory she'd only read about. But the dizzying scent of her sweet cunt filling the air, and the sight of her lush, naked body, made me want to toss away all Dom/sub protocol and fuck her senseless.

No submissive...hell, no woman had ever made feel so reckless and out of control before.

She's not a sub, reminded the voice in my head.

Not yet.

Emma knelt and peeled the jeans down my legs. The skim of her soft knuckles raking my flesh tested my resolve even more. Clenching my jaw, I tamped down the wild lust pumping through my veins. I'd promised her a taste of submission, and that's exactly what I was going to give.

Mentally gripping my Dominance in a stranglehold, I stepped out of my jeans and strode across the room. Emma didn't move, didn't say a word, but I felt her eyes raking from the top of my head to the soles of my feet before I turned and sat on the wing-backed chair beside the window.

"Crawl to me, little one."

The anticipation shimmering in her big hazel eyes instantly dimmed.

"Y-you mean...like a *d-dog?*" she asked, contempt dripping off every word.

"*Are* you a dog?"

"No."

"No what?"

"No, Sir."

"Then what's the problem?"

"I-I don't...crawling across the floor is just..."

"Demeaning?"

"Yes...Sir."

"What if swallowing your pride and crawling to me made me happy? Would you still find it demeaning?"

"Honestly?"

"If anything comes out of your mouth that isn't honest, this all stops, girl."

"Then, yes. Extremely demeaning, Sir." When I smiled, she furrowed in confusion. "You mean, you're not mad or disappointed I don't want to crawl to you?"

"No. Why would I be? I respect *all* your limits."

"Thank you, Sir. May I walk to you?"

"No." Based on the startled look on her face, I knew my curt reply confused her even more.

Good. I needed Emma off-guard, on edge, and unsure what command I'd toss out next. It was the only way I could gauge her true feelings.

"Rise and sit on the edge of the bed...facing me, then lie back."

As she timidly complied and lowered onto the mattress—like an all-you-can-eat buffet—my cock jerked, and my mouth watered. The sight of her heaving breasts and stony nipples reaching toward the ceiling with the shallow breaths filling her lungs made me want to howl.

There were a million reasons why she shouldn't, but everything about the little liar turned me inside out. Like a moth to flame, my gaze froze on the golden, glistening curls shrouding her cunt.

Unable to stop myself, I stood and strode to the side of the bed. Her milky-white skin—all but begging to be marked with my teeth and seed—glowed against the steel-gray comforter.

Though her dark, short hair was pretty, I selfishly wished Emma's long, golden hair was spilling like a halo across my bed...or cinched in my tight fist. But as her big hazel eyes—filled with curiosity, unease, and arousal—wildly darted between my face and my weeping dick, I honestly didn't give a fuck what her hair looked like.

I only wanted her watching me, while I watched *her*.

Cupping the back of one calf, then the other, I placed Emma's feet flat on the mattress. Then I cupped her knees and slowly parted her legs. I watched a crimson blush climb her chest and stain her cheeks while filling my lungs with her heady musk. Swallowing the saliva pooling in my mouth, I struggled to keep from staring at her proffered pussy and blindly guided her hand to her hot cunt.

"Is your pussy wet?"

"Yes," she whispered.

"Wrong answer," I tsk'd. "It's not your pussy tonight, little one. It's *mine*." Drinking in the tremor quaking her body, I arched a brow. "I'll ask again…is your pussy wet?"

"No, Sir, but *yours* is," she replied, eyes dilating with arousal.

My chest tightened. She'd caught on quickly…almost too quickly. She might not like humiliation, but I'd bet the ranch she'd lose her mind with role play. As kinky scenarios crowded my brain, a drop of pre-come slid off my aching crest.

"Show me," I demanded.

Scraping my gaze down her silky flesh, I locked a hungry stare on her pink, swollen folds. She was dripping wet. Warring with the demand to dive between her legs and latch my mouth over her flowing slit, I wrapped a fist around my cock and slowly started stroking.

Emma licked her lips as she watched my hand glide up and down my angry shaft.

"See what you do to me, little one? See how hard you make me?" I taunted. "Show me what I do to you. Spread those pretty, pouty lips and let me see how wet that juicy little cunt is for my fat cock."

Her eyes flared as she exhaled an excited whimper.

"Bladeeee," she moaned.

I didn't correct her for using my name. I was too busy drinking in the desperation lining her face and ringing in my ears.

I'd definitely tripped a trigger…a good one this time.

Jenna Jacob

Sweet, little Emma, the rich, pampered princess posing as my sister, gets turned on by dirty words. Oh, this is gonna be fun.

"I don't like repeating myself, girl," I growled, landing a light slap to her sodden cunt.

My cock jerked.

The feel of her coarse wet curls was as electrifying as the sound of her sharp gasp.

The only thing I liked better than sinking balls deep inside a lush, juicy pussy was spanking it. I didn't have many kinks, but landing an attention-grabbing spank against a woman's hot, wet, swollen folds flipped all my switches.

"Show me. Now!" I growled.

Emma mewled and parted her engorged folds...opening herself up for me, like a beautiful orchid. She wasn't wet, she was gushing. Her slick nectar was spilling onto the comforter like a river, leaving a dark, erotic puddle beneath her.

Shoving down the ache to coat my fingers in her slick cream and lick them clean, I locked my gaze on her clit. Her swollen nub, fully exposed from its protective hood—like a ripe pomegranate seed—sent a trail of pre-come dripping off my crest and down my fingers.

Raking my tongue along my teeth with a low, hungry growl, my mouth watered.

I couldn't wait to draw her plump, ready-to-burst berry between my lips while filling and stretching her narrow, wet slit with my fingers.

"Play with my flowing little cunt, girl. Show me how you make yourself feel good. Show me how your make yourself come," I whispered hoarsely, lifting a finger from her folds before guiding it back and forth over her pebbled clit.

Emma jerked, and gasped, and held me with a lust-soaked stare as I continued scraping a fingertip over her sensitive nub. The heat from her simmering core enveloped my hand and crawled up my wrist.

"I want to fucking fist you so bad," I growled.

"F-fist me?" she whimpered.

"You don't know what fisting is, do you?" I asked, fingers tingling. Emma shook her head. "It's exactly what it sounds like, little one. I start by working a finger inside you, then another, and another... thinning and stretching your tight little cunt."

When Emma shuddered and slowly rocked her hips, I knew my words had come alive in her mind. Knew she was fantasizing about my big hand invading her hot, wet pussy. I could practically feel her slick, silky walls softening and expanding around my fingers.

Cock screaming and dripping like a fucking sieve, I gripped my shaft harder and swallowed the ball of lust lodged in my throat, then continued.

"When I finally squeeze my last finger inside you, I'll tuck my thumb against my palm, and slowly press in and out of your flowing, wet cunt, inching deeper and deeper...filling and stretching you, while I fuck you with my long, thick fingers. You'll come, and keep coming...gushing all over my hand as I work my wide knuckles into your clutching core."

A full body tremor quaked through her. My balls tightened, and my heart raced.

"But I don't stop, little one. Oh, no, I keep shoving my hand inside you...all the way to my wrist. Then ball my hand into a fist and fuck you mindless as you come, screaming my name."

"Oh, god," she whimpered, trembling and softly panting.

"You'd like that, wouldn't you?"

"Yes," she moaned.

"Yes, what?" I growled.

"Yes, Sir."

"Good girl. Keep going," I instructed, grudgingly lifting my hand away to keep from living out the fantasy I'd just painted with my words.

Emma continued rubbing her clit, raptly watching me stroke my cock. Mesmerized by the pleasure playing over her face, and her flowing pussy, the need to hear and see her shatter grew like a crushing tsunami.

Fisting myself faster and harder, I lifted my free hand and skimmed my fingers up the insides of her silky thighs. A needy moan spilled off her lips as the muscles in her legs bunched and quivered.

I'd been with several women in my life, but never one as sensually responsive, and erotically uninhibited, as Emma.

She made my blood boil.

Made me wish for things I'd vowed to never have in my life.

Still, I couldn't turn down the chance to gorge on her forbidden fruit.

"I can't wait to latch my mouth over your hot little cunt," I bit out in a gravelly growl. "Can't wait to stab my tongue in your glistening slit and drown on all that sweet juice flowing from inside you."

Whimpering, Emma's fingers moved faster, punishing her clit.

"You'd like, that wouldn't you…like to ride my tongue and come all over my face?"

"Yes, Sir," she mewled, bucking her hips against her busy finger.

"I'd like that, too, my sweet slut."

Her eyes widened in shock as another full-body tremor rolled through her. Fearing she'd taken the word as an insult, I was about to explain it was a term of endearment when flames ignited in her eyes. A quivering cry tore from the back of her throat while she thrust her other hand to her pussy, plunging a slender finger deep inside.

My mouth watered. My balls churned, and my cock grew impossibly harder.

"Oh, you're a dirty little slut. You like hearing my filthy words, don't you?" I taunted, savoring the desperate sounds rolling from her throat, and the shameless nod of her head. "You're so fucking gorgeous. That's it, my naughty little slut, finger fuck my hot, juicy cunt. Fuck it fast and deep."

Emma stabbed another finger inside her narrow slit. The stream of needy whimpers pouring from her lips fused with the sexual energy humming in the air. It was all I could do to keep from shoving her hands away and taking over…for hours.

"Are you pretending those fingers are my cock, girl?"

"Yessss," she hissed, wildly bucking her hips.

The sight of her furiously strumming her clit and fingering her wet slit shredded my resolve.

I'd never been so fucking turned on in my life.

"You want my fat cock inside you...filling and stretching your hungry little cunt?"

"Oh...yesss. Pleaseeee," she wailed.

"No," I growled, forcing the word off my tongue. "You haven't earned it yet."

Her wail of frustration went straight to my balls.

"You haven't come for me yet. But you're going to. You're going to come hard for me, aren't you, my sexy, dirty slut?"

"Yes. Yes. Yes," she chanted, whimpering breathlessly.

Me too, gorgeous. Way too soon, if I'm not careful.

Careful?

Why start now?

I'd been anything but careful since meeting the wild, erotic beauty writhing and keening in desperation before me.

Like an idiot, I'd invited the beautiful con artist under my roof... and now into my bed.

Ever since I'd watched Emma masturbating in the shower, I'd been possessed with an inhuman demand to drive balls deep inside her and claim her. She was like a drug constantly pumping through my veins. And though it scared the living fuck out of me, I was completely addicted.

Determined to fuck her out of my system, I released my cock with a growl and grabbed a condom from the nightstand drawer beside me. After sheathing my throbbing dick, I made another careless decision and knelt in close beside the edge of the bed.

Gazing at the frantic rhythm of Emma's glossy fingers driving in and out of her flowing slit, I filled my lungs with her erotic pussy perfume as her urgent keening cries echoed in my ears. I bit back a depraved snarl, then dragged my lips and tongue up the insides of her silky, straining thighs. Her coarse curls tickled my nose, and the wet heat of her sweltering pussy singed my face as I nipped the sweet flesh around her gyrating mound.

"Please, Bla...Sir, please," she begged.

"Please what, my needy little slut?"

"Lick me. Suck me. Fuck me with your tongue, your cock, your fingers...*anything*. Just please...put out this fire. I-it's too hot."

Like a cyclone, her bold and desperate, breathless plea twisted and swirled inside me, obliterating my resolve.

With a feral roar, I brushed her hands away and wedged mine beneath her ass cheeks. Lifting Emma's hips off the bed, I latched my mouth over her juicy, red swollen cunt. My tastebuds exploded as I sucked, lapped, and gorged on her tart, flowing nectar.

"Yes...yes," she panted.

Sinking her hands in my hair, Emma brazenly grinded her pussy against my face as she chased the bliss building inside her.

"More...more. Oh, pleasseee...moreeee."

Like a shot of morphine, her anguished wail of need wended through my veins.

I wanted more, too.

Wanted to prolong her sweet suffering.

Wanted to keep Emma riding the razor's edge as long as possible.

Purposely steering clear of her pebbled clit, I stabbed my tongue deep inside her quivering core...lashing and scraping her wet, velvety walls.

"H-help...m-me," she shrieked.

When she lowered her hand and tried to wedge her fingers beneath my lips to strum her clit, I tore from her succulent cunt with a feral roar. I pinned her with an angry glare, but she couldn't see past her unfocused glassy stare. No problem. There was more than one way to get her attention.

Lowering her ass to the bed, I raised my hand and landed a sharp slap to her glistening cunt. Her hot, slick juices splattered and coated my hand, sending fingers of lightning splintering through my system. Unable to stop myself, I spanked her saturated slit again.

Crying out in bliss, Emma arched her hips high in the air, silently begging for more.

What. The. Actual. Fuck?

My cock lurched.

My heart clutched.

The air froze in my lungs.

She's fucking perfect, roared the beast inside me.

"P-please...m-more." She bucked as tears spilled from the corners of her eyes.

Emma's tears, and my duty as a Dom, kept me from focusing on the shocking and terrifying fact she ached for my specific kink.

Determined to give her what she needed...what we both needed, I bestowed a succession of stinging slaps. She arched into each spank, crying out in ecstasy as pleasure and pain rippled across her face while her body quaked and quivered.

As Emma panted, screamed, and murmured incoherently, I watched her pretty pink pussy darken to a ball-churning shade of crimson.

"Come for me, my dirty, little pain slut," I growled before stabbing three fingers deep inside her blistering cunt.

Launching her hips higher, Emma's muscles turned to granite. A guttural groan tore from her throat. And her narrow, slick walls clutched at my digits as I stretched and filled her.

Fighting the urge to keep her suspended between agony and ecstasy, my screaming cock and selfish greed won the war. Wrapping my lips around her stony clit, I drew it deep inside my mouth and lashed the engorged pebble with my tongue.

I felt the brutal orgasm roar through her and swallow her whole as Emma bore down on my face and fingers, and screamed my name.

The beast within bellowed as her silky walls rapidly convulsed around my fingers.

Fire raced down my spine and coalesced in my balls.

Tearing my mouth from her throbbing clit and my fingers from the liquid lava of her clutching cunt, I stood and gripped Emma's waist. She was still quaking and coming as I dragged her to the center of the bed, kneed her legs apart, and slammed my cock into her tight, contracting core.

Her eyes grew wide, and her scream—a combination of surprise and pain—vibrated through me as I stilled inside her gripping tunnel. Engulfed by her blistering heat, my eyes rolled to the back of my head.

"T-too big...too full...t-too much. I-it b-burn," she panted, wriggling beneath me.

I clenched my jaw and dragged my cock back, keeping my bulbous crest inside her.

"Yes...yes," she whispered.

"I've got you, little one," I murmured, reaching between us before gently strumming her berry-hard clit.

Emma quivered and purred, then rocked her hips. Watching the pleasure erase all traces of pain from her face, I took my time and slowly fed inch after throbbing inch back inside her softening core.

"Did you enjoy your first taste of submission, sweet slut?" I whispered.

A sated smile tugged the corners of Emma's mouth as she blinked the smoky haze of orgasm from her eyes. "Yes, Sir. It was...amazing. But...we're not done yet, are we?" she asked lowering her gaze to my cock gliding in and out of her sweltering core.

Suddenly, an idea stormed my brain. Blinded by the opportunity before me, I refused to ponder the fallout.

Cock screaming in outrage, I clenched my jaw and peered down at her, shaking my head. "Your lesson is over for today, but we're not finished. Not by a long shot...*Emma*."

Panic replaced her soft, sated expression.

"Y-you...y-you know who I am?" she stammered as every muscle in her body tensed.

"Oh, I definitely know who you are, *Emma Tolliver Bishop*. What I don't know is why you're pretending to be *Aubrey Elizabeth Holden*," I bit out, dragging my cock in and out of her heavenly pussy.

"Get off me," Emma barked, uselessly shoving my chest. "Stop fucking me."

"Oh, no, darlin'. That's not how this is gonna work. See, I'm gonna keep sliding my cock in and out of your hot little body...make you shatter over and over again, until I finally fuck the truth out of you."

Chapter Twelve

Emma

No. No. *This isn't happening.*

Trapped on an elevator ride from heaven to hell, my heart leapt to my throat, and my stomach bottomed out. Panic pumped through my veins, and tears stung my eyes, but I blinked them back. There was no way in hell I was going to let Blade see me cry.

He'd known. The whole time he'd known exactly who I was and didn't say a freakin' word. Why? Why the hell had he chosen now—with his thick cock inside me—to say something?

Because he's playing you, the voice in my head barked.

And doing a damn good job of it because I'm letting him.

No more!

Welcoming the anger building inside me, I tried to ignore the sweet hum still singing through my body. Clearly, my hormones hadn't gotten the memo I was sleeping with the enemy. That, or they were still in a coma from the massive orgasm he'd wrecked me with. Either way, it didn't matter. I let my dented pride and mounting fury take the wheel. My libido could catch up later.

"In your dreams," I bit out, defiantly lifting my chin. "If you think I'm going to lie here and let you rape me, you're out of your fucking mind. Get your dick out of me, and let me up, now, Blade."

A deviant chuckle rumbled deep in his chest as a cocky smirk tugged his lips. "Forgive me, I haven't formally introduced myself to you yet, darlin'. My bad. Blade's my club name. My real name is Grant…Grant *Holden.*

Mind seized by a powerful vacuum, I was suddenly sucked back in time.

Aubrey burst through the door of our dorm room wearing a dazzling smile.

"You aced your test, didn't you?" I asked, closing my textbook and hopping off my bed.

"Like a boss," she beamed, dancing in a little circle.

"And you were worried," I drawled, rolling my eyes, catching sight of the envelope on my bed. "Oh, I almost forgot. You got another letter from Grant."

Aubrey let out a delighted squeal and snatched the envelope from my fingers before frantically tearing it open and plopping down on my bed.

"Come on, let's see what dangerous crap my big brother's doing now."

Joining her, I leaned over Aubrey's shoulder—as usual—and read the bold, masculine written words.

"Oh, no. He's in the hospital again," she groaned.

"Relax. He says it's just a flesh wound." I grinned, pointing to the little sketch of a man in armor with no arms or legs from the classic Monty Python movie.

"You don't know my brother. His guts could be dragging behind him in the middle of the desert and he'd still say it was just a flesh wound," Aubrey groaned.

"Well, he's obviously healthy enough to send you the letter. That's all that matters, right?"

"Yes." She smiled and squeezed my hand. "Oh, Em, I wish you could meet Grant someday. He's the most amazing man on the planet. You'd instantly fall in love with him."

Fall in love with him.

Fall in love with him.

As her words gonged through my mind, my heart clutched and my stomach pitched.

I already had, at least, partially.

Another burst of panic rolled through me as Blade, err...Grant rocked his hips, dragging his masterful cock through my still tingling core. Struggling to dismiss the goosebumps peppering my flesh, I clenched my jaw and shot him a furious glare. "Why didn't you tell me you were Aubrey's brother?"

"Why are you pretending to be my sister?" he countered, thrusting deeper, lighting up the bundle of nerves beneath my pubic bone.

"Get the fuck off me, Grant. I'll tell you everything you want to know, just...not like this."

"Give me one good reason why I should believe you, darlin'?" He arched his brows.

"Because I haven't lied to you about anything else since you brought me here."

"You mean since I *kidnapped* you outside the fucking house Aubrey. And. I. Grew. Up. In?" he asked, emphasizing his last few words with deliberate and spine-bending thrusts of his glorious, thick cock.

Like sandpaper and silk, guilt and lust collided inside me.

"Yes," I hissed, swallowing my pride. "Now get the fuck off me."

A mischievous flicker skipped across his blue eyes. "I already told you. You're not in charge, darlin'. This is *my* bed. We play by *my* rules here."

"I'm not playing anymore."

"You sure?" he asked, flashing a dirty grin before he dipped his head and latched his sinful mouth over my left nipple.

I tried not to respond, but when he pulled on the aching stiff peak —with the perfect amount of suction—and pressed it to the roof of his hot mouth, my body betrayed me. While shards of lightning ignited my clit, I rocked my hips against his driving shaft as a needy whimper escaped my lips.

"Mmm," he groaned, releasing my aching peak with an audible pop. "I knew you'd change your mind."

With a sexy wink, he lashed my glistening peak with his tongue, sending another sizzling current of lightning to my throbbing nub. Unable to quell the tremor quaking through me, I didn't know whether to scream or moan.

"Why are you pretending to be Aubrey?" he asked again, circling my other nipple with the pad of his finger.

"It doesn't matter," I murmured, shoving at his big body, wriggling beneath him—not in sexual splendor, but self-preservation. "Please. Get off me. I'll pack my things and go."

"Oh, it matters. It fucking matters a whole lot," he said, narrowing his eyes. "You're not going anywhere until I get some answers, princess."

"Don't call me that," I spat.

Grant arched a brow and thrust balls deep inside me. "Let me get this straight. You love it when I call you my dirty, little slut, but hate me calling you princess?"

My cheeks burned. Like fire and ice, lust and embarrassment swirled through me.

"Shut up. Just shut up, and get off me."

"Not until you start giving me some answers, my dirty, little slut," he growled, dragging his thick shaft and swollen crest toward my fluttering opening.

"Then start asking them already, and get off me," I huffed, inwardly cursing my traitorous hormones.

"I have. *Twice.* Answer the fucking question," he snarled, thrusting his hard cock deep again.

His maddening, salacious rhythm, and piercing blue eyes—sending sparks pinging through me—made it nearly impossible to rub two brain cells together.

"Stop fucking me so I can think," I barked.

"Not a chance, darlin'. I'm going to peel away your layers of lies… one stroke at a time."

As a brutal tremor quake through me, my pussy clutched.

Fire flashed in his eyes.

"Answer me," he demanded in a gravelly growl.

Sinking his teeth into his bottom lip, Grant savagely shuttled in and out of my quivering core.

"I needed a new identity," I shouted.

"Why?" he asked, slowing to the same seductive and vexing rhythm as before.

Realizing there was no way to escape his wicked and unorthodox interrogation, I shoved my pride down deep and sucked in a ragged breath.

"Because I had to run away."

"From?"

Doing my best to block the arousing ebb and flow of his steely cock, I fixed my stare on the etched glass globes of the ceiling fan above the bed.

"I'm probably going to be breaking dozens of FCC laws, but—"

"You already broke a few federal ones by cashing that check," he stated.

My stomach twisted as I pinned Grant with a panicked stare. "I have?"

Not missing a single spine-bending thrust, a lopsided grin tugged his lips. "Don't worry, I'm not going to call the feds and turn you in. It'll be our little secret, okay?"

I swallowed tightly and nodded.

"Continue," he instructed in that buttery Dom voice.

Continue? I couldn't remember where I'd left off.

"FCC," Grant prompted, as if reading my mind before nipping the tip of my nipple.

"Oh, right," I breathlessly nodded, forcing myself to focus on the ceiling fan again. "My parents are, or were…I'm not sure what's happening since I left, in the middle of a huge merger with Fairchild Media. I didn't know, until recently, they'd spent years separately growing their empires, secretly planning to merge them one day, and corner the media market. If the merger goes through, my father and Ted Fairchild will pocket an obscene amount of money in new stock acquisitions alone."

Pausing, I drew in a deep breath. The sparks assaulting my system from the ceaseless scrape of Grant's pubic bone against my clit were ramping my hormones up again.

"So, you ran away because you're going to inherit more money than God someday?"

His incredulous tone doused the flames licking my spine like a fire hose.

"No. I ran away because my parents were forcing me to marry a criminal."

"I'm not sure how to tell you this, but you're a grown woman. Nobody can force you to do anything...unless you let them."

I knew he wouldn't understand. How could he? Grant hadn't grown up in the cold, calculating, and manipulative environment I had. He'd been raised by the same warm, loving, and supportive parents Aubrey had adored with her whole heart.

"Oh, really?" I quipped dryly, deflecting the pangs of envy seeping inside me. "You're forcing me to fuck you right now."

Grant reared back and shook his head. "I'm not forcing you to do anything, my dirty little slut. You're *letting* me."

"Only because I can't shove your big body off me. How many times have I told you to get your cock out of me?"

"Several."

"And yet, you're still plowing in and out of my pussy, like you own it. Why?"

"Because you haven't used your safeword yet, darlin'."

It took all the willpower I possessed to keep from slapping the cocky smirk off his face while white-hot flames of rage scorched my soul.

"Tornado, you fucking asshole," I bit out between clenched teeth.

"See? That wasn't so hard now, was it?" he taunted, slowly

dragging his thick cock from my core before climbing off the bed, taking all his sinful body heat and erotic sensual scent with him.

Mourning the unfamiliar emptiness in my core, as well as my soul, I sat up and watched him stride to the bathroom before peeling the condom off his beautiful, thick cock with a growling hiss.

Oh, hell. He never came.

My heart sank. Grant's magical tongue and fingers had destroyed me with the most intense orgasm of my life, but he never finished himself off. Why? Why hadn't he orgasmed before he dropped the mega-ton bombshell and called me Emma?

Why do you care? He's done nothing but play you since day one, chided the voice in my head.

Clinging to my fraying threads of anger, I bounded off the mattress and gathered up my clothes as Grant strolled from the bathroom carrying a white, fluffy robe.

"Here, put this on," he commanded, thrusting the garment toward me.

"Sorry, *Sir*. We're not playing that game anymore."

"No, we're not. But if you ever call me an asshole again, I'll turn you over my knee and paddle your ass crimson, *little one*."

"You won't get the chance," I said, defiantly lifting my chin. "I'm leaving."

"No, you're not. Not until you finish telling me why you stole Aubrey's identity."

"What are you gonna do? Tie me up?"

"If I have to." He shrugged. "It's not my first choice. I'd rather we sit down and talk like adults, but…it's up to you."

"Fine. Let me get dressed, and we'll talk," I said, shoving the robe back at him.

"No. Put the robe on, Emma."

"Why? Why can't I just get dressed?"

"Because you're less likely to run away wearing nothing but a robe."

"Trust me. If it wasn't pitch black outside, and I wasn't in the middle of nowhere, I'd run away from you naked."

"I'll get the rope," he announced flatly.

Clearly, I didn't convince him enough to change his mind.

Stubborn asshole.

"Fine," I growled, yanking the robe from his fingers.

As I tugged it on and angrily tied the sash, Grant dragged on a pair of sweatpants. After carefully tucking his red, mouthwatering, and still fully engorged cock beneath the gray fabric, he waved an arm toward the door.

"Where are we going?"

"To the porch, so we can finish our wine, look at the stars, and... talk."

As Grant silently followed me down the stairs, I mentally slapped a thick shield of armor around me.

Fully encased and ready for battle, I stepped onto the porch. The air had grown cooler. As I plopped down on the swing, I was grateful for the warmth the robe provided, but would never tell him that.

After topping off my glass, he handed me my wine. Instead of sitting beside me, Grant leaned his butt on the edge of the white porch railing across from me. Regarding me over the rim of his glass, he took a gulp, then cleared his throat.

"Before you continue, I need to tell you I've spent hours researching you. There wasn't a single website or social media post about you and a wedding."

I took a sip of wine, then flashed him a brittle smile. "You can come right out and call me a liar. I don't care." Actually, I did. His insinuation cut like a knife, but I refused to let him see me bleed. "Except, I'm *not* lying. Somewhere out there you might find the announcement on some obscure website, but don't count on it. My father and Ted Fairchild...father of Wesley Fairchild, the felonious, disgusting little weasel I was supposed to marry, scrubbed the web clean. I know, because I looked several times on my way to Texas."

"They can do that?"

"They have the power and money to do anything they want. That's why I ran."

"Tell me more about the felonious, disgusting little weasel." Grant smirked.

"Ugh," I grunted. "I'm sure there are women out there who find him, or rather his fat bank account, attractive, but not me. He's a clone of his father—skinny, pale, short, and dull. He doesn't eat meat. He has zero sense of humor. He hates sunshine. Hates to travel. Hates pretty much everything but strip clubs, Scotch, and hanging out with his frat buddies from college. We have absolutely nothing in common."

"Does he hate Twilight Zone marathons?" Grant quipped.

Hiding his grin behind the rim of his glass, he couldn't mask the knowing sparkle in his eyes. The same sparkle that left a giant dent in my armor.

"He loathes television, which makes no sense for a future heir of a multi-media empire." I shook my head and scoffed. "Four weeks before the wedding, Wesley's mother, Lydia, hosted a bridal shower for me. Right before everyone was supposed to arrive, she asked me to find Wesley so he could greet the guests. Being an inch taller than him, he loathed me towering over him in heels, so I'd purposely worn a pair of flats. Little did I know that decision had been nothing short of divine intervention. The shoes didn't make a sound on the hardwoods as I strolled to his office. I was inches from the doorway when I heard him talking on the phone with a high-ranking congressman about the merger. Wesley's tone was so…menacing, the hairs on the back of my neck stood up. I'd never heard him sound like that before. Instead of waltzing into his office, I pressed my back against the wall and listened."

Memories of that terrifying, life-altering day rolled through my brain like a bad horror movie.

"He offered to wire the congressman ten million dollars to an offshore account if he'd pressure the FCC Advisory Committee to vote in favor of the merger. When the congressman balked, Wesley started threatening the man."

An icy chill ran down my spine.

The glass of wine in my hand trembled.

"What was the threat?" Grant asked, squatting down, eye-level in front of me, before lifting the quivering glass from my fingers.

"He gave the congressman a choice," I said, staring at my hands. "He could either go along with their *arrangement*, or Wesley would k-kidnap his daughter and *use* her like he did other *little girls*. She's only six-years-old, Grant," I softly wailed, wiping a tear from my cheek.

The gut-wrenching terror I'd locked deep down inside me that day broke free. Panic and fear careened through my system, leaving a trail of violent tremors quaking through me.

"Of course, the congressman agreed after that. But before Wesley ended the call, he warned the man if he told anyone, or if anyone found out about the payoff, he'd k-kill them all."

When I lifted my head and peered up at Grant, his eyes were dull and lifeless. Every muscle in his body had turned to stone, and the potent waves of rage rolling off him slammed me like a tsunami.

Suddenly, the glass in his hand shattered.

I jolted and yelped, then jumped off of the swing.

"Stay back," he snarled. "You're barefoot, and there are shards all over the place."

"But your hand," I said, nodding to the blood blossoming on his palm.

"It's just a flesh wound." He smirked as he stood and cinched his non-bloody hand around my waist.

Lifting me off the porch, he stepped over the glass and carried me to the welcome mat before easing me onto my feet. I opened the door, then followed him into the kitchen. Grant pointed to a cabinet that contained a first aid kit. I quickly retrieved the kit, then sat at the table. While I laid out the medical supplies, Grant stood at the sink, rinsing the blood from his hand and plucking out glass fragments.

When he joined me at the table, I cupped his fingers and gently dabbed the blood while picking out the remaining slivers with the tweezers.

"Why on earth did you crush that glass with your hand?"

"It was an accident." He shrugged.

"I'm sorry you cut yourself, but I'm glad I finally get the chance to pay you back and bandage *you* this time."

"Stop being so worried about paying me back. I don't want that."

"What do you want?"

"Exactly what you're finally giving me, darlin'...honesty."

"I'm sorry I didn't tell you the truth from the beginning."

"You're telling me now, that's all that matters." A soft smile tugged his lips before he sobered. "I need to know *why*, after finding out what he was capable of, you agreed to marry Wesley."

It was going to be impossible for Grant to understand, but I had to try if I ever wanted him to forgive me for pretending to be Aubrey... which I truly did.

"She'd spend hours telling me about you, your parents, about growing up in Richardson, and about how much you loved each other."

Grant nodded and swallowed tightly as sadness filled his eyes.

"I hounded Aubrey relentlessly to tell me stories about your family."

"Why?"

"Because I grew up without a morsel or a half-a-grain of sand of the love and affection your family shared. When I was a teenager, I started secretly reading risqué romance novels. I used to pretend I'd been conceived in the heat of passion, in a room bathed in candlelight, with rose petals on the bed, and a standing, silver ice bucket teeming with champagne. But the cold, hard reality is I'm probably nothing more than an unfortunate accident."

"Why would you say that?"

"Because my parents never gave me any reason to think otherwise. My whole life they've been totally self-absorbed, cunningly manipulative, and incapable of loving anything but amassing money, maintaining appearances, and clinging to the upper wrung of the elite social ladder. Since the day I was born, they groomed me, heaped unrealistic expectations on me, manipulated and controlled me. I tried to be what they wanted...tried to earn their approval, but I was never good enough. I was always so defeated I didn't know how to break the cycle or fight back. I never knew my own mind, power, or strength until they backed me into a corner and demanded I marry Wesley."

As Grant nodded in understanding, relief swept through me.

Maybe he truly understood why I'd tried to reinvent myself as Aubrey.

Seconds later, my hope faded when his brows furrowed and he peered up at me. "You're telling me no one's ever loved you before?"

"One person did." I swallowed the ball of emotion lodged in my throat.

"Who?"

"Aubrey. She loved me like a sister, and I loved her right back. She was my best friend...the only *real* friend I ever had." My voice cracked, and a tear slid down my cheek.

"I loved her, too," Grant whispered thickly as he reached up and caught my tear on the pad of his thumb. "Listen, Emma, I'm sorry I pulled that asshole move on you upstairs. I know you're probably still pissed at me, but you can't leave. Not until the merger goes through. It's too dangerous."

My heart swelled, and my chest tightened.

"I'm not pissed at you anymore, Grant. Embarrassed, yes, but not pissed." He didn't bother trying to hide his relief and blew out a billowing, cheek-puffing breath. "But I don't even know if they're still trying to push the merger through. I was supposed to marry Wesley in order to secure the commission's vote. Well, that and the ten million dollars."

"I've got connections in DC. I'll find out the status. Just promise me you'll stay so I can protect you."

The angst of packing my things and leaving, of spending days, weeks, maybe even years looking over my shoulder, vanished. I would definitely take Grant up on his offer. Who better to protect me than Aubrey's bad-assed brother and former SEAL? Still, I was floored, He wasn't kicking me to the curb for pretending to be his sister. Which begged the question...

"Why is protecting me so important to you?" I asked, smearing the ointment over the cuts on his hand. When he didn't answer, I glanced up. The guilt reflecting in his face and eyes broke my heart. "Oh, Grant," I whispered. "You couldn't have saved her. None of us could. It was a random—"

"Act of violence. Yeah, I know. I memorized the police report."

"Then you also know—"

"I know that cocksucker raped and tortured her before he killed her. I also know he suffered tenfold for what he did to Aubrey."

The hairs on the back of my neck stood on end. "How do you know that?"

He pinned me with a *bitch, please* expression and quirked a brow. "My sister told you what I did for a living back then, right?"

"Yes. Aubrey shared every letter you sent with me."

"Then it should come as no surprise I'm the sadistic prick who slit his throat when I was through exacting my revenge and listening to his screams."

Chapter Thirteen

Grant
Friday, July 28th

"Keep those hands behind your back, girl. You do *not* have permission to touch me," I warned, peering down at Emma bobbing her hot, unholy mouth over my swollen cock.

It had been a week since she'd agreed to stay until the merger was finalized. I'd been relieved and stupidly ecstatic. While I still wasn't thrilled she'd assumed Aubrey's identity, I no longer thought Emma a thief, but a victim of her parent's warped expectations and heartless inability to love. She certainly wasn't a victim now.

Through sheer will, determination, and an impressive amount of creative planning, Emma had escaped their cruel world. The sight of her discovering who she was, deep down inside, was like watching a bird freed from its cage take flight.

Though still vigilant about protecting her, after Emma spilled her truths, I let my guard down around her. It surprised me, but also scared me a little, how quickly we'd fallen into an easy routine. Even Mack busted my balls, saying I'd been in a better mood since my *new wife* moved in. Yeah, it chafed, but he wasn't wrong. I *was* happier…more centered and content.

It hadn't all been smooth sailing. After stupidly confessing to the torture and death I'd inflicted on Aubrey's killer, Emma seemed more cautious and noticeably distant around me. Determined to re-earn her trust and prove she had no reason to fear me, I used the lifestyle to redirect her focus. To my delight, and the delight of the come now boiling in my churning balls, it worked like a charm.

The sunrise inching over the horizon beamed through the window, casting her beautiful face and lush naked body in a golden glow. On her knees, staring up at me with a smoky, lust-filled stare, she looked like a fucking angel straight from heaven.

But looks were deceiving. Prowling beneath her innocent facade was a seductive, uninhibited, sexual siren. Lucky for me, I'd discovered all the naughty buttons and nasty words that turned her inside out.

"That's it, my dirty, little slut. Worship my cock. Suck it all the way down your filthy throat. Gag and cry. We both know you want to. You love choking on my cock," I growled, scraping my thumb down her hollowed cheek while filling my lungs with her spicy arousal saturating the room.

With a needy whimper, Emma complied. Leaning forward, she devoured every hard inch before burying her nose in my coarse curls. Her throat convulsed, compressing and surrounding my fat crest in her wet, velvety softness. Sparks ricocheted down my spine, but the tears spilling down her cheeks set my blood on fire.

From day one, my gut told me Emma's mouth was made for sin. I'd been right. Two nights ago, when she'd first wrapped her plump lips around my cock, I was ready to sell my soul to the devil and chain her to my bed until the end of time.

Dragging her mouth off my dick, Emma gazed at my angry, glistening cock while gulping air into her lungs. Her red, swollen lips shimmered in the sunlight as she rocked her hips, trying to alleviate the needy burn assaulting her neglected clit. A mischievous flicker skipped across her eyes as she parted her lips and swirled her wet tongue over my purple crest. When she circled the underside, flicking the tip of her tongue at my sensitive flesh, streaks of lightning slammed my balls.

She was teasing me…toying with me.

Clearly, my little minx had forgotten who was in charge.

Gripping her head in my hands, I tilted her chin back. When Emma's jaw dropped open in surprise, I took advantage and shoved my cock to the back of her throat with a snarl.

"I didn't give you permission to play with me, little girl. Suck it. Suck it 'til you choke on my come, you dirty slut."

A fervent wail rolled off the back of her throat—vibrating the entire length of my cock—as Emma's eyes rolled to the back of her head. Wildly rocking her hips, she whimpered and complied, sucking so deep and hard on my dick black dots formed behind my eyes.

"Hello? Anybody awake yet?" Mack yelled from the floor below.

"Fuck," I hissed as horror crawled across Emma's face. When she instinctively started to lift from my cock, I cupped her nape and held her in place. Turning toward the door, I yelled over my shoulder, "We just climbed out of bed, Mack. Fix yourself some coffee. We'll be down in a few."

"Will do," he replied.

Inwardly cursing Mack's unexpected early arrival, I scrubbed my plans of scalding Emma's throat with my seed before drowning on her spicy, slick nectar. Grabbing a condom off the nightstand, I tore the foil open with my teeth and eased from her wicked mouth.

After rolling the latex down my shaft, I plucked Emma off the floor, kissed her hard, and tossed her on the bed.

"Hold on, little one. This is gonna be fast and hard," I warned with a dirty grin.

Shoving her legs apart, I gripped her hips and impaled myself on her hot cunt.

Biting her lips together to muffle her scream, Emma sank her nails into my biceps as I jackhammered in and out of her hot cunt. Meeting my feral thrusts, her blistering tunnel sucked at my shaft while muted whimpers and moans raked my ears.

"You're so fucking perfect," I murmured, sliding my thumb to her pebbled clit.

With a smothered scream, Emma jolted as a gush of hot silk drowned my driving cock. I strummed her engorged nub, drinking in the sound of her stifled keening cries as I hammered into her softening core.

The hum of release vibrating through me quickly grew to a deafening roar.

Lightning slammed down my spine, and my balls drew tight.

"You ready, girl?" I growled.

Eyes hot and wild, she frantically nodded.

Leaning in close to her ear, I tersely whispered, "Come for me now, my sweet, hot slut."

Body bowing beneath mine, Emma's walls clamped around my stabbing cock like a vise. As she tossed her head back and parted her lips, I slammed my mouth over hers. Feasting on her screams of ecstasy, I thrust deep and grunted as the brutal orgasm swallowed me whole.

Both of us panting like porn stars, I pressed my sweaty forehead to hers. "Sorry, darlin', that wasn't at all what I had planned this morning."

"Never apologize for something that amazing, Sir," she breathlessly replied.

I pulled out of her with a hiss, then rolled out of bed and staggered. Emma smirked, then scooted to the edge of the mattress. When she stood, her legs wobbled, too. Grabbing my arm for support, she shook her head and smirked.

"The things you do to me, I swear." She softly chuckled.

"Are you complaining, little one?" I teased.

"Never."

Fifteen minutes later, showered and dressed, we joined Mack in the kitchen. While Emma poured us each a cup of coffee, I started fixing breakfast.

"Didn't mean to barge in on you two so early," Mack apologized as Emma began setting the table.

Something about his tone was off.

Stirring the scrambled eggs, I glanced over my shoulder and studied the former sniper.

"It's fine," Emma said, waving his apology away.

The affable smile he sent her didn't quite reach his eyes.

Something was wrong. Staring at him a minute longer, Mack never looked my way. His focus was pinned on Emma. Alarms and buzzers blared in my brain.

The day after Emma had finally come clean, I told Mack about Wesley's bribery and threats. He promised to stay hyper-vigilant and note anything suspicious.

My gut told me he had.

Tamping down the angst rising inside me, I finished cooking the eggs, then poured them into a bowl. As usual, Emma was standing beside me, waiting to carry them to the table. The thought of having to identify her body, like I had Aubrey's, sent waves of panic rolling through me. Slamming a lid on the urge to fly to New York and put a bullet between Wesley's eyes, I handed her the bowl. Then I cupped her elbow and pressed a soft kiss to her lush lips before following her to the table.

Like he did every morning, Mack commented on how good the food looked and smelled while we loaded our plates. But unlike every morning, he didn't once look my way.

Instead of allowing the plethora of ball-shrinking scenarios of losing Emma to continue running wild in my head, I set my fork down and turned to him. "So, why *did* you?"

"Why'd I what?" Mack asked, finally looking at me.

"Why *did* you come over so early?"

"Grant," Emma gasped. "That's...rude."

"No, it's not," I replied, holding Mack with a penetrating stare. "Spill it. What's happened?"

"You still got it, don't you?" A humorless scoff slid off Mack's lips as he reached inside the pocket of his shirt.

"Got what?" Emma asked, clearly confused.

"A sixth sense. He always knows when something's not right. I'm not saying it's a bad thing. Lord knows, it kept us guys in his unit from coming home in body bags, but it's unnerving as fuck sometimes," Mack explained, handing me a small piece of paper. "It's a license plate number."

"I can see that. Start talking."

"It's probably nothing," Mack said, glancing at Emma. "But I was up late last night...couldn't sleep." Because he, like most of the other guys in our unit, struggled with bouts of PTSD from time to time. "I was sitting out by the side of the barn when I saw a car creeping down the road...way under the speed limit. I darted inside the bunkhouse, grabbed my Glock, and stepped outside to find the car stopped on the side of the road, near the driveway."

My heart rate tripled, and my mouth went dry. Making a mental note to install some motion sensor alarms and cameras around the perimeter of the ranch, I arched a brow at him.

"And you didn't call and wake me up?"

"So you could what...use a set of bolt cutters on him like you did that—"

"Shut up," I growled, pinning him with a glare.

"Sorry," Mack muttered. "I didn't want to wake you until I did some recon to find out if we had a problem. Sticking to the hedgerow beside the barn, I snuck in behind the car. After memorizing the license plate, I hunkered down and crept to the open window of the driver's side door. Then I popped up and pointed my gun in the guy's face behind the wheel and told him to step out of the car when he was done shitting himself."

Emma softly gasped and clasped her hands together.

"You get a name?" I growled, blood boiling.

"I got better than that. I have a picture of his driver's license on my phone."

After opening the app and tapping the image, Mack slid the device across the table to me.

Emma stood and peered over my shoulder at the photo of Matthew Carter, a surfer looking dude, from Hollywood, Florida.

"Have you ever seen this guy before?" I asked her.

"Never."

Tendrils of relief wended through the flames of fear blazing in my veins.

"What was he doing here?" I asked, knowing full well Mack had interrogated the kid for me.

"Said he drove up to surprise his grandparents for their anniversary, but took a wrong turn and got lost."

"You believe him?"

Mack shrugged. "He didn't smell like a PI."

"What's a PI smell like?" Emma asked.

"Coffee and desperation." Mack smirked. "This kid was smoking a joint, drinking *Red Bull,* and listening to *Pink Floyd.*"

I still wasn't convinced. "See any weapons, paperwork, or extra wallet?"

"Nope."

"Thanks for covering my six," I said, picking up the piece of paper and Mack's phone as I stood.

"Where are you goin'?" Emma asked.

"To make sure Matthew is who he says he is."

"What about your breakfast? I-it's gonna get cold."

I leaned down and smiled. "Darlin', I don't give a fuck if my breakfast turns to ice. All I care about is keeping you safe."

As her chin quivered in my palm and she blinked away the tears filling her eyes, I pressed a raw, possessive kiss to her pouty lips. I flashed her a wink, then turned and raced up to my office.

After doing some digging, I confirmed Matthew Carter was indeed who he claimed, and that his grandparents truly did live four miles north of me.

Finally able to breathe again, I quickly checked out a few security companies. I wanted to get cameras and motion detectors installed immediately. I was comparing prices when my cell phone chimed. Dragging it from my pocket, I semi-cringed at Dalton's name on the caller ID. I hadn't been to the club or barely talked to him since the day of the tornado.

"What's up, boss?" I answered.

"Just making sure you're still alive, man. I haven't seen you in weeks."

"I know. Sorry. I've been super busy," I lied.

"Well, you need to get un-busy. The subs at the club are missing you like crazy...we *all* are."

"It's kinda hard to get away at the moment."

"You on the bounty hunting trail again?"

"No, not right now," I said, scrubbing a hand through my hair. "Remember the woman I was with after the tornado?"

"Of course, I do." Dalton paused, then chortled. "You didn't take her home did you...well, not to *her* home, right?"

"I tried, but...It's gotten a little complicated."

"If she's still at the ranch, I'd say that's a good complication."

"Sort of."

"Did you show her how you like to...play on the dark side?"

"You could say that."

I tamped down a groan as visions of Emma, on her knees sucking my cock to the back of her throat, flashed in my mind.

"So, am I correct to assume she likes a kinky slice of life, too?"

"In a big way."

"Well, hell, man, bring her to the club. Help her spread her wings, unless you think she's not ready."

"She probably is, but..."

I trusted Dalton, but I wasn't going to out Emma. A, it wasn't my place to spill her secrets. And B, the fewer people who knew her true identity, or that she was with me, hiding from a deranged psychopath, the better.

Of course, I'd immediately shared Emma's secrets with Mack. He was more than a brother from another mother. He was my brother in arms. We'd spent years crawling through deserts and jungles watching each other's backs. I knew he was more than capable of doing whatever it took to help me keep Emma safe.

Safe.

Suddenly, I had an epiphany.

"I'll talk to her about it. But first, while I've got you on the phone.

Do you know who installed the security cameras at the club?"

"Sorry, I don't. But funny you should ask. After a couple of the monitors in my office glitched out the other day, Mika—*the actual owner of the club*—wants to update the entire security system."

"Awesome. Do you know who he's gonna use?"

"As a matter of fact, I do. Our friends, and fellow Doms, Ian and James are flying in from Chicago to do the install. They own a PI company in Chicago and just finished upgrading the club there for Mika." Dalton's voice turned low with concern. "Why? What's going on? You need their help with something?"

I did. But friends of Dalton's or not, I wasn't gonna let two private investigators—who might have already been contacted, or God forbid, hired by the Bishops and Fairchilds—anywhere near Emma.

"No. Everything's fine…just getting overrun by coyotes out here. They're thick as flies this year and stressing out the cows," I lied.

"That sucks."

"Meh. I'll run them off."

"Sounds good," Dalton replied. "Look, I need to fly, but seriously, man…talk Aubrey into coming to the club. It'd be good to see you again."

Aubrey. Fuck!

Hearing him call Emma by that name made my stomach knot.

If in fact she wanted to go to Genesis, we'd have to come up with a club name for her.

"It'd be better for her to find out I'm not as sadistic or demanding as other Doms," I scoffed.

"Don't try telling me you only want her there for purely educational reasons, my friend. I know better." Dalton chuckled.

"I wasn't saying that." I grinned.

After ending the call, dozens of ball-churning images of Emma—cuffed to a cross, tied to a spanking bench, and covered in elegant Shibari knots swaying beneath a suspension frame—crowded my mind as I hurried back to the kitchen.

If she showed any interest in going to the club, which I suspected she would, I'd need to take her shopping again.

Chapter Fourteen

Emma

My heart had been pounding ever since Grant returned to breakfast and asked if I'd like to visit Club Genesis with him. Of course, I said *yes*, without thinking twice. But now, inside the lobby of an actual *BDSM club*, waiting in line beside him while he chatted with the people around us, my heart was practically beating out of the rhinestone and lace covered corset hugging my chest.

As soon as breakfast was over, Grant had taken me shopping at an actual fetish store. I knew shops like them existed, but I'd never been brave enough to visit one.

The minute we'd crossed the threshold, I'd felt like Alice in Kinky Wonderland.

Covering the walls, every implement of pleasure and pain were grouped in sections. I recognized some of the things, like paddles, floggers, dildos, vibes, cuffs, and rope. But there were a lot of things that were a mystery to me.

The one thing that wasn't were the racks and racks of clothing filling the center of the store.

After asking my size, Grant prowled the latex, leather, spandex, and lace, plucking out dresses, corsets, skirts, and a few barely there pieces of lingerie and draped them over his arm. When he was finished, we followed the salesclerk to a dressing room, where Grant did as he'd threatened...sat and watched me model every stitch.

I'd barely wiggled into the first dress when I noticed his cock straining beneath his jeans.

And when I slid on the black, silk-lined lace skirt and fastened the metal clasps of the rhinestone and lace corset, Grant growled and unzipped his fly.

Mouthwatering, I watched him furiously fist his cock before he raised his other hand and pointed a finger to the floor in front of him.

Thankfully, the salesclerk hadn't interrupt and asked if we needed any help.

On our way to Genesis, the only instruction Grant gave me was to call him *Blade* or *Sir*.

When we finally arrived and he escorted me through the door, I was shocked to find the lobby packed with members. They were crazy happy to see Grant, greeting him with smiles and clapping him on the back before raking me with their stares. Most were welcoming, some curious, and a few—younger women dressed to the nines in sexy fetish wear—were hateful and rude.

Feeling like a bug under a microscope, I didn't know what to do or say, so I simply lowered my gaze to the carpet and tried to calm my frazzled nerves.

It didn't work.

I grew increasingly anxious and insecure by the second.

As if sensing my unease, Grant tucked me against his side tighter, then flashed me a reassuring smile. Like magic, the knots in my stomach dissolved.

"This is the first time Breeze has ever been to a private club like ours," Grant said to Sir Indigo, the young, blue-eyed Dom he'd introduced me to a few moments ago.

Breeze.

Hearing my club name spill off Grant's lips made my heart flutter. Not because it was a light, airy, and beautiful name, but because of the reason he'd chosen it for me.

While I was cleaning up the kitchen from breakfast, he'd eased in behind me and nipped the lobe of my ear.

"You know you can't stroll into the club as Emma tonight, right?"

"I know."

"Bad thing is, you have to sign a waiver, and show ID before you can enter the dungeon. I don't want you flashing your fake ID there, Emma. I won't risk compromising the club in any way."

"Then what am I supposed to do?"

"Nothing. I'm gonna ask Mack to work the podium tonight...to check in the guests and sign you in without an ID."

"Wait. Mack's a member of Genesis too?" I gaped.

"You didn't hear him tell Dalton he'd see him at the club the day he dropped us at the ranch, after the tornado?"

"If I did, it didn't register. It does now. Wow."

Grant chuckled. *"We need to come up with a club name, one that will protect your anonymity when I introduce you to people."*

"What kind of name?"

"What do you think about Breeze?"

"I think it's beautiful."

"I do, too, and it's fitting."

"Fitting? How?"

"Well, you did *breeze into my life on a tornado, little one."*

And just like that, Grant stole another piece of my heart.

"Oh, I love when we get to sacrifice a virgin," Indigo teased with a playful wink.

"S-sacrifice? H-how?" I stammered as we inched closer to Mack and a pretty young blonde standing behind a tall, wooden podium near a set of swinging saloon doors.

Panic surging through my veins, I jerked my head toward Grant.

"He's teasing, little one." He chuckled. "No one's touching you but *me.*"

135

Jenna Jacob

"Shit, Blade. I'm sorry. Sorry to you, too, Breeze," Indigo apologized. "I was only teasing."

"It's fine, Sir. I'm just a little nervous."

"Don't be. You're among friends here, girl," the young Dom assured with a tender smile before turning to talk to someone behind him.

Grant cupped my nape, then leaned down and nuzzled his lips close to my ear.

"Relax, sweet slut. We're not playing tonight. I have no desire to strip you down, put you on display, and scene with you in front of everyone. I'm a greedy bastard. The sight of your hot, naked body is for my eyes only. I brought you here to watch how the subs interact with their Doms."

"Yes, Sir." I nodded.

He'd calmed my fears, but his wet breath skimming down my neck, and his deep possessive growl vibrating the shell of my ear, ignited a needy throb low in my belly.

As we slowly made our way to the podium—and Mack's knowing smile—Grant kept his hand cupped to my nape, gently strumming his thumb along the side of my neck...silently reassuring me.

"Well, well...look what the cat dragged in," Mack boisterously exclaimed when we finally reached the podium. "It's a good thing you showed up when you did, we were fixin' to put a search party together."

"I've been a little busy," Grant replied.

"I bet you have been," Mack drawled, turning his focus on me with a little wink. "And who's this stunning, sexy thing beside you?"

Um, the same woman you had breakfast with this morning.

The snarky retort singed the tip of my tongue, but I swallowed it down. Clearly, the fact Mack lived and worked on Grant's ranch was a secret.

What happens in the club, stays in the club.

Grant's words rolled through my brain as he smiled and pressed his hand to the small of my back.

"This is Breeze. Breeze, this is Master Savage," he introduced, reaching into the pocket of his pants before palming something in his hand.

"Pleasure to meet you, Breeze. Welcome to Genesis."

"Thank you, Master Savage, it's a pleasure to meet you."

With a barely perceptible nod of approval, Mack turned to the blonde beside him. "Aspen, be a good girl and get me a bottle of water, please?"

"With pleasure, Sir." She beamed, then turned and quickly disappeared through the swinging saloon doors, sending the scent of leather and sex wafting through the air.

Mack smiled at Grant, then without moving his lips muttered, "Let's do this."

Grant calmly placed his driver's license and a light-colored credit card on the podium.

While Mack pretended to copy Aubrey's information off the credit card onto a sheet of paper, my heart drummed against my ribs.

Guilt and paranoia sluiced through my veins. I nonchalantly glanced at the ceiling, looking for security cameras. I didn't see any, but it did little to quash my shame. If I had known I'd be putting both men in such a risky position, I would have declined Grant's offer to come to the club.

Heart in my throat, I watched Mack shield the license and credit card in his big, calloused hands before placing them in Grant's waiting palm.

"You two have fun now," Mack said, flashing a carefree smile.

"Oh, we will," Grant wolfishly replied, smoothly sliding them back into his pocket.

As he pressed his palm against my spine—seemingly unfazed by the subterfuge that had just taken place—and led me toward the swinging doors, guilt had destroyed every bit of the crazy excitement I'd felt since breakfast.

Twenty days ago, when I'd pulled out of my parent's garage, I'd been so damn confident—after weeks of meticulous planning—that I'd covered every conceivable contingency to start my new life. Never once did I imagine being literally swept up into Aubrey's brother's rugged arms, or sheltered by his steadfast determination to protect me. If I had, I would have chosen a different alias and saved Grant the trouble and risk of exposing me to his friends.

Drowning in the guilt flooding my veins, I peered up at him and whispered, "I'm sorry, Sir."

With one hand on the swinging doors, Grant paused and narrowed his eyes at me. Then, without a word, he lowered his hand and quickly ushered me to a secluded corner, opposite of the waiting members. Pressing his palms flat on each wall, he caged me in and silently studied me for several-nerve wracking seconds.

"If you think I'm mad or upset about the little trick Mack and I just pulled, I'm not."

"But I am," I softly replied.

"Why?"

"Because I put you two in danger."

A corner of his mouth kicked up with a crooked grin. "Trust me, sweet slut. Mack and I have been in hundreds of situations a hell of a lot more dangerous than this."

"I know, but none of them were because of *me*."

Lifting a hand from the wall, Grant softly stroked my cheek. "You don't get it yet, do you?"

"Get what?"

"That I'll do anything, to anyone, at any time, in order to keep you safe." Slanting his lips over mine, he claimed me with a toe-curling, nipple tightening, clit throbbing kiss that erased all my guilt. "You feel better now, little one?"

"Definitely, Sir."

"Good. Come with me," he said, threading his fingers through mine. "And I'll introduce you to your wildest fantasies."

The hungry gleam in his eyes kickstarted my excitement again. With a nod, I dragged in a deep breath as Grant pressed his wide hand to the small of my back. Then ushered me through the saloon doors and past a thick, black velvet curtain.

The sights and sounds of the dungeon not only overwhelmed but also annihilated all the preconceived notions I had from reading BDSM books.

Tingles raced up my spine.

My nipples drew impossibly tighter, and my pussy clutched.

"Wow," I whispered.

Beside me, Grant chuckled as I struggled to take in everything at once.

Suddenly, cheers and applause echoed through the dungeon.

"Aw, fuck," Grant muttered with a sheepish grin.

"What's going on?" I asked, realizing all eyes were on us.

Grant opened his mouth to explain, but before he could get a word out, a man with dark hair and dark eyes raced up and wrapped him in a bro-hug.

"Damn, Blade. We thought you'd fallen off the face of the earth, for shit's sake. Where the fuck have you been?" the man asked with a grin. Suddenly realizing Grant wasn't alone, he did a double-take at me before his grin widened. "You don't need to answer. I now know where you've been, and who you've been doing." Turning his full attention on me, he gave me a wink so dramatically flirtatious and wiggled his brows, I nearly laughed. "Well, hellooooo, sweet thing. Where you been hiding all my life?"

"Back. The. Entire. Fuck. Off. JJ...Now!" Grant menacingly growled.

"Whoa, damn." JJ raised his hands in surrender and laughed. "Easy, Rambo. You know I was just messin' around."

"Mess around with your own sub, fucker," Grant bit out.

JJ reared back and blanched.

Clearly, I wasn't the only one shocked by his murderous tone. However, I was totally confident the fingers of lightning pulsing between my legs thanks to Grant's possessive caveman demeanor were mine alone.

"It finally happened, didn't it?" JJ murmured as a nostalgic smile tugged his lips. Turning toward me, he bowed his head slightly. "Forgive me, little one. I meant no disrespect. I'm Master JJ. Welcome to Genesis."

"Thank you, Sir. I'm Breeze. It's a pleasure to meet you," I replied, darting a glance at Grant to make sure I wasn't stepping on his Dominant toes. Based on the pride flickering in his eyes, I wasn't.

"With Blade's permission, of course, I'd like to introduce you to my girl this evening."

Grant heaved a heavy sigh, dragged his hand from my spine, and shook his head. Leaning in toward JJ, he dropped his voice. "Cut the formal bullshit, for fuck's sake. I'm sorry. I lost my head."

"Forget about it," JJ replied as they each stepped back. "With a girl as pretty as Breeze, I'm sure you lose *both* heads...one place or another, on a regular basis."

"True." Grant smirked. "And yes, I'd love for Breeze to meet Alli. But first, we're gonna grab something to drink."

"No rush. She keeps pestering me to scene. I figure I'll let her suffer a couple more hours, only because I love to watch her squirm." With an evil laugh, JJ turned and strolled away.

Why would he be so mean to his sub? Scowling, I watched him disappear into the crowd.

"If a submissive always gets what she wants, who's she submitting to?" Grant whispered, reading my mind...*again*.

The mental aspects of the lifestyle were far more confusing to me, than the physical ones.

Guiding me toward the back of the club to a long, sleek bar, his steps were slow and even. He let me drink in all the sights and sounds as he quietly explained the type of exchanges playing out in the numerous stations lining the walls. Dungeon Monitors, dressed in black tees, with the word SECURITY emblazoned on their backs, kept watchful eyes on both the Doms and the reflections of their subs in the mirrors attached to the wall at each station.

Unable to peel my gaze off a Dom landing a thick flogger over his sub's glowing backside, I slowed to a stop. It wasn't so much the Dom who intrigued me, but the reflection of pure, unadulterated peace etching his sub's face.

Easing in behind me, Grant leaned in close to my ear. "Are you curious to know what she's feeling?"

"Yes," I nodded with a breathy whisper.

"I can show you when we get back to the ranch, if you'd like."

Arousal and fear collided. "Will it hurt?"

"Not unless I want it to."

I anxiously peered up at his wolfish grin. "*Do* you want it to?"

He chuckled and shook his head. "No, sweet slut. The only time I'll *want* to give you pain is when you beg for it."

"You mean if?"

"No, I mean...*when*. If you continue exploring your submission, I guarantee you won't be where you're at tonight for long. Your need to please, as well as your desires and curiosities, will continue to grow. The things that scare you now, you'll likely crave somewhere down the road."

I knew his words were meant to give me hope, but once the merger was completed, I'd be moving on. The fact Grant wouldn't be the Dom fulfilling my desires and cravings down the road made my heart shatter and the ground crumble beneath my feet.

Chapter Fifteen

Grant

The minute the words fell from my tongue, waves of sadness rolled off Emma. As a sinking feeling landed in my gut, I knew exactly what she was thinking. I was now thinking the same thing. As soon as the merger was finalized, Emma would pack her things and leave...start her new life as Aubrey.

And there won't be a thing you can do to stop her, whispered the voice in my head.

An internal howl of regret and sadness screamed inside me while a desolate hollowness I hadn't felt since burying Aubrey and Mom spread through my soul.

I'd find a way to keep her. I'd do whatever—

"It's about time you crawled out from that hole you've been hiding in, Blade," Mistress Magic chided from behind the bar with a grin.

Flashing the tall, willowy blonde a forced but friendly smile, I tabled my plans to keep Emma on the ranch and gently clasped her elbow.

"Come, little one. There's someone I want you to meet."

Emma grudgingly peeled her coveted gaze from Master Creed's scene with his sub, Meadow, and nodded before I guided her to the bar. After helping her onto a vacant barstool, Magic darted a curious glance between me and Emma.

A shit-eating grin tugged the Domme's lips as she thrust her hand out to Emma. "Hi, precious. Welcome to Genesis. I'm Mistress Magic." At the same time, her sub—and bar back—eased in beside her with an armful of soda cans. While shaking Emma's hand, Magic sank her other fist into her boy's dark curls and yanked his head back. "And this insolent little shit is my boy, Knotty."

Emma tensed and forced a smile, warily watching Magic.

I knew she didn't grasp the dynamic playing out before her. Skimming a palm down her back, I did my best to reassure her as she studied the silver collar around Knotty's neck.

Visions of fastening a delicate collar around hers crowded my brain, igniting a blazing brushfire of longing to actually own Emma. Unwilling to analyze the bizarre craving, I introduced her to the couple, then arched a brow at Knotty. He was a sweet young man, but he had a penchant for Topping from the bottom. "What did you do *this* time, boy?"

Sticking out his bottom lip with an exaggerated pout, he sighed. "I disobeyed Mistress."

"You jacked off without permission...*again*, you horny little bastard," Magic railed, releasing his hair before landing a hard slap to his ass.

Knotty jolted, then smiled with a dreamy purr before pressing a contrite kiss to her cheek. "Thank you, Mistress."

"Suck up all you want, boy. You're light-years from getting on my good side," Magic warned, then turned to us with a grin. "What can I get you tonight?"

"Two colas, please." I chuckled.

While Magic fixed our drinks, I felt the tension melt from Emma's body. I leaned my hip against the bar and bent close to her ear. "Tell me what you learned from Magic and Knotty's exchange, little one?"

Emma pursed her lips and pondered my question briefly. "That Mistress will, at some point, punish Knotty for his...transgression. But I also see and feel the bond they share. It's strong. I can tell they love each other very much."

My heart and chest swelled at once. "Yes. They've been together for several years. You're very observant, my sweet slut."

Emma's proud smile was all but blinding.

As we sipped our drinks, I watched her reactions to the various scenes playing out around us.

She shivered and glanced away as Master Memphis painted his sub Moonlight's backside in long, red stripes with his single-tail.

When she locked an enthralled stare on Indigo, reddening un-owned sub Sutton's ass with a wicked rubber paddle, curiosity and hunger burned in Emma's eyes before she turned her attention on Master Gray Wolf. The older Dom had an un-owned sub, Luna, draped over his knees. One arm was tightly bound around her waist, holding her in place, while he firmly spanked her wiggling backside with the open palm of his other.

Emma's eyes shimmered with longing as she nibbled her bottom lip.

Without a doubt, I was going to introduce her to some impact play once we got home.

Home.

As the word echoed in my brain, I realized I'd never once called the ranch or the house sitting on the land, *home*. In my heart, home was the familiar structure on a quiet street, nestled between big, shady oaks. The place I'd grown up with laughter and love. The house on my ranch had never felt like home until Emma stepped through the—

"Well, I'll be a son of a bitch," Dalton barked, clapping me on the back, saving me from the ball-shrinking ramifications of my disquieting epiphany.

I flashed him a smile, then politely nodded to the two men flanking him.

"If I'd known it would only take a phone call to get you here, I'd have rung you up days ago." Dalton chuckled.

"Yeah, yeah," I drawled, studying the two, dark-haired, dark-eyed strangers.

"Fuck, where are my manners?" Dalton drawled. "Ian and James, this is Blade. Blade, this is Ian and James...my friends from Chicago. Yanno, the ones I told you about who are going to update the security system."

The private investigators.

My heart stopped.

The air in my lungs turned to sand.

And a hot knife twisted in my gut.

Struggling to keep from sweeping Emma into my arms and sprinting out of the club, I forced a placid smile and quickly sized up the pair. The one closest to me, gazing at Emma with a too-sharp, too-assessing stare without doubt, posed the biggest threat.

Keeping my affable smile in place, I extended my hand to purposely draw his focus off her. "Nice to meet you..."

"Ian," the shrewd prick supplied with a sturdy handshake and a reciprocal smile. "Same."

The first rule of conducting a successful interrogation was observing body language. The second was dissecting your target's answers. Ian's one-word response told me he was astute, smart, and kept his emotions and all intel locked in a tight little box. He didn't slip up, at least not often.

Neither do I, fucker.

Casually turning, I fixed my cemented smile on the other man and extended my hand again. "That means you must be James. Nice to meet you."

Liar.

"I am. Good to meet you, too." He grinned. James was exponentially less of a threat. He was laid-back relaxed, and a million times more affable than Ian. "Mika asked us to tell you he sends you his best wishes, and thanks you again for keeping the club running while Dalton and Blair moved down here."

"Please return my best wishes to him, and tell him it was no trouble at all."

"Will do." James grinned.

"Did you bring Aub—"

"Yes, and she's going by Breeze here, bro," I said, purposely cutting him off.

I didn't want to give Ian or James a morsel of information they could sink their teeth into.

"Where is she?" Dalton asked.

Poking her head around me with a giggle, Emma waved her fingers. "I'm right *here*, Sir."

I held my breath as James and Ian smiled and nodded at Emma. But as Ian's stare lingered, studying her face with a razor-sharp gaze, it took all the strength I possessed to keep from gouging his eyes out.

"Damn, girl!" Dalton barked, stealing Ian's attention off her. "I didn't recognize you. What happened to your hair?"

"I cut it off, and—"

"She wanted a new style," I explained, interrupting Emma before she could mention dying the color. "I like it. I think it looks sexy on her."

Dalton blinked at me in surprise as a knowing smile speared over his lips. "I do, too. You're beautiful, as always...Breeze."

"Thank you, Sir." She blushed, before taking a sip of her soda.

Turning ever so slowly, I surreptitiously blocked their view of Emma with my body before addressing Dalton. "So, when's the new install starting?"

"Tomorrow morning," he replied. "Which reminds me. We should probably head up to my office and look at the blueprints before it gets too late."

After James and Ian voiced their agreement, we said our goodbyes.

As the trio disappeared down the hallway of private rooms, I mentally shoved the tension pinging in my system away. I turned and studied Emma, now completely engrossed, watching Master Cruz skillfully bind his sub, Brooke, in stunning Shibari knots.

Though I could only see her profile, Emma didn't look a thing like she had the day we'd taken shelter from the tornado.

Still, my sixth sense was screaming.

Long seconds later, she turned and licked her lips. "Can I ask you a question, Sir?"

"You can ask anything, little one."

"Why did Ian and James make you so...uncomfortable?"

Fuck! I really had gone soft and lost my edge.

If Emma had picked up on my angst, there was no way Ian hadn't as well.

I couldn't tell her the truth. Not here. Not now. If I did, she'd freak out and run...run as far and as fast as she could.

The thought of not being able to protect her terrified me as much as never seeing her again.

Gut twisting and heart racing, I knew I had to get my shit together, like I'd been trained. Had to wire it tighter, stronger, and tougher than I had while leading my unit through hell and back.

Though it scared the living fuck out of me, deep down, I knew life without Emma—without her smile, her laughter, and her sassy tongue that did things to me no mortal woman had ever before—would be a kind of hell I might not survive.

As I peered into her hazel eyes, brimming with trust and faith, I banished the fear scraping my psyche. It was too late to save myself. I'd already fallen too deep and hard to ever let her go.

I shrugged. "They're strangers. I'm always cautious around people I don't know, at first."

It wasn't a lie.

"You weren't cautious around me at first," she said with a playful smile. "You were a big, brave, bad-assed Boy Scout."

I threw back my head and laughed, then cupped her nape and brushed my lips over hers. "Wait 'til you see the badge I earned in rope tying."

"You mean, you can tie rope like that?" she asked, discreetly pointing to Master Cruz.

While Mack's Shibari skills surpassed everyone else's in the club, mine didn't suck. Just the thought of binding Emma's soft, naked flesh in linear lines and rows of knots made my cock stir.

"I can."

Her eyes smoldered as a quivering breath spilled from her lips.

"In fact, when we—"

"Excuse me, Blade. I'm sorry to interrupt," fellow Dom and DM Axel apologized.

"No problem. What's up?" Though alarm bells and buzzers were roaring through my head, I smiled.

"Dalton just called down," Axel explained, pointing to his headset. "He asked if you could stop by his office before you leave."

Ian recognized Emma.

My biggest fear had become a reality.

I forced myself to remain calm as my heart clutched and sputtered before slamming against my ribs. And nodded. "Of course. Radio back and tell him I'll be there as soon as I find someone to watch Breeze."

"I'll do it for you," Magic offered with a helpful smile. "I'll keep the wolves off your girl."

I whipped my head toward Emma, searching her eyes. "You okay with that?"

"Of course." She smiled. "I'll be sitting right here until you get back."

"Swear to me you won't go anywhere," I said, somehow keeping the fear shrinking my balls from my voice.

"I swear," Emma replied, eyeing me suspiciously.

"Relax, Blade. I'll tie her down myself if I have to." Magic grinned, then in a stage whisper said to Emma, "I'm just teasing, Breeze. No one here, including me, is gonna touch you."

"I know, Mistress." Emma chuckled.

Though I knew Magic would keep her word, leaving Emma alone and unprotected made me want to howl. But I couldn't stand here with my dick in my hand. I had to find out just how big of a threat Ian was.

"Thanks, doll," I said to Magic, then nodded to Axel. "Tell him I'm on my way, please."

After pressing a soft kiss to Emma's lips, I promised I'd be right back, then forced myself to step away. I strolled toward the hallway, focusing on slowing my heart rate, then clearing my mind.

Though I knew Emma wouldn't leave her barstool, I had no clue how she'd react if this meeting went to shit and I was forced to toss her over my shoulder and sprint to my truck.

Like every mission I'd been on, I hoped for the best, but prepared for the worst.

I climbed the stairs to the second floor, racking my brain for some place safe to hide Emma from Ian and James...hell, from the whole fucking world. Mack had a cabin in the Missouri Ozarks. I knew he'd let us hole up there if needed until I found something better. The hard part was gonna be alluding the two pricks in Dalton's office long enough to get Emma there.

As I cleared the last step, I drew in a deep breath, clenched my jaw, and knocked on the door.

"Come on in," Dalton called.

Wiping all emotion from my face, I turned the handle and stepped inside.

"Thanks for coming up, Blade. Please, have a seat," Dalton said, sweeping his hand toward the empty chair in front of his desk between Ian and James.

When I sat down, Dalton opened his mouth and closed it a couple of times. With frustration written all over his face, he scowled and shook his head. "I'm not sure how to tell you this, man, but Aubrey isn't who she says she is."

"I know."

Dalton blinked, jaw dropping open. "You *know*?"

"Exactly, what *do* you know?" Ian asked.

"I know you recognized Emma. I know her rich, pathetic, heartless parents hired you to find her, so they can sign her fucking death warrant. And I know if you try to take her from me, you're not getting out of this room alive," I bit out with a low snarl.

"Whoa. Whoa. Hold up," James said, raising a hand in the air. "Ian didn't recognize her, I did. And trust me. We're *not* taking her anywhere. We're not working with the Bishops."

"Then you're working for the Fairchilds. Either way, you're not taking Emma," I growled.

"Easy, man," Ian whispered, showing an unexpected solicitous side. "We're not working for *either* of them, but a fuck-ton of other PIs are."

"How many?"

"After the families offered their reward?" James shrugged. "Hundreds...maybe thousands."

"What reward?"

"This one," Ian replied, calmly handing me his cell phone.

Willing my hand to stop shaking from the dread charging through me, I gripped the device. A photo of Emma, eyes sparkling and a blinding smile stretched across her lush lips, filled the screen. The need to touch her...to shield her with my body and get her out of the club rode me like a desperate whore.

Instead, I slowly dragged my thumb up the screen and began reading.

The headline: MISSING was in big bold letters like a flyer for a fucking lost dog.

As I digested the words on the screen, my anger spiked and continued climbing. The heartfelt, emotional plea for Emma to: *"Please, come home, darling. We miss you,"* quoted by her mother, Roslyn Tolliver Bishop, made me want to vomit.

But when I saw the amount of money the Bishops and Fairchilds were offering as a reward for Emma's *safe* return, a murderous, unholy rage unleashed inside me.

The rich cocksuckers had no problem dropping ten million in the pocket of a corrupt congressman. Yet they could only bear to part with a measly two million to get Emma—their daughter, future daughter-in-law, and the mother of their possible grandchildren—back.

"I've read enough," I bit out, shoving the phone back to Ian.

"You need to get Emma out of here, before someone else recog—"

"I know," I roared at Dalton, rage rolling inside me. Turning my focus to Ian, I cocked my head. "Two million dollars is a lot of money. Why aren't you and James hunting Emma?"

Ian arched a brow at James. "Go ahead. Tell him."

Whipping my attention to the man I'd foolishly assumed the lesser threat—*because you're slipping, man*—I ignored the voice in my head and waited impatiently.

"Back in the fifties, my great-grandfather started a TV station in Cedar Rapids, Iowa. It's an independent, family-owned station that my Uncle Jack—who I talk to every week—runs now. Several years ago, the Fairchilds approached my uncle and offered him an obscene amount of money to purchase the station. He turned them down, but they've continued to keep hounding him." James took a deep breath and continued. "About a month ago, Jack called and told me there were rumors the Bishops and Fairchilds were gonna make a merger and corner the media market. Essentially, drive my uncle out of business. So, I asked a friend of mine, who's got a lot of connections in DC, about it. Long story short, there are certain *agencies* watching this merger closely. They have reason to believe bribes and threats are being made to push the thing through, but you didn't hear that from me."

I didn't have to; I already knew the rumors and threats were true. But I was stumped why my contact in DC wasn't privy to the same intel.

"You're right. Two million dollars is a lot of money," James continued. "But we want nothing to do with either family."

"You're right not to." I nodded.

"You know more, don't you?" Ian asked.

Way more, but I would not draw an even bigger target on Emma's back.

"I know I'm leaving, and taking Emma home where I can keep her safe," I announced, rising from the chair.

"Listen, we know how to keep people alive, too. If you want our help, we'll be here for a week…longer if you need us to stay," James offered as he stood and extended his hand.

"Thanks. I appreciate that, man. I got experience, too." *Killing bad guys.*

I shook his hand first, then Ian's when he, too, stood.

"If you have to get Emma out of Dallas, I can get you aboard a private jet in under an hour," Dalton offered, not bothering to mask his worry. "I'll get you whatever you need to go and set up after you get there. Just say the word."

He could. I'd been to the man's house…er, rather, his mansion. Even though Dalton was richer than God, his offer warmed my heart.

"Thank you, man. Thanks, all of you." I nodded before bolting out of the office and racing down the stairs.

Chapter Sixteen

Emma
Saturday, July 29th

S unrise streaming through the windows pulled me from sleep. Not ready to get out of bed, I turned to my side, blindly inching toward Grant. I wanted to snuggle his hard, naked body and catch some more z's. But he wasn't there. The sheets were cold where he was supposed to be. Sitting up, I blinked against the morning light, as confusion and worry tightened my chest.

Something was wrong.

I'd first sensed it when Grant returned to the bar after his meeting with Dalton. But simply dismissed it as club business. I hadn't noticed anything off on the ride home, but of course, I hadn't been paying attention. I'd been too busy trying to calm my hungry hormones. After watching all those erotic scenes at the club, I'd been hornier than hell, dreaming of him taking me over his knee and spanking my ass, or tying me up in rows of pretty knots.

However, once we were home and getting ready for bed, he was so preoccupied and distant, I'd asked him what was wrong. Grant said he had a headache. I'd offered to massage his temples, neck, and shoulders, but he declined and popped some ibuprofen. He'd then climbed into bed, kissed me good night before snuggling me against his chest and, falling sound asleep.

As he snored beside me, I'd laid awake for hours, replaying the entire night in my mind searching for anything I might have said or done to upset him. But I couldn't think of a single thing. Only after convincing myself whatever upset him, or caused his headache, had happened in Dalton's office, I'd finally been able to fall asleep.

But waking up alone—something I'd never done since moving in with Grant—my worries roared back to life. Determined to find out what was bothering him, I rolled out of bed. After completing my morning ritual, I tossed on my clothes and strode downstairs.

As I neared the kitchen, Grant and Mack's deep voices filtered through the air.

"I know you want to nab this drug dealer. You've been after him for almost a year."

"I do," Grant growled. "He's pissing me off."

"That little maggot isn't what's got you pissed, and we both know it," Mack chided. "Look, I'll be happy to meet with the snitch for you. Hell, I'll grab the fucking drug dealer, too. Just say the word."

As I stepped into the kitchen, waves of tension slammed me.

That wasn't what stopped me dead in my tracks.

No, what stopped me cold was seeing Grant.

Though he sat in his usual spot at the table, there was nothing usual about his posture.

His elbows were pressed against the glossy wood, and his forehead was resting on the base of his palms. Mack sat beside him, face lined with concern, leaning in close with his focus glued on Grant.

"I appreciate the offer, man, but the snitch is a paranoid little rodent. If you show up at the meet point in my place, he'll freak out and slink back into the sewer." Grant heaved out a heavy sigh. "Why? Why'd the fucker have to crawl out now, when all hell's break—"

Mack gave him a little nudge while he cleared his throat. Stopping mid-sentence, Grant raised his head before our three gazes collided.

Quickly wiping the haunted look off his face, Grant smiled at me. For the first time, it didn't reach his eyes. "Morning, little one."

"Morning, you two," I said. Painting on a smile as I breezed into the room, pressing a kiss to Grant's cheek before continuing straight to the coffee pot. Intuition told me I was going to need a whole lot of caffeine this morning.

"How's your headache?" I asked, filling my mug.

"Oh, it's gone. Did you sleep well?"

"Not really, but I can grab a nap later," I replied before taking that first glorious sip. "Sounds like you're gonna do some bounty hunting today."

"Maybe. I haven't decided if I want to leave the ranch."

"Why not?"

"Sit down, Emma. There's something I need to tell you."

His serious expression and apprehensive tone sent a foreboding chill down my spine.

"What's wrong?" I asked, easing into the chair beside him before setting my mug on the table.

Holding me with a tormented gaze, Grant cupped my hand and sucked in a deep breath.

As he relayed the horrifying details of his conversation with Ian and James in Dalton's office, panic and fear roared through my veins. My heart bounced off my ribs and my entire body quaked while I frantically tried to draw air into my constricting lungs.

"Easy, Emma," Grant murmured, strumming his thumb over the back of my hand. "Don't freak out on me, sweetheart."

Too late.

"James was the only one who recognized you last night, and he will not breathe a word," Mack reminded, trying to talk me off the ledge as well.

"That we *know* of," I snapped, while the voice in my head hysterically screamed, *Run! Run!*

My fight-or-flight reflex kicked in with a vengeance. Unable to fight assumptions I couldn't see, I bolted out of my chair, sending it crashing to the floor. I had no clue where I was going, only that I had to run and hide. But as I turned to race up the stairs and gather my things, Grant launched from the table and cupped his strong fingers around my arm.

"What are you doing?"

"Leaving," I firmly stated.

"No, little one. You're not going anywhere. You're staying right here where I can protect you."

"You can't protect me from everything, Grant."

"Watch me."

"What if someone else recognized me at the club last night?"

"They can't say anything without violating their contract. What happens inside the club stays—"

"Stays inside the club. Yeah, I know all that. But let's get real, Grant, two million dollars is a lot of money," I said, impatiently pointing out the obvious. "Plenty for someone tired of working forty hours a week, living paycheck to paycheck, to stop and think…You know what? Screw my membership. I want a new house, a sports car… a boat."

He and Mack exchanged a grim glance. They didn't argue, which made my skin crawl even more.

"You're right." Grant nodded.

Guiding me back to the table, he helped my into my chair before easing back into his, and pulled out his cell phone.

"Who are you calling?" I asked.

"No one. I'm texting my informant to tell him I won't be at the meet point."

Guilt, thick and oily, mixed with the fear and panic pulsing through me, made it even harder to breathe.

"No," I blurted, gripping his fingers to keep him from typing. "You can't blow off your meeting to stay here and babysit me."

"I can do whatever the fuck I want, darlin'," he said in a low, controlled growl, lifting my hand off his phone.

Okay, so telling a Dom what to do wasn't getting me anywhere.

Fine. I could easily change tactics.

"Yes, I know you can. But I'm asking…no, I'm *begging*. Please don't cancel your meeting. Mack has the same SEAL skills as you do, right?"

Grant clenched his jaw and slowly nodded. Yeah, he hated the idea of leaving me alone. But I hated him thinking I was too weak or stupid, to save myself more.

Turning to Mack, I arched my brows. "You'll be here. You'll protect me, right?"

"With my life," he ground between clenched teeth.

"Dammit, Emma. I don't want to leave you," Grant roared, unwilling or unable to mask the conflicted emotions clawing through him.

Rising from my chair, I climbed onto his lap and straddled his hips. Ignoring the fact that Mack was sitting right beside us, I cupped Grant's cheeks and stared into his tormented blue eyes.

"I know you don't want to leave me. But I'm not a porcelain doll you can keep in a glass case on the shelf. I trust *your* trust in Dalton, Ian, and James to keep their mouths shut. And I trust *your* trust in Mack to keep me safe."

Grant's nostrils flared and his chest expanded as he gripped my nape and slammed his mouth over mine. As he plunged his tongue past my lips with a raw, urgent kiss, I tasted the fear, desperation, and the inner war churning inside him. Aching to ease his turmoil, I draped my arms around his neck and melted against his steely frame with a soft moan. His cock—lengthening and straining beneath his jeans—throbbed against my swelling clit and wet core.

"Looks like breakfast is gonna be a little late this morning," Mack drawled.

Mouths still melded together, and tongues swirling madly, Grant and I silently chuckled before he grudgingly pulled back and ended the kiss.

"There *are* more important things than food, fucker," Grant snarled with a smirk.

"I know, like meeting your tweaker friend and getting the

information you need," Mack replied with a pointed stare.

"Fine," Grant grumbled, scrubbing a hand through his hair. "I'll go get the intel, but I'm hauling ass back here and ordering the motion detectors and security cameras."

"Good. I'll help you install them when they get here." Mack curtly nodded.

As the choking tension in the room lessened, I drew in a deep breath before climbing off Grant's luscious, thick erection and easing onto my chair. He tucked his phone away, then took a sip of his coffee.

"Aren't you gonna start cooking?" Mack asked impatiently.

"In a minute."

"What are you waiting on, man?"

"For my cock to deflate, if you must know," Grant said with an irritated scowl.

As Mack burst out laughing and shook his head, I pinched my lips together and held back a giggle.

"Dude, unless it's so big you can't belly up to the stove, I don't give a fuck about your junk." Mack chuckled.

"What if it is?" Grant countered.

"Then you shouldn't be raising cattle. You should be starring in porn movies," Mack drawled.

I slapped a hand over my mouth and shook with silent laughter as relief wended through me.

The giant elephant of fear and uncertainty was still in the room, but Grant and Mack refused to keep feeding the beast. Instead, they'd shoved it into a corner and invited a sense of normality back into our lives with their zany banter.

Grant muttered a curse, then stood and pinned Mack with a fake glare before striding to the stove.

Minutes later, as usual, I carried a stack of French toast to the table before we filled our plates. Like always, Mack complimented Grant's cooking. Though none of us attacked our food with much gusto, we laughed and talked, and made a concerted effort to pretend it was an ordinary morning.

At least, until Grant stood to leave.

As if a switch had been flipped, the oppressive tension filled the room again, making it hard to breathe. After wrapping me in a fervent hug, Grant pressed a passionate kiss to my lips—drinking me in like a life-force—then pinned Mack with a pleading stare.

"With my life, bro," Mack vowed, clapping Grant on the back.

Grant's stare held me prisoner for several long seconds. Then he nodded his head and flashed me a crooked smile. "I'll be right back, darlin'."

"I'll be right here," I promised as he turned and walked out the door.

Mack and I wordlessly stood in the kitchen until the rumble of Grant's truck faded away.

"So, what do you want to do? Play poker or clean up?" Mack asked, severing the suffocating silence.

"Clean. I have no idea how to play poker."

He blinked in surprise, then flashed a wicked grin before rubbing his hands together. "I'll teach you."

"Teach me, or take all my money?"

"Depends. How much you got?" He playfully winked.

"I'll stick with the dishes. They're a much safer bet."

"Fine," he drawled dramatically. "But only if you let me help."

"I'll get them. I'm sure you've got plenty of chores to do."

"They'll keep."

"Mack, you don't have to stay here and babysit me."

"Yes, I do. I enjoy saying *alive*. I'm not stepping foot outta this house until the boss comes back."

"Fine," I huffed, rolling my eyes. "You can help."

"And I will, just as soon as I get another cup of coffee in my system." He smirked, filling his mug and jerking a nod toward the table. "Join me?"

"Why not? If your chores can wait, so can mine."

Doing my best to ignore Grant's absence, I sipped my brew while Mack and I talked about benign things like the ranch, cows, and weather.

Long minutes later, when our mugs were empty, we tackled the kitchen.

We continued talking about surface stuff while I rinsed the dishes and Mack loaded them into the dishwasher. I appreciated his help, but his unusual presence only amplified the fact Grant was gone. Not out in the field tending to the cows, or inside the barn, but gone-gone.

An icy chill slid down my spine.

Though it wasn't, the house felt empty. And I suddenly realized; yes, Grant was a big, burly man, but his presence was a thousand times bigger…and filled every room.

"Do you think we're all worrying about nothing and simply getting carried away with paranoia?"

"If we are, so what?" Mack shrugged. "Better safe than sorry."

"I know, I just hate the idea of him wasting his money on surveillance equipment because of me."

Mack scoffed and closed the dishwasher. "Sweetheart, he'd buy the sun, moon, and stars, and part with every penny he owned to keep you safe."

Because he feels guilty he wasn't able to save Aubrey.

"I know, but putting so much pressure on himself isn't healthy," I said, strolling back to the table.

"Health has nothing to do with it," Mack said, sliding into the chair across from me. "I've known Grant a long time. I know he hasn't told you. Hell, he probably hasn't even told himself, but that man is in lo—"

The blare of a loud alarm cut Mack off. Launching out of the chair, he darted across the kitchen and yanked open the pantry door. Silencing the scream with a curse, he raced to the back door and pressed his head against the glass.

"What's going on? What was that?" I asked as he peered toward the barn.

"Fire alarm. Smokes rolling out of the barn," he bit out, gripping the doorknob.

Suddenly, he froze and glanced at me over his shoulder.

"What are you waiting for? Go. Try to put it out. I'll call—"

"It's a trap…a diversion."

162

"You don't know that. What if it's not? You're not going to let the whole barn burn down while you stand here babysitting a grown woman, are you?"

"Damn right, I am," he said, releasing the knob. "I'm not leaving you in here alone."

Gaping at him in disbelief, I wanted to scream as he yanked out his cell phone and punched in 9-1-1.

"Call Grant. Tell him we might have a situation," Mack said, waiting for the operator to answer. "Tell him to get his ass back here, pronto."

While Mack calmly recited the address of the ranch and requested the fire department, I tugged my phone from my back pocket. Holding the device in a death-grip, I quickly scrolled for Grant's number.

After ending his call to 9-1-1, Mack breezed past me and disappeared inside the pantry again. I tapped Grant's number and pressed the phone to my ear. Impatiently waiting for the call to connect, I softly gasped as Mack emerged from the pantry gripping a dull, black handgun.

"Emma?" Grant's voice was as sharp as a blade.

"The barn's on fire. Mack thinks it's a trap," I blurted, as he leaned over the sink, and peered out the window. "He says you need to come—"

"Fuck," Mack snarled. Jerking back from the sink, he cinched a strong arm around my waist, and shoved me to the floor behind him, and barked, "Stay down."

A surprised yelp tore from my throat, as I skidded across the hardwoods.

"Emma? Emma?" Grant barked, voice thick with panic and rage.

"I saw a shadow. I think we've got incoming, Master Chief," Mack barked as the back door exploded with a thunderous crash.

Suddenly, everything that had been moving at the speed of light slowed to a heart-stopping, gut-churning crawl.

Raising his weapon, Mack spun toward the door as Wesley stepped inside...holding a gun of his own.

"Emma! Fucking talk to me," Grant bellowed in my ear while

simultaneous gunshots thundered through me.

Blood splattered outward from the front of Mack's body.

Time slowed even more as a bone-chilling scream tore from my throat.

I was still screaming as Mack clutched his chest and staggered backward. Tripping on my legs, he stumbled sideways. Blood flowed from between his fingers pressed to his chest, and the gun slipped from his other hand before skidding across the floor.

"Mack. Oh God, Mack, no!" I shrieked as he toppled backward, ripping the phone from my hand before landing on top of me with a gut-churning grunt.

"Mack...Mack, get up. Please get up," I begged, frantically shoving his big body while bucking and wiggling for freedom.

Tears blurred my vision. The scent of hot copper filled the air and stained my tongue. Still struggling to push him off me, all I could think about was grabbing his gun to finish the job for him.

But before I could pry his heavy weight off me, Wesley gripped my arm and brutally yanked me from beneath Mack's body before hoisting me onto trembling legs. Blood dripped from a gash at his temple. Mack's shot had gone wide, merely grazing the maniac.

"Hello, darling," Wesley said with a demented grin. "Did you miss me?"

Body quaking and mind numb with fear, I struggled to think of a way to escape the madman.

There was no way I was leaving with Wesley.

No way I'd leave Mack to bleed out on the kitchen floor.

And no way in hell I was leaving Grant.

"No. Sorry, not sorry, I haven't missed you at all," I replied, hoping I could stall for time and keep Wesley talking long enough for Grant to get back home and rip him limb from limb with his bare hands.

"I didn't miss you either, cunt. But you're still coming home with me because I have to marry your pathetic ass," Wesley snarled, slamming the butt of the gun against the side of my head.

Like sharp ragged fangs, pain ripped through me before everything went black.

Chapter Seventeen

Grant

Accelerator pressed to the floor; I sped down the highway.

Terror, rage, and adrenaline scorched my body and brain. Emma's voice, Mack's warning, and the sound of gunfire—that turned my guts to liquid—echoed in my ears. Honking the horn and weaving around cars like a hornet, I dipped onto the shoulder several times to pass assholes who refused to get out of my way.

Though Emma had suddenly gone silent, a fact that sent blinding rage vibrating through me, the call was still connected. I strained, praying to hear a breath, a whisper...even a scream, but the only sounds coming through my Bluetooth were Mack's moans and groans. Clearly, he'd taken a bullet. I just didn't know where. Since Wesley hadn't outright killed him, I clung to the hope Mack would pull through.

Veering off the highway, I turned onto the two-lane leading to the ranch. Glancing at every vehicle I met, I took a mental snapshot of the driver inside. I knew who I was looking for. I'd done a deep dive into

Wesley Albert Fairchild's pampered life, the day after Emma spilled her secrets on the porch. Unfortunately, like other deranged degenerates, there were no flags, no signs, no warnings to indicate how insane or brutally dangerous he truly was.

The monster, doing God knows what to Emma, was a devious, cunning psychopath.

Roaring a string of curses, impatience clawed deep...shredding my soul with every impotent second that ticked by.

In the distance, smoke billowed, rolling up into the sky. I didn't give two fuck's about the barn. All I cared about was getting to the ranch to make sure Emma and Mack were all right. The cows were safe in the field, the ATVs and everything else was insured. Mack's belongings could be replaced...if he fucking lived. My heart squeezed and my chest tightened as I blew past the firetruck—lights flashing and sirens wailing.

"If that motherfucker has touched one hair on Emma's head..." I growled, gripping the steering wheel tighter.

As the bloodthirsty rage continued boiling inside me, I knew the suffering I'd put Aubrey's killer through would pale in comparison to the torture I planned to inflict on Wesley. By the time I was through, there's be nothing left of the lunatic to identify.

When I finally reached the ranch, the barn was fully engulfed. Acrid smoke hung in the air. Barely lifting my foot from the accelerator, I whipped into the driveway, kicking up dust and gravel. As the truck fishtailed, I steered onto the grass before skidding to a stop in front of the porch.

The firetruck's siren wailed in the distance as I retrieved my Glock from the glovebox and bounded out of the truck. Using the open door as a shield, I quickly glanced around the property, searching for Wesley's vehicle, but didn't find it. That, coupled with the fact I wasn't being pinned down with a hailstorm of bullets, filled me with dread.

I drew my weapon and crouched low. Sweeping my gaze, and the gun's muzzle, back and forth, I quickly darted to the side of the house. It would have been faster to barge through the front door, but since everything had gone down in the kitchen, I hoped to sneak up on

Wesley and take him out there. Yeah, I wanted to make him suffer, but blowing his brains out would net the same result—the cocksucker's death.

After reaching the back of the house, I darted my head around the corner, but no one was there. Quickly and quietly, I crept to the back door. Crouching low again, I studied the splintered frame and pieces of wood and glass littering the floor. The prick had kicked his way in. I remained still for several gut-churning seconds, listening for voices or movement. But all I could hear was the crackling fire, the siren growing louder, and Mack's faint, agonized groans.

Raising my gun, I bolted upright and swept the room. Mack lay on the floor in a puddle of blood, blinking up at me with a glassy gaze.

"Emma?" I mouthed to him.

"Gone," he rasped in a hoarse whisper, face twisting with guilt.

My heart shattered.

My whole world caved in.

The ground beneath me disintegrated, sending me tumbling back into a blackened, searing hell I'd sworn I'd never revisit.

I'd failed her...failed Emma, just like I had Aubrey.

Biting back a howl of rage, regret, and shame, I forced myself to focus on my fallen teammate. I tucked my gun in the back of my jeans, grabbed a handful of towels from the drawer, and knelt down beside Mack. As I ripped open his shirt to assess his wound, the kitchen melted from my periphery, replaced by the hot, Iraqi desert. My knees no longer pressed against the hardwoods, but sank into the fine Fallujah sand as I poured clotting compound inside the hole in Mack's arm.

"Sorry," he wheezed, yanking me from the flashback.

"Stifle that shit, soldier," I growled, blinking fully into the present.

"It's s-sailor, you...p-prick."

It was the exact response I'd wanted to hear.

"Fuckin' right it is. Now shut the fuck up. I know you were ambushed. There wasn't a damn thing you could do. I'm just glad you're still alive, man."

Though he wouldn't be if Wesley's bullet had been two inches lower, into his heart.

Mack murmured something but I couldn't hear him over the siren coming up the drive.

Steeling myself for what had to be done, I drew in a deep breath. "Okay, brother, you know the drill. I'll do it fast...get it over with quickly. All right?"

He groaned, then nodded and clenched his teeth.

As the sirens abruptly stopped, I rolled Mack onto his side, then quickly brushed his blood-soaked shirt aside. Exhaling with a low grunt, his body trembled. When I spied the exit wound, relief rolled through me.

After placing several towels against the hole in Mack's back, I carefully eased him onto the floor again. He blew out a ragged breath, then held me with an anxious gaze.

"In and out, brother. You're gonna be fine," I said, praying it wasn't a lie.

As expected, jostling him around had the wound bleeding in earnest. I quickly folded several towels before pressing them firmly against his chest. Mack grunted and cursed, then grunted again. If we'd been on a mission, I would have torn into my IFAC (Individual First Aid Kit) and at least stemmed the flow of blood. But we weren't, and Mack needed far more help than I could give him.

Outside, the sound of Kirk Reyes—my dad's old golfing buddy, and the fire Lieutenant—barking out orders filtered through the open door. Lifting Mack's good arm, I placed his hand on the towels.

"Hold down tight on this, brother. I'll be right back."

Wincing, he did as I'd instructed.

Racing out the back door, I yelled and waved my arms as I sprinted toward Kirk. "I need a medic. Mack's inside...he's been shot."

"Shot? What the..." Kirk blanched before anger lined his face. "Simpson, grab your jump kit and get your ass inside the house. We got a gunshot victim in the..." Kirk paused, quickly glancing at me.

"Kitchen," I called out.

"Who the hell would shoot Mack, and why?" he asked bewilderedly.

"Not a clue," I lied.

"This whole fucking world has gone to hell."

And then some.

With a grim nod, I turned, then sprinted back into the kitchen. I knew the Simpson guy wouldn't be far behind. Dropping down alongside Mack again, I kept my voice low. "Listen, man. There's gonna be a lot of people asking you a shit-ton of questions. I need you to cover my six. Tell them you don't know who shot you...don't know what they looked like. Hell, tell them you don't remember a fucking thing. Got it? That's an order, sailor."

"Affirmative," Mack groaned. "Go...get Em...back."

"I will. I'm already working out a plan."

"Wish I could...h-help you k-kill him," he wheezed.

"You'll be with me in spirit, brother. I'll make the cocksucker suffer extra, just for you."

A weak smile tugged Mack's lips as Simpson raced into the room.

I stood and stepped away, giving the medic space to work. I watched him long enough to become confident he knew what he was doing, then strolled down the hall and washed the blood off my hands in the bathroom.

With my focus no longer diverted, helping Mack, flames of rage and agony burned through me. Based on the last actual words that had come from my Bluetooth, I knew the lunatic was taking Emma back to New York. Knew he, and their fucked-up families, were going to force her to marry him.

But I also knew Emma...surprisingly well for the short time we'd been together. She wouldn't go quietly. If she was able, she'd raise hell. She'd kick and scream, and cause a scene. If the prick was smart, which I suspected he was—that or incredibly fucking lucky—he couldn't risk flying her out someplace public, like DFW or Love Field. No, he'd force her onto his private jet—pay off his employees to keep their mouths shut—and fly her to New York.

Taking the stairs two at a time, I raced to my office. After a few illegal keystrokes, I scanned the flight plans registered for the closest private airport. It only took a couple seconds to find the Gulfstream IV, bound for Teterboro, New York.

Hope soaring, I glanced at the clock. Instantly, my heart sank.

The plane was scheduled to take off in fifteen minutes. Even if I drove like a bat out of hell, I'd never get to the airport in time to stop the prick and rescue Emma.

Pounding my fist on my desk, I threw back my head and roared... drowning out the dozens of sirens screaming outside my window. No, I wouldn't be going anywhere until the police were through interrogating me about the shooting. But unlike Mack, I didn't have to lie. I truly hadn't *seen* a fucking thing, and I was drowning in guilt because of it.

Shoving my shame down deep, I shut down my computer.

I needed to check on Mack. As I bounded down the stairs, out of the blue, Dalton's offer charged my brain. *I can get you aboard a private jet in under an hour.*

For the second time since stepping through the demolished back door, hope soared.

"I'll definitely take you up on that, brother, just as soon as I wrap things up here," I murmured to myself..

I rushed into the kitchen and skidded to a halt. My jaw dropped open as Cody Tanner, aka Sir Indigo, strolled through the door behind another male EMT. Gaping at me with the same shocked expression, Cody did a little stutter-step, then quickly banked his surprise.

While running the club before Dalton arrived, I'd grown close to the core members who donated their time to keep the place open. I knew Cody was an EMT, but never expected to see him working my neck of the woods. He lived miles away in the small town of Haven.

As Simpson stood and stepped away, Cody's eyes grew wide, and the blood drained from his face, as he realized he was staring at the man he knew as Master Savage.

"My friend Mack was shot. Upper chest...in and out," I supplied, using his real name.

I didn't want to risk Cody outing himself to his partner by calling Mack, Savage.

Shaking off his shock, Cody hurried past me before dropping to Mack's side as four police officers—three I knew well—stepped through the door.

Simpson had done a fine job, wrapping the wound in thick layers of gauze, but the fact blood was already seeping through worried me. It obviously concerned Cody and his partner, as well. Within minutes, they rolled in a gurney and lifted Mack onto it.

"Anyone else injured" Cody asked, curiously scanning the room.

I knew he was looking for Emma.

"No," I said, nonchalantly dragging a finger over my lips.

With a subtle nod, Cody and his partner rolled Mack toward the door. As he passed me, I reached out and squeezed Mack's hand. "I'll meet you at the hospital as soon as I can."

"No," he whispered tersely. "Take care of what you need to."

As Mack disappeared out the door, the cop I didn't know slid a suspicious sidelong glance my way.

"Damn fool. He's more worried about the fucking cows than he is himself," I scoffed with a shake of my head.

Determined to quash any and all speculation from the start, I invited the officers to take a seat at the kitchen table, then spent the next hour and a half telling them...*nothing*. After what seemed an interminable lifetime, Kyle and his men finished putting out the hot spots where the barn had been and drove away.

Finally alone, I tapped in Dalton's number and gave him a rundown of the morning's epic clusterfuck. When I asked if his offer for the private jet was still on the table, he told me to pack a bag. He assured me Mack would have plenty of visitors and asked me to check in when I could. After profusely thanking him, I hung up and raced upstairs.

The second I stepped inside the bedroom, the scent of Emma's erotic perfume and the rumpled sheets on the bed nearly took me out at the knees.

I should have stayed in bed and woken up beside her.

Staggering to the mattress, I sank onto it and grabbed her pillow.

Jenna Jacob

Pressing it to my face, I breathed in her scent as muffled screams of failure, fear, and heartache tore from my throat.

Two hours later, I was high above the world in a plush Bombardier Challenger 350, dissecting every morsel of Wesley Albert Fairchild's life on my computer.

Chapter Eighteen

Emma
Tuesday, August 1st

Throat parched, and head pounding, I rose from the inky darkness...*again*. With an inward whimper, I tried to roll over, but the biting ropes around my wrists and ankles held me in place. A rush of panic rolled through me as threads of gut-twisting memories, strung together like spider webs, filled my drug-altered mind.

I had no clue what day it was, where I was, or how many times Wesley had shoved a drug-filled needle in my arm, forcing me in and out of consciousness. Fuzzy memories of him hauling me to the bathroom, feeding me soup, and filling my mouth with water stirred in my mind like dust bunnies. But the glorious dreams of Grant, that always kept me company in the inky darkness, were fresh and clear. So was the never-ending raw ache to see, touch, and taste him again.

Please find me, Grant. Please, somehow find me, and get me out of here.

Heart aching, I kept my eyes closed and worked to clear my brain while listening for the sound of Wesley's breathing. I knew he was near. The sickening stench of his designer cologne cloyed my senses and churned my stomach.

"You can stop pretending. I know you're awake. Your breathing has changed," he boasted, as if he actually cared. "Open your eyes, bitch," he barked, slapping my face impatiently.

"Stop," I snarled in a dry, brittle voice, fighting the restraints as I opened my eyes and glared at him. "Don't touch me."

"Oh, come now, Emma," he tsk'd. "I know what kind of club you were in the other night. I'm delighted you like pain, because I enjoy… *giving* it."

He'd been watching me? How long? When had he found me… and how?

His confession and the fact he had me bound to the bed, helpless to escape any kind of insidious pain he enjoyed inflicting, made my heart race. Though grateful he was merely mind-fucking me and not physically assaulting me, I didn't know *why* he was suddenly talking to me. All the other times Wesley had been in the room with me, he'd barely spoken more than two or three words.

While I didn't relish the thought of having a heart-to-heart with the man—mostly because I knew he was a heartless prick—it might keep him from sticking that fucking needle in my arm again.

"W-what do you mean, you *know* what kind of club?"

"God, you're as oblivious as you are stupid," he chided. "I've been following you…watching you for days."

Days? That didn't make sense. Grant and I hadn't left the ranch in over a week.

"H-how did you find me?"

"Did you actually think I wouldn't after you ran out on our fucking *wedding*?" he roared.

I didn't bother responding. Not because his question was rhetorical, but because I was afraid of saying anything for fear of pissing him off more.

Like the flip of a switch, his rage disappeared as fast as it came, and a proud, cocky grin stretched his lips.

"It was a stroke of genius…my genius, to be exact," he unabashedly boasted. "An acquaintance of mine works for a secret alphabet department in DC. I simply gave him your photo, and a fat stack of cash—*because bribery is the only way you can achieve anything*—to upload your image into a special computer. What happened next was *magical*. Here, let me show you."

With an excited giggle—reinforcing how completely unhinged he truly was—Wesley hurried across the room. The blasé, boring, self-involved frat boy I'd known since forever was gone. In his place was a scary, unpredictable madman who'd clearly lost all grip on reality.

While he continued his trek toward a tall dresser near the door, I skimmed a glance over my surroundings. Except for the bed and dresser, there wasn't any other furniture to be found. I didn't recognize the room as any inside Wesley's Central Park South townhouse, but the darkened ensuite at the foot of bed was very familiar. Though my memories were foggy and disjointed, I knew there was a toilet, vanity sink, and possibly a shower—which I desperately needed—beyond the portal.

"I knew you'd be curious, so I kept this within reach," he preened, dragging a piece of paper from the dresser before striding back to the bed.

He gazed at the page as if it were a certificate of achievement, then flipped it over and shoved it in my face.

"So stupidly oblivious," he chortled.

The shock permeating my system deflected Wesley's insult as I gaped at the image of myself, sitting in the stylist chair—admiring my new do—at the salon in Richardson. Based on the angle, whomever had captured it had been sitting beside me. Though it chafed, Wesley was right. I had been stupidly oblivious. I'd never even suspected someone had taken my picture.

Memories flooded my mind.

"Miss Holden, I'm ready for you," the stylist announced.

Grant stood before my butt had left the waiting room chair.

"What are you doing?" I asked.

"Coming with you."

"No. You're going to sit here, thumb through all these girly magazines, then tell me how pretty I look when I come back out."

"You already look pretty," he murmured with a wolfish grin.

"Then you can tell me I look prettier." I smiled, then quickly sobered. *"I don't need a babysitter to get my hair done. Honest."*

"Fine. I'll wait here and tell you anything you want to hear when you're done. But I'm not thumbing through any girly magazines."

The blinding smile he'd flashed me still glowed in my mind.

My heart ached, and crumbled.

I knew he was beating himself black and blue for leaving me at the ranch.

Oh, Grant...it's not your fault. I'm fine. Okay, well...I'm alive. Alive and missing you with all my heart. Please, come find me...please.

Tears burned my eyes, but I quickly lowered my chin to hide them from Wesley.

"After I'd finally convinced our stupid parents to offer every PI on the planet a reward—using *my* email address as the point of contact, of course—*this* little gem appeared in my inbox one morning." He pulled back the paper and smiled. "It's poetic justice, don't you think?"

"Mmm," I softly nodded.

I'd seen mentally disturbed people wandering the streets and subways of New York, but I'd never been up close and personal with one...until now. Common sense, and self-preservation, told me to act as passive and compliant as possible...to do everything in my power to pacify the deranged demon prowling Wesley's mind.

"Of course, I haven't told them I found you, or brought you home. That's *our* little secret."

The malevolent gleam in his eyes made my stomach twist.

Though millions of questions still crowded my mind, he'd answered the one most pressing. I was back in New York, though I had no memory of how I'd gotten here.

"Why haven't you told my parents?"

"Are you questioning my decision?" Wesley yelled, tossing the photo to the floor.

"No, of course not," I replied as contritely as possible. "I was just…curious."

"Be careful. You know what curiosity did to the cat, right?"

It wasn't a question. It was a threat.

Masking the wrecking ball of panic plowing through me, I kept my expression neutral and nodded.

"I didn't tell them, because it's not time, yet," Wesley bit out cryptically.

Dozens more questions I was too afraid to ask spooled through my brain.

As he eased onto the mattress beside me, my pulse rate tripled and every muscle in my body turned to stone.

"I can't play the role of hero and tell them I found you, yet. They'd ask a million questions if I showed up with you on my arm looking like we'd been through a war zone. The scab on my head where that cocksucker's bullet grazed me, and the pretty little gash on yours has to heal before I can carry out the rest of my plan." He grinned.

As Wesley stroked a finger over the throbbing, tender spot where he'd knocked me out, I forced myself not to flinch and stayed statue still.

"Not gonna lie. The sound of my gun when it thudded against your skull and the sight of you blacking out got my dick hard."

His sadistic smile, and the perverse gleam in his eyes, made my stomach churn, and bile burn the back of my throat. But when he slid his finger down my cheek and to my chest before inching closer and closer to my nipple, I nearly threw up.

Clenching my jaw, I lurched as far away from him as the ropes would allow and growled, "Get your fucking hands off me."

Fury crawled across his face as he jerked his hand back and balled up a fist.

As he drew back his arm, time slowed again.

Though I knew I couldn't escape his wrath, I thrashed and tugged against the biting rope before whipping my face away from him and pressing my cheek into the pillow. Then I squeezed my eyes shut and tried to steel myself for the impact.

Jenna Jacob

As his brutal punch connected with my mouth, fireworks exploded behind my eyes. Blades of white-hot agony sliced through my flesh, blood, and bone. My futile fight had been for nothing.

The taste of blood stained my tongue as an inhuman wail of pain tore from my throat.

Tears spilled from my lashes. The blistering sparks of pain were still ricocheting through me when I felt Wesley launch from the bed.

Terrified he was off to find something more vicious than his fist, I ignored the pain still hammering through me, and the blood spilling down my chin and pooling at my neck. Blinking at the tears blurring my vision, I watched him pace back and forth across the room, muttering to himself, and dragging a hand through his hair.

While Wesley conversed with the gremlins in his mind, I gingerly swiped the tip of my tongue over my burning lip. When I discovered a Grand Canyon sized gash in my flesh, I nearly retched. Using my teeth, I scraped the blood off my tongue and let it flow down my chin with a shudder.

Wesley suddenly paused. Nostrils flaring, he held me with a hateful glare before storming to the ensuite. Then, clutching a towel, he returned to the side of the bed.

"Great. This is just great," he bit out. "Look what you made me do. You're bleeding again. Now I have to keep you here longer, you stupid cunt."

What I made you do? I didn't make you do shit, you demented fuck.

The words seared the tip of my tongue, along with the urge to spit a wad of blood in his face.

When he tossed the towel on my chest and pulled a knife from his pocket, raw terror slammed through me. Total insanity had finally swallowed him whole.

This was it.

I was going to die.

Die in this chamber of horrors without ever seeing Grant again. Without ever touching, kissing, laughing, or making love to him again. Without ever telling him...*I love you.* Fighting the sobs burning the

178

back of my throat, I closed my eyes and waited, waited for the glistening blade to stab my heart.

Instead, the rope attached to my left wrist tightened. I opened my eyes, and in disbelief, I watched Wesley slice through it. My arm—numb from lack of blood flow—dropped to the bed like a tree limb while my forearm and hand flung over the side of the mattress, bobbing in mid-air.

"Clean yourself up, you stupid bitch," Wesley barked. Leaning in close to my face, he sneered. "You do anything to fuck up my plans... I'll slit your throat."

His threat ricocheted through me as he turned and stormed out of the room, slamming the door behind him.

I blinked at my free hand, dangling off the bed, as shock and excitement bled the fear from my system. Eyeing the door, I prayed Wesley was mentally too far gone to realize he'd fucked up. When he didn't return after several long seconds, I let the embers of hope sparking inside grow into flames.

Shaking my arm to bring life back to my hand, I rolled to my side and stretched toward my tethered arm. My fingers were still tingling and partially numb, but I managed to untie the rope and free my other hand. After rubbing and squeezing, working life into it as well, I wiped the blood from my face, chin, and chest, then worked to free my ankles.

The rope had rubbed my skin raw, but I didn't care. I was free.

Biting back a howl of delight, I climbed out of bed. My legs wobbled and my feet were numb, but that didn't stop me from shuffling across the carpet to the window and whipping back the drapes.

Confusion charged through my brain.

I was in New York all right, but nowhere near my Central Park South home. My bird's-eye-view of the Hudson River and Statue of Liberty told me I was somewhere in or near Battery. While I had no idea whose penthouse or apartment I was in, the mystery of my location was solved.

Turning from the window, I tore through the room, looking for

Jenna Jacob

anything I could use as a weapon. I never considered myself a violent person, but I couldn't wait to bash Wesley upside his demented head, knock him out, and punch *him* in the mouth.

I was so stupidly excited about the prospect, I feared his crazy had rubbed off on me.

"All the more reason to get as far away from him as possible," I muttered, opening the drawers of the dresser to find them completely empty.

Turning in a slow circle, I studied the room. The walls were bare. There were no paintings or pictures I could bash over his head, and no knickknacks of any kind. Even the curtain rods had been screwed into the walls.

Frustrated but undaunted, I hurried into the bathroom. Again, no pictures. Inside the cabinet beneath the sink were two rolls of toilet paper. Determined to find something to use to my advantage, I pulled open the vanity drawers. But all I found was a flimsy plastic toothbrush, a travel-size container of toothpaste, and a basic black comb. Hope dwindling, I turned my attention to the shower. A couple bottles of hotel-size shampoo and conditioner, along with a bar of soap, sat inside a recessed marble ledge. Draped over the glass shower door was a thick white towel and washcloth. When I noticed the towel bars had been removed, my heart sank.

The lunatic had stripped the entire room. Though Mack had nearly stopped him, Wesley had meticulously planned to find me and bring me here all along.

To do what?

An icy shiver slid down my spine.

The door burst open, and Wesley raced in holding the wicked hypodermic needle in his fingers.

My shiver turned into a full-body tremor.

"I knew you'd try to escape." A sinister smile speared his lips as he prowled toward me like a rabid dog.

"No. I-I just needed to use the restroom," I lied, somehow keeping my voice soft and even. "I assumed you'd left the room so I could untie myself and go pee in private."

180

"That's right. I did. You think I'm stupid enough to leave one hand untied so you could try to run away again?"

And do exactly what you just accused me of? No, you're not stupid. You're fucking INSANE!

"Never. You're the smartest man I know." Unable to look him in the eye for fear he'd see right through me, I glanced at the needle. "Please don't drug me anymore, Wesley. I won't run away."

Two can play your demented mind games, you sick fuck.

"Liar!" he roared. "You ran away the first time…left me standing at the altar with my dick in my hand. You embarrassed me, bitch!"

"I know…and I'm sorry. I'm so sorry," I said, forcing a contrite tone I didn't feel. "I-I was scared…scared you didn't love me."

"I don't…I don't love anybody." He laughed, striding into my personal space. "All I love is *money*. Marrying you…temporarily, of course, is nothing but a necessary part of my plan."

Temporarily?

My gut told me Wesley didn't mean to divorce me…but kill me.

"You actually thought I was in *love* with you?" As fast as the strike of a snake, he gripped his hand around my throat. "You're a stupid bitch. So stupid, you didn't realize I have cameras everywhere in my penthouse. I saw you standing outside my door…listening that day I bribed Congressman Swanson. And you damn well know exactly what I have to do to anyone who found out about it, too."

My heart leapt to my throat.

As panic unfurled inside me, Wesley stabbed the needle in my neck before filling my system with poison.

"After your fucking face heals, you're gonna play an ignorant, simpering wife. If you play your part good enough, I *might* let you live," he snarled before darkness swallowed me whole again.

181

Chapter Nineteen

Grant

When I'd landed in New York, three days ago, Dalton had arranged a rental car and a luxurious hotel suite near Central Park. Either by fate or design, he'd literally set me up in the Bishops' and Fairchilds' backyard.

Though I was beyond ready to escape the mass of humanity, and breathe in some fresh Texas air, I wasn't returning to the ranch without Emma.

I'd spent the first twenty-four hours staking out the building where Wesley lived, as well as the one beside it that his parents owned. I studied the security guards inside the doorways, as well as the occupants coming and going. Of course, Wesley and Emma weren't among them. I hadn't expected to see them. I'd known the prick wouldn't parade her out in I public. He couldn't risk exposing her.

The only way I would have been able to find and rescue Emma was to get inside the building.

After the sun came up on the second day, I'd scouted a couple of thrift stores and searched a few alleyways. Then I'd stopped at a hardware store and picked up a few *supplies* before I'd returned to my hotel suite.

I'd showered and dressed, and donned my new *uniform*, then I'd waited in the shadows of the tall, manicured shrubs beside Wesley's building. A few hours later, two delivery trucks pulled to the curb. When the drivers hurried toward the door, I'd quickly darted in behind them, carrying a box I'd plucked from the alley and re-sealed with tape.

"What have we got today, gentlemen?" the security guard asked.

I let the two men in front of me rattle off the names of the occupants receiving packages.

After the guard waved them through, I stepped up and smiled. "This one's for..." I paused, pretending to read the original address sticker on the box. "Wesley Fairchild."

"I'll take it," the guard announced, extending his hand.

Fuck! Was Wesley's ego so huge he didn't want a lowly delivery driver near his door?

"Sorry, man. No can do. My instructions are he's gotta sign for it."

"I'm afraid that's impossible. Mr. Fairchild is out of town."

Out of town? No. No. If he's not here, that means Emma's not here. Where the fuck is she?

Keeping my expression neutral, I swallowed the ball of panic lodged in my throat, and frowned.

"If you tell me when he's coming back, I'll note it on the ticket."

"I'm sorry. I don't have a clue."

"No problem." I shrugged. "Have a good one."

I'd hurried away, pissed that I'd been forced back to square one, and returned to my suite. Then I'd dialed up Dalton to check on Mack and pick the new club manager's brain.

We'd become close since he'd moved to Dallas. While it wasn't common knowledge, I knew he'd made his fortune in the stock market. I also knew I'd never find Emma in the vast sea of humanity outside my door thinking like a farmer or a former SEAL. Of course, the skills I'd obtained from the latter would be quite useful when I found

Wesley. In order to find the demented prick, I'd had to think like someone filthy rich.

"What else could someone invest in besides the market?" I asked.

"Lots of things," Dalton replied. "Gold, silver, cryptos, commodities, businesses…real estate."

"Real estate. Real estate!" I barked. "That's it. He's got her stashed someplace else…a warehouse or building or something. Thanks, man. I'm gonna dive down that rabbit hole and see what I find. I'll call you later."

After we'd hung up, I'd spent the next fifteen hours slamming coffee and wandering through the labyrinth of multiple LLCs and shell companies Wesley had his fingers in.

Eyes burning and acid churning my stomach, I leaned back in my chair and glanced at the clock. It was three in the morning. My body was stiff and my brain numb from lack of sleep. Though I couldn't afford to waste precious minutes resetting my own clock, I tapped the alarm on my phone for one hour, then closed my eyes and drifted off.

Strolling hand-in-hand with Emma in the field, her long, blonde hair—like the day we'd met—shimmered in the sun and billowed in the breeze.

Her hazel eyes sparkled like diamonds as she paused and peered up at me.

"Help me, Grant," she wailed, crumpling to the ground.

Terror gripped my throat.

When I bent to pick her up, she was gone.

The field suddenly morphed into a dark and eerie dungeon. Emma was still screaming for me to help her, but I couldn't find her. Racing down a narrow hallway, I was lost in a maze of stone walls and flashes of flame randomly shooting from the mortar between them.

Bellowing her name, I bounced off the hot bricks at each dead-end, cursing and roaring while frantically retracing my steps.

Without warning, the walls disappeared and a blinding white light pierced my eyes.

Blinking past the pain searing my retinas, I saw Emma…naked, bound, and writhing on a white marble altar. When she turned her head and looked at me, I could see, taste, and feel the panic and fear exploding inside her.

At the end of the altar, near her feet, Wesley flashed me a maniacal grin, then raised a razor-sharp Damascus sword over his head.

"No!" I roared, sprinting toward them.

I glanced at Emma, but instead of seeing her beautiful, loving face, my eyes locked onto Aubrey's bloody, beaten, lifeless body.

Jerking awake with a heart-pounding jolt, I gasped for air and blinked the nightmare away.

"No. No. I'm not letting her die, too," I growled, scrubbing a hand over my face.

With staunch determination, I studied the document on my computer. When I read the words, *Lease Agreement,* I'd almost closed it out and moved on.

But the hairs prickling the back of my neck made me pause and ponder...

"Why would Wesley lease an apartment when he could just buy the whole building?" I muttered.

I jotted down the address, then scrolled to the end of the document and froze. Wesley had signed the agreement the same day I'd met Emma.

Struggling to tamp down the hope rising inside me, I bolted from my chair and grabbed a quick shower. After dragging on my bogus delivery uniform again, I grabbed the box and hurried out the door. I knew it would be hours before I could attempt to talk my way past another security guard. Since I hadn't eaten much the last few days, I stopped at an all-night diner, and forced myself to choke down some food. Then drove to Wesley's newly acquired apartment and watched the sun rise behind the Statue of Liberty while I scoped out the sleek, modern high-rise.

As the minutes ticked by like hours, my sixth sense—the one Mack had teased me about—hummed with certainty. I knew, beyond a shadow of doubt, Emma was on the sixty-fourth floor of the building... inwardly screaming for me to help her.

"I'm coming, little one. I swear," I murmured.

Fighting the urge to burst into the lobby, press my Glock to the security guard's head, and demand he give me his master key, I gripped the steering wheel tightly. Though I loved the idea of going in guns blazing—if only to calm my raw, scraping nerves—the chances of making it to the elevator before being tackled and detained, or shot dead, were slim to none.

"Stick to the plan, fucker," I grumbled, searching for any sign of a delivery truck.

Forty-five interminable minutes later, a brown cargo van pulled to the curb.

Heart bouncing off my ribs, I grabbed the box and hopped out of the car before following the real delivery driver up the stairs. Like the time before, I painted on a placid smile and waited for the guard to wave the other guy through. Then I stepped up and announced I had a package for the evil cocksucker.

"One moment, please." The guard smiled as he lifted a phone from his belt.

I fucking knew it. The cocksucker is here. Emma better be, too. If she's not, if he's stashed her somewhere else, I'm going to rain down a world of hurt on that prick-assed motherfucker. Make him suffer every unimaginable pain known to man.

Though bloodthirsty vengeance pumped through my veins, I remained calm and cool on the outside.

"He said for you to leave it here and he'll pick it up later," the guard relayed, holding the phone away from his mouth.

"Sorry, man. No can do. My instructions are he's gotta sign for it," I said, repeating the same line I'd used before.

When he apprised Wesley of the condition I could hear the cockbag screaming and cursing through the damn phone. Anger crawled across the guard's face. Clearly, he wasn't a fan of Wesley, either.

I flashed him a sympathetic cringe, then leaned in as close to the mouthpiece as I dared and said in a loud voice, "If he doesn't want to sign for it, I'll just take it back."

The guard grinned and gave me a thumbs up before ending the call. "He'll be right down."

"Works every time." I chuckled, darting a glance at the huge, decorative clock behind him.

Under the pretense of making room for the next guy, I stepped to the side until I had a clear view of the elevators. The weight of my Glock, tucked in the back of my slacks and pressing against my lower spine, made my fingers twitch. I had no clue how long it would take before Wesley stepped out of the elevator. All I knew was I had to distract the guard before the prick made it across the lobby.

Thankfully, it was a big-assed lobby.

Each second ticking by felt like an eternity. Anticipation and anxiety ate a hole through me. I was overanalyzing everything. If I didn't quit and get my shit wired tight, I was liable to fuck up my on-the-fly plan.

This isn't a plan, it's an op...the biggest mission of your life, supplied the voice in my head.

It was. And I needed to prepare for it, exactly as I had every other assignment I'd led my men through.

Dragging in a deep breath, I cleared my mind and mentally donned my combat gear.

Focused on every sound around me, I kept my head on a swivel—tracking the elevator, the guard, and the people outside passing the building.

The soft ding of the elevator gonged through my ears.

Stare glued to the conveyance, I held my breath as the doors opened and exhaled as Wesley stepped out.

Show time.

I glanced at the guard, lost in some paperback, then gasped dramatically and rushed toward him.

"Holy shit, did you see that?"

"See what?" the guard frowned.

"Some dude just snatched some old lady's purse out there," I screeched, pointing toward the sidewalk.

"Oh, hell. Not on my watch," he growled, running toward the door.

"Hurry. Go get him. I think he knocked her down."

As the guard rushed out the doors, I pinned Wesley with a fake smile and quickly ate up the distance between us.

"Sorry about the signature, man...but rules are rules," I said, tucking the box under my arm with my left hand while retrieving my Glock with my right.

"I didn't order anything," he bit out impatiently, tilting his head to read the address label. "Hey, what the fuck's going on here? That's not me, you idiot. You've got the wrong name *and* the wrong address."

"Oh, I got the right name and the right place," I replied with an ugly smile as I shoved the barrel of my gun against his side.

As the blood drained from his face, Wesley glanced down at the gun, then back up at me.

The abject terror in his eyes paled in comparison to the rage thundering inside me.

"Shhh. Don't say a word, or make any sounds," I instructed in a low, even whisper. "Just turn around nice and slow, and I won't blow a hole through your bowels or cause sepsis to dissolve your organs."

"W-what do you—"

When I pressed the barrel harder to his pasty flesh, he snapped his jaw shut. Body trembling, and panic shimmering in his eyes, he slowly turned.

"Good boy," I replied in a patronizing tone and guided him inside a waiting elevator. "We're going back upstairs, to your new apartment, to have a little...*chat*, cockbag."

As the doors closed, I dropped the box. Standing close beside him to conceal the gun from the cameras in the corners, I punched the button for the 64ᵗʰ floor.

Wesley's eyes widened in surprise.

"I did my homework." I smirked. "Be a good boy again and reach into your pocket...nice and slow. Then hand me the key to your apartment."

"W-who are you?" he stammered, but complied.

"I'm your worst fucking nightmare," I growled, plucking the key from his palm.

Like acid, the urgency to get to Emma burned my veins. Clenching my jaw, I shoved all thoughts of her aside. I couldn't afford to let emotions invade my mission. I had a job to do, and an enemy to take care of first.

As the elevator slowed to a stop, I nodded toward the box. "Pick it up...nice and slow, Wesley."

"What's in it?" he asked, doing as he'd been told.

"Toys," I said with an evil grin.

A brutal wave of panic exploded from his body.

"Don't kill me. Please don't kill me," he whined as tears trickled down his cheeks. "I have money. I'm rich...real soon, I'll be a whole lot richer. How much do you want, I'll—"

"I don't want your money," I said, cutting him off as the elevator doors opened.

"Then w-what do you want?"

"For you to shut the fuck up until we're inside your apartment," I hissed, jabbing the gun harder before guiding him into the hallway.

Ratcheting my senses up another notch, I paused when we reached his door. If the prick grew a pair and made a move against me, he'd do it now...before I got him alone.

A split-second later, a flicker of defiance skittered over his face.

I shook my head and tsk'd. "Don't even think about it," I warned, opening the door. "I'll be happy to leave you here, bleeding out on the floor, like you did my friend."

Wesley gasped and blinked at me. As an incredulous expression settled over his face, I shoved him inside the apartment, then closed and locked the door.

"That's what this is about?" he yelled, whipping around to face me before tossing the box to the floor. "You want payback because I shot the prick who was with *my* Emma?"

She's not your Emma, you stupid son of a bitch!

"And a whole lot more," I snarled, gripping him by the throat and lifting him off the floor.

Gasping for breath, Wesley kicked his legs and clawed at my hand.

I raised the gun, and pressed the barrel between his eyes, then arched a brow in warning.

He instantly stopped fighting and closed his eyes.

Like an approaching summer storm, I could feel Emma's energy sizzling in the air.

Not yet. I gotta deal with this cocksucker first.

Using my foot, I dragged a carved wooden chair from beneath a glossy oak table before shoving Wesley onto its seat. As he choked, coughed, and wheezed, I grabbed the box and ripped it open.

Grabbing a bundle of rope and a roll of duct tape, I went to work.

"No. No. Please don't tie me up, I-I'll lose my mind."

"You lost your motherfucking mind a long time ago," I scoffed, yanking his arms behind his back before tying them in rope...all the way to his elbows.

They weren't pretty Shibari knots. In fact, they weren't pretty at all, but the bastard wouldn't escape.

"Stop, you son of a bitch," Wesley snarled. The change in his demeanor was like flipping a light switch. "Untie me right *now*, motherfucker, or I'm gonna add you to my hit list."

Ignoring his ramblings, I tied his ankles, legs, and thighs to the chair's thick, wooden legs.

"I'm going to kill you, right along with my mother, father, the Bishops, and, of course, Emma, after we tie the knot. I'm going to slaughter them...bathe in their blood, then inherit every fucking penny they own."

Over my dead body...which you'll never get the chance to touch.

Wesley let out a demented giggle, then continued—in horrific detail—all the things he was going to do to me, Emma, her family, and his. No doubt, Wesley was beyond insane and would likely have tried to carry out his plan, but I'd heard enough. Peeling off a strip of duct tape, I slapped it over his mouth. Then turned and strode from the kitchen.

"Emma!" I roared, storming into the living room.

Rounding the couch, I spotted a bag of syringes and vials of liquid sitting on the coffee table. Stopping dead in my tracks, I grabbed a few of the vials and read the labels.

Ketamine and Ativan.

I clenched my jaw as a red haze of rage clouded my periphery.

Turning slowly, I pinned Wesley with a death glare and raised the bottles in my hand. "You've been shooting her up with this shit?"

Wesley lifted his chin defiantly and smiled behind the duct tape.

My blood boiled.

"You sick, twisted fuck! I'm going to make you wish you'd never been born," I growled.

Slamming the vials on the table, I charged out of the room.

"Emma! Emma!" I roared, storming down a long hallway.

Pausing, I kicked in the first door I encountered.

It was a bathroom.

The next was an office.

Claws of anger and desperation shredded my soul.

When I kicked in the third door, my heart stopped.

The ground crumbled beneath me.

There she was...pale, naked, and bound to the bed—just like my nightmare.

"Emma. Oh, Emma, baby," I groaned.

Blinking at the tears stinging my eyes, I tucked my gun away and sprinted to the bed.

Repeating her name like a mantra—trying to coax her awake—I stared at the wicked wounds the motherfucker had inflicted...

The angry, red cut—caked in dried blood—on the side of her head.

The jagged gash on her bottom lip, still oozing red.

The streaks of blood staining her chin, neck, and chest...

All ripped my heart in two.

Unable to contain the volcanic rage erupting inside me, I threw back my head and unleashed a thundering roar.

Panting wildly, I eased onto the mattress beside her and gently stroked her hair.

"Come on, baby...wake up. Please, wake up," I begged.

"Grant," Emma whispered.

"I'm here, little one. I'm here...I got you," I croaked, biting back a sob. Yanking a pocketknife from my pants, I began sawing through the scratchy rope binding her to the bed. "Talk to me, little one…keep talking to me."

But Emma didn't respond.

Making every slice count, I quickly freed her wrists and ankles. Then I gently removed the rope binding her red, raw and—in several places—bleeding flesh.

"You fought back, didn't you? Yes, I know you did. I can see how hard you struggled, my love," I praised, vigorously rubbing her limbs, working the blood flow through them.

"Grant," she groaned, lashes fluttering against her pale cheeks.

"I'm here, love. I'm right here. Open your eyes. Open your eyes and look at me, baby girl," I commanded, but she was still too drugged to comply.

I had no clue how much poison the bastard had shoved into her veins. All I knew was I wanted Emma to wake up and open her eyes so I could tell her…*I love you.*

Jolted by the realization, I inwardly chuffed. For the first time in years, the notion of letting someone into my heart…and returning their love, didn't sail me into a terrified panic.

Somehow—in the few short weeks we'd been together—Emma had climbed inside my cold, dead heart and brought it back to life.

The urgency to get her out of this…torture chamber…this prison, out of Wesley's apartment, and back to the ranch rode me hard. Refusing to let her out of my sight again, I gathered the dirty, blood-stained sheet around her, then gently lifted her into my arms.

Clutching her close against my chest, I pressed a soft kiss to her forehead.

Emma's lids fluttered open.

As she blinked—struggling to clear the drug-induced fog, and focus on me—I swallowed the ball of emotion lodged in my throat and sent up a prayer of thanks.

"Morning, sunshine." I smiled. "I've missed the hell out of you."

Chapter Twenty

Emma

Convinced I was merely dreaming again, I blinked to bring the blurred image of Grant into focus. Seeing him in my mind, like this, ripped me apart. Yet it also soothed me...filled me with hope he was somewhere out there searching for me. I savored the warmth and love shimmering in his blue eyes, yet something wasn't right. The way his voice vibrated through me and the familiar heat and scent of his body confused me. Grant had never appeared in my dreams this *real* before.

When he drew me closer to his chest, I could feel his heart beating.

Like watching the glowing orange sunrise slowly peek over the horizon back at the ranch, I realized it wasn't a dream.

Grant really is here...holding me in his arms.

Lifting my hand, I gently cupped his face. As the warmth of his skin slid over my fingers and into my palm, I buried my face in his chest and breathed him in before I burst into tears.

"Shhh, baby. It's all right. He'll never hurt you again. I've got you," Grant murmured, pressing his lips to the top of my head.

"You found me. Y-you really found me," I sobbed, clutching his shirt in my fists.

"Of course, I did, gorgeous. I would never stop looking for you."

"Oh, Grant...I love you," I whimpered, letting all my emotions spill free.

Softly cupping my chin, he gently tilted my head back and stared into my watering eyes.

"I love you, too, Emma," he said in a thick, low voice before skimming a feather-soft kiss over my throbbing lips.

My heart swelled with such pure and unbelievable happiness, it nearly burst from my chest.

"Take me home...back to the ranch, please," I begged.

"Soon, baby. I'm gonna take you home real soon."

As he glanced at what was left of the door, his muscles tensed as he clenched his jaw.

"He's out there, isn't he?"

"Yes. And I need to deal with him before we go."

"Please, don't leave me in here."

"Baby, I'm never letting you out of my sight again," he vowed. After carrying me out of the room, Grant paused in the hallway. A pained expression lined his face. "Things are about to get very... *unpleasant* for Wesley. I don't want you out of my sight, but I don't want you to see my dark side, either."

The night he'd confessed to killing Aubrey's murderer, Grant hadn't shared graphic details with me. He didn't have to. I knew, from his letters and the things his sister had told me, Grant possessed a dangerous dark side, and savage skills for inflicting horrific and unimaginable kinds of torture.

Still...I'd never once been afraid of him.

"I can handle it."

"I don't think you know how truly evil and ugly my dark side is, baby."

"I don't care. I know there's light inside you, too...and it's

blinding. It shines with all the care, compassion, and understanding…
and a million other things inside your big heart that made me fall in
love with you."

"You do understand there's no way Wesley is coming out of this
alive, right?"

"I know, and thank you."

Grant blanched. "You're *thanking* me for what I'm about to do to a
man you've known forever?"

"He's not a man. He's a deranged monster…a dangerous rabid dog.
Someone needs to put him out of his misery…someone like you."
Grant looked at me like I'd lost my mind, too. Maybe I had, but I
couldn't think of any other way to stop Wesley's madness. "I want to
know one thing before he dies."

"What?"

"You have your cell phone, right?"

"Yes."

"Good. If I can get Wesley to give the details about his big *plan*, I'd
like you to record it."

"Oh, he'll tell you what you want to know, or I'll force him to.
Either way, you're gonna get your answers, and I'll record every word.
After the hell he's put you through, he owes you that much."

Grant's decadent body heat warmed me to the bone. But when he
carried me into the living room, the sight of the syringes and drugs on
the table, coupled with Wesley tied to the chair with a strip of duct tape
over his mouth, didn't stop a chill from quaking through me.

Striding to the edge of the open kitchen, Grant gently eased me
onto my feet—a generous and safe distance from Wesley—before
tucking the sheet around my naked body. When he was done, he
reached behind his back and pulled out a gun. Pinning Wesley with a
penetrating stare, Grant dragged a sturdy, thickly padded, wooden chair
from the kitchen table and set it beside me.

As I eased onto the soft surface, Grant strolled back to Wesley
before checking the ropes binding his arms and legs.

"Emma is going to ask you some questions." Grant's voice was low
and commanding, but sounded nothing like the Dominant tone he used

on me. No, this one had a brutal, arctic quality to it. He raised the gun and pointed it at the crazy man still glaring daggers at me. "You're going to answer them, politely and respectfully. Understood?"

Wesley didn't respond, simply slid his angry glare from me to Grant.

A humorless chuckle rolled off Grant's throat as he strolled to the kitchen, returning a few seconds later gripping a large knife. Without a word, he slammed the blade deep into the wood between Wesley's splayed legs.

Wesley's eyes widened and muffled cry of terror leaked behind the duct tape.

"Listen up, shit for brains. You got two seconds to decide if you want to play games, or answer questions," Grant growled.

Whimpering, Wesley frantically nodded toward me.

"Wise choice," Grant drawled before ripping the duct tape off his mouth.

Sucking in a hiss, Wesley narrowed his eyes on me. "What do you want to know, bitch?"

As fast as a flash of lightning, Grant's fist collided with Wesley's mouth.

His head snapped back, and blood spilled down his chin as his screams of pain filled the air.

I don't think you know how truly evil and ugly my dark side is, baby.

Grant was right, I didn't. And though the high-pitched screams bouncing off the walls made my stomach swirl, something dark, and evil, and ugly wended through my veins.

Getting a taste of your own medicine isn't fun, is it?

"I said *politely* and *respectfully*, cockbag," Grant barked, yanking the knife from the chair before slowly oscillating it in Wesley's face. "You insult her again, I'm gonna start cutting off your fingers. Understood?"

"Yes. Ask your question...*Emma*," Wesley snarled, blood dripping from his chin.

Grant stepped behind him and silently placed the knife down, then pulled out his cell phone. After tapping the screen, he nodded to me and placed the device—undetected on the table—behind Wesley's back.

"You said you were only marrying me because it was part of your plan. What exactly is your plan, Wesley?"

"It doesn't matter now. You've ruined it. You, and that asshole," he spat, glancing over his shoulder at Grant.

Inwardly reminding myself I was dealing with a complete nut-job, I tried to use it to my advantage.

"Not necessarily," I lied. "Tell us what it is…maybe we can help."

"Why would you want to help? I'm going to kill you."

His confession turned my blood to ice, but I refused to cave.

"Kill me? What good will that do?"

"Not just you, I'm going to kill them all…you, your parents, *and* mine."

Behind him, Grant shook his head in disgust.

"Why are you going to kill us all?"

I purposely worded my question as if he was still going to carry out his irrational plan. He wasn't, but…

"You can't be that…" Wesley paused and darted a glance back at Grant, then snarled. "For the money! For the power to rule the fucking world!" he roared, before a menacing laugh rolled from his chest.

"You wanna know how I'm gonna do it?" he taunted with an evil grin. Before I could respond, he continued. "Once your face heals up, I'm throwing you a little *welcome home* party. Since we can't risk you running away again, like you did the day of our *wedding*. I'm only inviting our parents. A big crowd might make you freak out, since you're still so mentally *unstable*."

Pot meet kettle.

"As soon as everyone arrives, I'll pop a bottle of champagne, then fill the glasses already laced with liquid ecstasy, and make a toast. Once you lambs have passed out, I'll prepare for your slaughter. First, I'll strip each of you ladies naked, then tie all the guests up, nice and tight. Once the drug wears off…my fun begins. I think I'll start with *your* mother first," he preened with a demonic grin.

As Wesley boasted about forcing everyone to watch the vile, horrific, and perverted things he planned to do—to me, my mother, and even *his own*—I wanted to grab Grant's gun and put a bullet in Wesley's head myself.

Of course, I knew Grant wouldn't let me. The fury blazing in his blue eyes could have set the entire building on fire.

When Wesley finished gloating and grinning while laying out his repulsive scheme—with delight dancing in his eyes—I stared at him in stunned silence for several long seconds.

"You *do* know you're certifiably insane, right?"

His eyes bulged and the smile fell from his face. As Wesley dragged in a deep breath—and held it—every muscle in his body grew taut. The air in the room instantly grew thick with tension while his face grew redder and redder.

Grant gripped his gun tightly, then stepped in front of him—completely blocking me from the maniac's view—before aiming the barrel at Wesley's head.

"Close your eyes, Emma," he instructed in a cold, flat, and deadly voice.

It was the first command I couldn't follow.

Staring at Grant's wide shoulders, I slowly stood. My body trembled, still weak from the drugs, so I gripped the back of the chair and peered around him.

The second I entered Wesley's line of vision, he locked his dull, lifeless eyes on me.

Then, with a demonic roar, he lurched forward.

Terror crashed through me as I watched the legs of the chair lift from the ground. Wesley wobbled, but instead of toppling over, he bore down on his feet and righted himself.

Bent over like a bull, he roared and frantically slammed the frame of the chair—and his body—against the heavy oak table, like a battering ram.

"I'm not crazy. I'm not crazy," Wesley screamed at the top of his lungs. "I don't give a fuck what those doctors or my parents, say...I'm not crazy!"

Before I could even process the ramifications of his shocking words, the crack of wood echoed like a gong as the chair broke apart.

Arms still bound behind his back, Wesley stood upright and shook the splintered wood from his body. Then, like some unearthly entity from a horror movie, he looked at me and flashed a blood-stained smile.

"I'm not crazy," he growled in a demonic voice, then licked his lips.

My heart sputtered and bounced off my ribs as an earthquake of terror shook my whole body.

"No, you're fucking *insane*," Grant scoffed, drawing his focus off me.

Whipping his evil glare to Grant, Wesley tossed his head back and screamed like a demon possessed. He then dropped his chin and pinned Grant with the same chilling, blood-stained smile before charging toward him.

With a feral growl, Grant pulled the trigger.

Slapping a hand over my mouth to hold in the scream clawing my throat, I squeezed my eyes shut——blocking out the carnage splattering the floor and walls—while the reverberation of the gunshot rattled my chest and echoed in my ears.

Blindly sliding back onto the chair, tears of relief and sorrow streamed down my face.

Relief that Wesley's torment was over.

Sadness that Grant had to be the one to put him out of his misery.

Like a lifeline, he wrapped his strong arms around me and silently drew me to his chest. Murmuring reassuringly, he stroked his fingers against my back in tiny circles as I completely fell apart. Long minutes later, Grant scooped me into his arms and carried me into the living room. He eased onto the couch and settled me over his lap.

I dropped my head to his chest, nuzzled my cheek against his heart, and worked to stem my tears.

"I'm sorry, Emma," he whispered. "I'm so sorry you had to see me kill him,"

201

He was beating himself up...still afraid I couldn't handle his darkness.

Silly man.

I lifted my head and cupped his cheek. "Don't apologize. He's not suffering anymore."

"Did you know about him seeing doctors for his...delusions?"

"No. I never had a clue. I'm still trying to wrap my head around the fact his parents knew he was crazy and never said a damn word. Why didn't they..."

"Why didn't they *what*?"

"Say anything," I scoffed. "But I already know the answer..." Easing back, I peered up at him. "You recorded everything, right?"

"Yeah. Why? What's going on in your gorgeous mind, darlin'?"

"I know we have to call the police—"

"And an ambulance. That lip of yours needs stitches. Plus, we need to find out what side effects you might have from the drugs he was knocking you out with."

"I know, but before we do all that, I'd like to call my parents."

Grant arched his brows in surprise. "Why?"

"I need them to see what he did to me, and hear his plan."

"All right," he nodded, pulling out his cell phone. "Under one condition."

"What condition?"

"I'm not leaving you alone with them for a single second."

"I don't want you to." I smiled, then leaned up and pressed a kiss to his cheek with the good side of my lips.

"I love you, Emma," he murmured, tapping the speaker option before setting the phone in my hand.

"I love you, too...*Sir*." I winked.

A low, sexy growl rumbled in his chest as I quickly punched in my father's number before I lost my courage.

"Hello?" he answered cautiously.

"Dad? It's me."

"Emma? Oh, thank fuck," he said in a shaky voice. "W-where are you, honey?"

Tears stung my eyes. He hadn't called me *honey* since I was six.

"I'm h-here...in New Y-york," I said, trying not to fall apart. "I need you c-come..."

Grant gently lifted the phone from my hand and cleared his throat.

"Mr. Bishop, my name's Grant Holden. Emma is fine...or rather, she will be, but there's been an...incident involving Wesley. The police need to be called, but Emma wanted to speak to you...and your wife, first. Can you two come to the Battery?"

"Yes, of course. Give me the address," my father impatiently demanded.

I wiped my cheeks and sucked in a deep breath while Grant rattled off our location.

"Got it. I'm sorry, who are you...how do you know Emma?" my father asked suspiciously.

"I'm Grant Holden," he replied, peering down at me with a sad smile. "Emma and my sister, Aubrey, were roommates at Columbia."

"Isn't that the girl who was killed?"

"Yes."

"My condolences," my father said with genuine sympathy.

In fact, he'd been surprisingly...warm and concerned through the entire conversation. A part of me wondered if our relationship would have been a whole lot smoother if I'd run away years ago.

"Please let Emma know we're on our way."

"Will do." Grant nodded and ended the call before worry lined his face. "Tell me why you were crying when you first started talking to him, little one?"

As I explained how the word *honey* had knocked the wind from my sails, and how his demeanor was so shockingly different, Grant simply stroked my back and listened.

"Maybe things can be different now." He shrugged.

"I'm not getting my hopes up. There's been a whole lot of water under the bridge between me and my parents."

"The thing about water is...when it flows away, new water takes its place." I slowly nodded and pondered his words. "You don't have to decide to make any amends with them today. But we do need to find your clothes."

"I don't know where they are. Hell, I don't even know when Wesley took them off. All I know is I need a shower."

"You can't take one until you've been checked out at the hospital, baby."

"Why not? He didn't rape me or anything."

"That you know of. You were naked and unconscious when I found you. He could have easily—"

"Don't," I said, cutting him off. "I don't even want to think about it. I never woke up feeling...violated."

"Sweetheart, that crazy cocksucker violated you the day he kidnapped you." Grant kissed the top of my head, then cradled me to his chest and stood. "Let's look for your clothes."

Chapter Twenty-One

Grant

Emma's shirt and yoga pants were draped over a chair in Wesley's bedroom...which could only be described as a chamber of horrors. Between the satanic symbols and statues, the altar teeming with voodoo-type offerings and little bowls of blood, I knew the reason for Wesley's dark, demonic soul.

Gaping at the unholy objects on display, Emma paled and darted out of the room. I quickly snatched up her clothes and followed, slamming the door behind me.

When I rounded the corner and stepped into the living room, the sheet was on the floor.

Visibly rattled, Emma muttered under her breath as she tugged on her yoga pants and yanked the blood-stained shirt over her head. My stomach knotted. She looked like she'd been in a wreck.

"Louder, little one. I want to hear what you're saying," I demanded, crossing my arms over my chest.

Slapping her hands on her hips, Emma jerked her head up. The anger lining her face and blazing in her eyes made me want to toss up a fist pump. When I'd found her bound to the bed, I feared Wesley had not only beaten her but also broken her spirit. He hadn't, and I was fucking ecstatic!

That's it, my little hellcat. Get as mad as you want...as mad as you can.

"You want louder?" she snapped. "Fine. I'll give you louder..."

Her sarcastic tone clawed my Dominant soul and made my palm itch. Tamping down the innate longing to drag her over my knee, I let Emma purge her rage.

"I can't believe my *own parents* set me up and arranged marriage between me...*Me*, their only child...their only *daughter*....their own fucking flesh and blood, and t-that devil worshiping lunatic!"

Emma tossed her hands in the air, then started pacing.

"Okay. Yeah, sure...*maybe* my folks didn't know Wesley was crazier than a shit-house rat. God knows, *I* didn't. But *his* parents did. They *knew* he was a dozen clowns short of a circus and didn't say a *word*! Not one fucking word. They played me, just like Wesley did. Played me, and nearly ruined my life, for nothing but...*money*," she yelled, slamming her fists on the arm of the chair.

As a tear slid down her cheek, I knew she'd burned through her rage. Before she could fall into a chasm of shame and tumble into the land of self-pity, I strode across the room and wrapped her in my arms.

"Oh, Grant, I'm such a fool," she moaned, melting against me.

I drew back my hand and swatted her ass. Emma jerked and sucked in a gasp, then glared at me.

"Wipe that look off your face, and don't ever belittle yourself again, sweet slut," I growled, caressing her orbs to ease the sting.

As if I'd waves a magic wand, her expression softened and she exhaled a tiny sigh.

"You may *feel* like a fool, but you have no reason to. You didn't need Wesley's family or yours to tell you a damn thing, little one. You knew in your heart and deep down in your soul marrying Wesley was a mistake. So, you plotted and planned, and escaped. You're a survivor, my love, not a victim."

"You're right." She nodded resolutely.

"I know." I smirked and winked. Emma rolled her eyes and shook her head. "I'm not sure you're aware, but your shirt's covered in blood, little one. If you want, I'll give you mine."

She glanced at her chest and cringed. When she raised her head, and looked at my shirt, she blinked at the logo in confusion. Leaning to the side, she looked down at my slacks.

"Umm, Grant, *why* are you wearing a delivery uniform?"

"I had to get inside the building somehow to save you." I shrugged. "You're not only gorgeous, but you're also brilliant."

"And you're not only sexy and brave, but you also stroke my ego... and *other* parts of me, just right."

A flicker of hunger danced in her eyes. "I want to go home."

"Ditto. As soon as we take care of things here, and get you looked at, I'll get us on a flight out of here. I promise."

A loud buzz sliced through the air, causing us both to jump.

"What the fuck is that?" I bit out, hating being caught off guard.

"It's the doorman. My parents must be here," Emma said, hurrying toward the front door, waving for me to follow. "You'll have to pretend to be Wesley and tell him to send them up."

After granting them permission, I ushered Emma back to the living room and helped her onto the couch. I grabbed the sheet off the floor and draped it over Wesley's body, then waited at the door to meet Emma's parents.

I didn't have to wait long before I heard a sturdy knock. Dragging in a deep breath, I turned the knob and opened the door.

"Mr. Bishop. Mrs. Bishop." I nodded to each of them and welcomed them in before extending my arm, barring them from going any farther.

"Where's Emma?" Rupert Bishop demanded, darting a disapproving glance at my arm.

"She's in the living room, waiting for you, but—"

"Then get out of the way, so we can see our daughter," he demanded.

Though I knew he was simply eager to clap eyes on Emma, it had been a long time since I'd taken orders from anyone. I didn't much like it then, and I hated it even more now. Striving for patience, I nodded.

"I will, but first, I need to try to prepare you for what you're about to walk into here."

As quickly and succinctly as possible, I explained everything… from the tornado to Wesley's dead body lying in the kitchen. As I'd expected, I was met with various degrees of shock, anger, and disbelief. I invited them to check out Wesley's apartment, to see for themselves, but the only thing the Bishops wanted to see was Emma.

"Don't look to your left," I murmured before escorting them toward the living room.

Emma stood—with her bruised flesh and short, dark hair matted and crusted with blood, bottom lip split, swollen and still oozing, wearing her dirty, blood-stained shirt—and confidently raised her chin to greet them.

Roslyn gasped in shock as tears welled in her eyes. Rupert simply groaned in horror and dismay. Agony lined their faces as they rushed to Emma at once and wrapped her in their arms.

I knew by the dumbfounded expression, and how stiffly she patted them both on the back, her parent's flourish of affection was completely foreign to her.

The need to save her clawed deep. Easing in beside the trio, I invited Rupert and Roslyn to sit on the loveseat, then I took Emma's hand, and together, we eased onto the couch.

"Thank you for calling us before alerting the police, Emma," Rupert softly said. "I wish there was a way to keep a lid on this, for all our sakes, but I'm afraid it will soon be out of our hands."

"Let them talk," Roslyn spat. "I don't give a shit anymore. Look at our daughter!"

Emma subtly started and blinked.

"Why didn't you say something?" her mother moaned, barely keeping it together. "Why didn't you tell us you didn't want to marry Wesley?"

Emma suddenly sat up, ramrod straight.

"I did! I told you *both*," she bit out. "You didn't want to hear it.

Neither of you cared what *I* wanted to do…or what would make *me* happy. All you cared about was binding the families to solidify the merger." Neither of them bothered to even try to hide their guilt. "Did either of you know Wesley had been mentally evaluated by doctors? Doctors who diagnosed him as crazy?"

"What?" Rupert gaped.

"No. No. What are you talking about?" Roslyn asked, clearly horrified.

Emma peered up at me and quietly asked, "Would you please play it for them?"

"Are you sure you can handle hearing this again?" I asked, dragging out my cell phone.

"No," she replied honestly. "But they need to hear it, so my father can decide what steps he needs to take to reclaim and protect his empire."

"Reclaim and protect?" Rupert frowned. "What are you talking about, Emma?"

"Just listen," I instructed, tapping my phone, then setting it on the table.

No matter how desperately I wanted to shield Emma from the sounds filling the air, or the horrific memories from flooding her mind, I couldn't. Instead, I wrapped my arm around her and drew her in close to my side, then gently stroked her arm.

Emma closed her eyes and lowered her head when Wesley's detailed description of what he'd planned to do to the women echoed through the room.

Rupert's body shook with rage, and he curled his fingers into tight, white fists.

Roslyn leaned over the arm of the chair and threw up on the floor, then softly sobbed.

But when Wesley began screaming about the doctors, and his parents, and about not being crazy, Rupert launched from his chair. His nostrils flared and his face turned crimson.

"Ted and Lydia knew their son was insane?" he roared, eyes wild with fury.

209

Emma quickly leaned forward and paused the recording.

"Yes. That's why I called you first, so you could contact your lawyer and stop the merger. You also need to subpoena Congressman Swanson. Under duress, he accepted a ten-million-dollar bribe from Wesley to pressure the FCC Advisory Committee to push the merger through."

My heart swelled with even more love and pride. I should have known Emma hadn't called her folks to rub their noses in the fact they'd arranged for her to marry a madman. Even after all they'd done, or rather hadn't done for her, she still wanted to save and protect them.

Rupert gaped at her, then cocked his head. "What kind of *duress*?"

Emma blew out a heavy breath and looked him in the eye. "Wesley threatened to kidnap his daughter, and I quote, use her like he did other little girls."

"No more. Please. It's too much," Roslyn sobbed. "I-I can't..."

"You can go to the other room and sit on the bed the son of bitch kept me tied to the past three days, if you need to, Mother," Emma replied coldly.

I nearly burst with pride.

My sixth sense told me this was the first time Emma had let her parents see her inner warrior.

Roslyn blinked and straightened her shoulders. Then she quickly wiped her tears and shook her head. "No, I'm fine. I'm sorry, Emma. I have no right to... I don't know how you endured and survived that madman, but you did. I'm so damn proud of you."

Physically taken aback, Emma bounced against my arm. Her eyes grew wide, then filled with tears.

"Is there more?" Rupert asked softly.

"Just him slamming himself against the table and breaking the chair I'd tied him to before he lunged at me and I shot him," I replied.

"I'll call the police," Rupert murmured before kneeling down in front of Emma. Tears glistened in his eyes as he pressed a soft kiss to her forehead. "I'm damn proud of you, too, but I'm so sorry...sorry about everything, honey."

As Emma broke down, like I knew she would—both from listening to the recording, and also from her father's long-overdue affection—I lifted her onto my lap and simply held her.

Rupert pulled out his cell phone, then strode toward the hallway. Roslyn stood and stared at the drugs and paraphernalia on the coffee table, then cast a sorrowful stare on Emma.

"What can I do to help her?" she asked, easing onto the couch beside us before softly strumming Emma's back.

"Exactly what you're doing right now," I said with a ghost of a smile, then nuzzled my lips close to Emma's ear and whispered, "It's okay to let the water flow away, my love. I think there's plenty of new water to take its place."

She lifted her head and nodded. "I think so, too. I love you so much."

"I love you, too, little one...love you with all my heart." I smiled, gently cupping her cheeks. Giving zero fucks her mom sat bedside us, I sipped Emma's tears, then pressed a tender kiss to the uninjured corner of her mouth.

Rupert returned, looking shaken and pale. "The police are on their way."

"Are you all right?" Roslyn asked him, still strumming Emma's back.

"No, I need a drink. I was just inside the room that monster kept our daughter prisoner in. Then I went into his room. He was beyond insane, Roz," he said, scrubbing a hand through his thinning gray hair. "He was a demon. I can't believe Ted and Lydia kept this from us and from Emma. It's more than inexcusable. It's unforgivable."

He paced for several minutes as if trying to outrun the images that were no doubt still searing his brain. Finally, Rupert flopped down on the loveseat and cupped his face in his hands.

Pressing a kiss to Emma's head, I savored the warmth of her soft body pressed against mine, as well as the precious moments of calm before the storm.

Four minutes later, the storm hit with a vengeance as dozens of police officers, detectives, firefighters, and a couple of EMTs poured into the apartment.

I let Rupert orchestrate the chaos while I did what I could to shield Emma from the circus. As expected, three detectives immediately began pelting us with questions. Roslyn and Rupert sat on the loveseat, eyeing the drugs on the coffee table. They listened to every word we said, while the flash from the coroner's camera strobed across their faces.

After the detectives finished their interrogation, I forwarded each of them the audio file on my phone before they announced we were free to leave. But before I could sweep Emma out the door, the EMTs moved in to assess her injuries. When she refused to let the medics transport her to the hospital, her parents' true, controlling colors popped out of the box.

"What do you mean you don't want to go? You *have* to go, Emma," Rupert demanded. "You're…you're a mess."

My blood was already boiling over his overbearing demeanor and choice of words when Emma bristled.

"She's not a *mess*," I bit out. "She's been beaten."

"I'm well aware of that," Rupert countered angrily.

"Stop," Emma snapped. "I *am* going to the hospital, but not in a damn ambulance. Grant is taking me."

"Don't be ridiculous. He's *not* a medical professional," Roslyn scoffed in an icy, pretentious tone. "You *are* going to the hospital, in that *damn* ambulance, then you're coming home with us, where you belong."

The rage rolling off Emma melded with mine. Easing her off my lap, I launched from the couch, and glared at her parents. "I need a word with you two…in private."

"Now, listen here. We're grateful you helped Emma, but you need to sit down and mind your own business," Rupert challenged.

"Emma *is* my business," I growled. Striding between the table and the loveseat, I glared down at them. "She's not staying with you or in this city. She's going to Texas…going *home*, with me."

"Over my dead body," Roslyn lashed out. "She's already been kidnapped once. You're not taking her from us again."

Lowering my ass to the edge of the coffee table, I pinned the haughty woman with a piercing stare. "No, I'm not. I'm taking her where *she* wants to go. Unlike both of you, I'll never *force* Emma to do anything. I'm not the enemy here...you two are. Instead of giving her the freedom to spread her wings and fly, you lock her in a gilded cage and keep her trapped."

"How dare you," Rupert growled, face growing redder by the second.

"With all due respect, which you definitely don't deserve, how dare *you*? Do you have any idea what your obsessive need to control and manipulate your daughter is doing to her?" Without giving either of them time to answer, I continued. "No. You don't. So let me clue you in. I'm taking Emma home with me, because she's asked me to. I'm going to put a ring on her finger and drown her in love until the end of time."

Behind me, Emma gasped. "Oh, Grant."

Though it wasn't the romantic proposal I would have planned, I glanced over my shoulder, then flashed her a wink and a smile.

"Are you seriously asking my permission to marry our daughter?" Rupert barked.

The happiness ricocheting through my system turned to anger.

"I'm not asking you shit," I bit out. "I don't need your *permission* for anything, and neither does Emma. She's a grown woman capable of making decisions for herself. I guarantee if you two don't stop forcing her down the life path you've created in your minds, and let her live the life *she* wants, you won't be a part of hers anymore. You won't get an invitation to our wedding. You won't kiss, hold, or even *see* the mess of grandbabies I hope we get busy making soon."

Ignoring the horror on Roslyn's face and the tears welling in her eyes, I glanced over my shoulder again and sent Emma—gaping in proud awe—a tender smile.

"I know your daughter...your only child, would never *choose* to turn her back on you, or banish you from her life. It would break her huge, warm, and loving heart. But if crawling out from beneath your thumbs and breaking the chains you're still trying to bind around her is the only way she can truly be happy, she will. So, yes... I *am* taking

Emma with me so we can grow old together, while I drown her in unconditional love. What you two decide to do…well, that's up to you."

As Rupert and Roslyn gaped at me in stunned silence, I stood and turned, then extended my hand to Emma weeping on the couch. She stared up at me with raw, unadulterated love shimmering in her tear-filled eyes. Then, with a watery smile she slid her slender fingers into my palm.

Easing her onto her feet, I wrapped her in my arms and drew her flush against my chest. I moaned in delight as her soft, lush body melded against me and nuzzled my lips against her ear.

"What do you think about changing your identity one last time to… oh, I don't know…maybe, Emma Holden?" I whispered.

She leaned back—face beaming like the sun—and nodded as a strangled sob-mixed-laugh rolled from her throat. "I think it sounds heavenly. Yes. Yes."

"I do, too. Now, let's get out of here," I murmured, kissing the upturned corner of her mouth.

Tucking Emma close against my side to block her view of Wesley's body, I weaved through the sea of cops and detectives and ushered her out the door.

Chapter Twenty-Two

Emma
Monday, August 21st

W hile the echo of air-hammers, saws, and other heavy sounds echoed from outside—courtesy of the construction crew building the new barn—I sat at the kitchen table, savoring another cup of coffee, thinking about all that had happened in the last few weeks.

After the doctor had checked me out and stitched me up at the hospital in New York, we'd stopped at Grant's posh hotel suite. While he'd ordered room service and packed his suitcase—saving out a clean tee for me to wear—I'd taken a long, hot shower. Two hours later, we'd boarded a luxurious private jet Dalton had graciously arranged and flew home.

When we'd stepped inside the house, I'd dreaded going into the kitchen. I'd been afraid Wesley's ghost would haunt me there forever. As if he'd sensed my reticence, Grant had simply threaded his fingers through mine, and together, we'd stepped into the room. Someone had cleaned up Mack's blood and installed a fancy new back door. When

Jenna Jacob

I'd asked Grant who'd taken care of everything, he'd smiled, and said it had to have been Dalton.

Climbing into bed that night, and snuggling against Grant's big, warm body, had been nothing short of nirvana. When I'd woken the next morning—after ten solid hours of blessed sleep—he'd been right there beside me. I'd realized not only how doggedly determined he'd been to find me but also grasped the depths of his unconditional love for me. Overwhelmed with emotion, I'd climbed on top of his rugged body, and while he held me...whispering loving reassurances—I sobbed like a baby.

Once I'd pulled myself together, he'd carried me to the shower, where he gently washed my hair and every inch of my battered body, then softly patted me dry. He'd dressed me, and fixed me breakfast, then we drove to the hospital to visit Mack.

When Mack and I clapped eyes on one another, we both nearly broke down. After a brief, gentle hug, we spent long minutes trying to ease our guilt and apologizing profusely to each other. Grant called a halt and reminded us Wesley was the one who bore the guilt. Then we sat for hours talking about Mack's surgery and filling him in on everything that had gone down in New York.

A couple of hours after Grant and I had returned to the ranch, I received a massive bouquet of beautiful red roses. Grant stood beside me when I'd pulled out the card and read the words: *We can change. We WILL change, because we love you with all our hearts, Mom and Dad.* I'd turned and melted into his open arms, and broke down sobbing again.

I hadn't cried since...at least, not tears.

I cried out in bliss nearly every night once the doctor—the one Grant insisted I see in Richardson—removed my stitches and told me I could resume my usual routine. Of course, there was nothing *usual* or *routine* about the ecstasy Grant loved dragging from my body. Just thinking of the spine-bending pleasure he'd drowned me in last night ignited a dull throb between my legs.

After I'd received the flowers, I'd called my parents to thank them, which sparked a long and difficult, but emotionally cleansing

216

conversation. After we'd cleared the air and mended most of our bridges, my folks had been keeping me updated on the fallout from the horrific nightmare in New York.

I learned that after Grant and I had left Wesley's apartment, it had turned into an even bigger circus when Ted and Lydia Fairchild arrived. According to my mother, after Ted finally confessed Wesley had some *mental issues*, the cops had to physically pry my father off Ted and restrain him. I also found out the ten million dollars Wesley had given to Congressman Swanson had been wired from an account Ted Fairchild had been hiding. Needless to say, the media mogul was quickly arrested and the merger was off.

The biggest shock for me was learning my parents were in counseling now. Not only were they learning how to love each other again but also learning there was more to life than money.

"Emma! Emma!" Grant bellowed, bursting through the front door.

A surge of panic, fear-charged adrenaline jolted me. Heart lodged in my throat, I launched from the chair and sprinted toward the family room. When I rounded the corner and saw Grant standing by the door, smiling from ear-to-ear, I wanted to slap him for scaring me half to death.

The second he saw the look on my face, guilt and pain replaced his smile.

"Fuck," he barked, eating up the distance between us before wrapping me tightly in his big arms. "I'm sorry, baby girl. I wasn't thinking. You're safe. I've got you, Emma," he murmured while I trembled against him, struggling to sweep the panic from my system.

"Let me help," he murmured, cupping my cheeks and claiming me with a raw, hungry kiss.

As he swept his tongue deep inside my mouth, pouring a deluge of passion and need into my system, my fears evaporated.

I clutched his shoulders and melted against him as he swallowed my kitten-soft whimper. All too soon, he slowly lifted from my mouth, then flashed a wolfish grin. "I'm damn glad your lip has finally healed so I can kiss you proper again."

Jenna Jacob

"I'm damn glad it's finally healed so I can wrap them around your cock and finally suck you proper again," I said with a cheeky smirk.

"I like the way you think," he growled, then grinned excitedly. "Close your eyes. I have a surprise for you."

I lowered my lids and heard him step onto the porch. Anticipation spiked. A few seconds later, I felt and smelled him stride past me, heading toward the family room before he gently cupped my elbow and guided me in the direction of the couch.

"Keep your eyes closed."

"I am."

"You're never gonna believe this," he chuckled, slowing to a stop. "Okay. Open them."

I lifted my lashes and blinked in shock at the suitcases—that had been in the trunk of my rental car—lying, open, side-by-side on the couch.

Gaping at Grant, I babbled, "How? Where? What the hell?"

His whiskey-smooth laugh flowed over me as I stared at the clothes, shoes, handbags, and toiletries I thought were lost forever.

"Where did you find these?" I asked, finally able to string a full sentence together.

"While I was in town to get groceries, I saw a guy who hangs out with the snitch I went to meet the day…"

"Go on," I urged before Grant could drown in a river of guilt.

"I offered him a couple of twenties if he'd tell me where my snitch was at. He told me the paranoid little prick was lying low in an abandoned farmhouse northeast of Denton. He didn't have an address, but he gave me the name of the street. So, I took a drive. I didn't find the farmhouse, but I found your rental car…beat to shit. I knew it was yours when I saw the license plate."

"That's crazy," I murmured, gazing at all my things.

"Anyway, the trunk was still sealed, so I grabbed a crowbar from my truck and popped it open. And like they say…the rest is history."

The pride on his face and excitement in his voice collided with the strange, prickly sensation crawling beneath my skin.

"What's wrong? You don't look one bit happy."

218

"I-I am…I mean, I think I am. I'm not sure," I whispered, dragging my fingertips over the silky, black and gold fabric. It felt as luxurious as I'd remembered, but… "I'm not sure what's wrong. This was my favorite blouse from my Versace collection, but it feels strange…like it belongs to someone else."

Grant grunted and nodded thoughtfully. "Touch the others."

Rummaging through the suitcases, I realized the clothes I'd once coveted didn't ignite even the tiniest spark of joy or happiness I'd felt buying and wearing them back in New York.

Thoughts tangling, I stepped back and scowled.

"Talk to me, little one," Grant instructed in that deep, commanding voice I couldn't refuse.

"I'm sorry, I know you're excited you found them, but…" I cringed. "I-I don't want them anymore."

"Why not?" he asked, arching his brows in surprise. "They're expensive designer things, right?"

"Yeah," I nodded. "All of them. I spent a small fortune on those clothes, shoes, and handbags. It's just…"

As he drilled me with an expectant stare, the corners of his lips twitched. Without a doubt, Grant knew why I didn't want them. He was simply waiting for me to figure it out for myself.

Brows furrowed and lips pursed, I lowered my chin. As I stared at the little pink flowers adorning the sundress I'd picked up from a quaint little clothing store in Richardson, it suddenly dawned on me.

"Go on. I can see it in your eyes…tell me, little one."

"I'm not her anymore," I said, pointing to the suitcases. "Everything in there isn't…me."

A wide, blinding grin lit up Grant's face as he dragged me flush against his chest before suddenly turning serious. "I was afraid this was gonna happen."

"Afraid of *what*?"

"Afraid once I introduced Central Park South Emma to Wally World, you'd never be the same again…and you're not."

Grant struggled to hold back a laugh, but failed miserably.

"Oh, you are so…grrrr," I grinned, swatting his shoulder and trying to wiggle out of his grasp.

"So what?" Grant challenged.

"Evil."

"Evil, huh?" he repeated with a dirty grin.

Without warning, he lifted me off the floor and tossed me over one wide shoulder. I let out a surprised yelp, then giggled and kicked my feet as he carried me up the stairs…playfully swatting my ass. I squeezed and groped his butt cheeks, laughing like a loon as we went.

"I'll show you *evil*, my dirty, little slut," he growled.

His hot breath skipping down my thighs sent a shiver racing up my spine.

As he turned and entered the bedroom, my laughter withered to a whimper.

Since returning from New York, Grant and I had spent many nights sipping wine on the front porch, discussing the lifestyle…and ways it could encompass our daily life.

While Grant's Dominance was hard-wired into him—something he couldn't turn off and on like a light switch—my submission was new. I didn't know yet if it was hard-wired inside me, too. When we talked about a twenty-four-seven Dom/sub relationship, it sounded spectacular…at least, in theory.

After spending my whole life being controlled—albeit in a non-consensual way—the thought of conforming, day in and day out, to someone else's wishes again…even Grant's, left a sour taste on my tongue.

When he explained his job, as my Dom, was to provide for and protect my emotional, physical, and mental well-being…before his own, he promised never to lock me in another gilded cage. Grant wanted to give me the freedom I'd never had growing up, freedom to spread my wings and fly. He wanted me to explore the world and experience the satisfaction of making my own choices. But mostly, he wanted me to grow…to know and love the woman inside me as much as he did.

I was, and discovering so many new things about life and myself was beyond glorious.

But even more glorious was the decision we'd made together. Inside the bedroom and at Club Genesis, Grant was my Dominant and I was his dirty, little slut.

Before he'd even hoisted me off his shoulder, I closed my eyes and let the seed of submission unfold like a lotus blossom within me.

The instant my bare feet sank into the carpet, I dropped my chin and lowered to my knees in front of him. When Grant dragged in a deep, ragged breath, in my mind, I saw his chest expand and his nostrils flare.

Simply hearing him breathe had me wet, throbbing, and aching to please.

"Stand and strip, my sassy, succulent slut."

His hot growl slid over me. Goosebumps peppered my flesh as I quickly rose and yanked the sundress off over my head.

Raking a hungry gaze over my nearly naked flesh, Grant's stare stilled on the scrap of white lace between my legs. He licked his lips, sat down on the edge of the bed and widened his thighs. His cock was already straining inside his jeans as he crooked his finger, silently motioning me closer.

Anticipation spiked.

I could already taste and feel his thick, hard cock dragging over my tongue. Heart racing, and butterflies fluttering wildly in my stomach, I sent him a sensual smile. Purposely putting an extra sway in my hips, I made my way to him and paused between his legs.

"For a little girl who just called me evil, you're awfully brave...and naughty," he murmured, sliding a thick finger beneath the string of my thong. Then he slowly dragged his warm digit up and down the flesh of my hip.

Grant loved it when I got a little sassy—within reason—if only to *put me in my place again.*

I lifted my chin defiantly. And though he hadn't given me permission to touch him, I dragged my fingernails through the prickly, wheat-colored scruff framing his chin.

"I'm not sure about being brave. As for being naughty? Well... maybe I just got tired of waiting for you to show me your so-called *evil*...Sir."

When fire leapt in his eyes, instead of disapproval, I smirked, knowing my sassy reply was *within reason*.

Snapping his teeth together like a wolf, Grant slid his gaze to my thong. "Why are you wearing these, slut? You know you're not allowed to wear panties inside this room."

Ahh, he wants to play the damned if you do, damned if you don't game.

Lowering my chin, I peered up at him with big, sad puppy-dog eyes and pursed my lips. "I wiggled and wiggled over your shoulder as you hauled me up here, Sir, but they didn't come off."

Though Grant's expression remained neutral, I didn't miss the glint of laughter skittering across his eyes.

"Would you like me to take them off, now, Sir?" I asked with feigned innocence.

Flames ignited in his erotic blue pools again.

Grant clenched his jaw, then cinched his finger around the thin band of silk before ripping the thong from my hips.

"No need, little one," he assured with a dirty grin. After tossing my tattered thong over his shoulder, he gripped my hip in one hand, then dragged the pad of his thumb along my saturated slit. "Did I give you permission to get wet for me, sweet slut?"

"No, Sir, but I can't help it. I can't control it." I sank my teeth into my bottom lip, then slowly scraped a stare down his body, stilling at his straining cock. "Just like you can't control...*that*."

"That *what*, girl?"

"That thick, hard cock, all throbbing and weeping, and ready to burst from your jeans, Sir," I purred, licking my lips.

"Yes, my cock is thick, hard, throbbing, and weeping because of *you*."

"I know," I said, flashing him a cocky grin.

With a feral roar, Grant cinched his hands around my waist, and flipped me over his knees.

I yelped and tensed.

I'd crossed the line. I'd gotten too sassy.

"I'm sorry, Sir. I'm sorry," I whimpered, sending him a pleading stare over my shoulder.

"What are you sorry for, slut? For making me hard?" he scoffed. "Every time I look at you, I get so hard all I can think about is fucking you senseless."

My pussy clutched and my nipples tightened as the vision of Grant driving his fat cock in and out of me roared through my brain, colliding with the crippling failure thundering in my veins.

"No, I'm sorry for crossing the line...for being too mouthy. I didn't mean to let it get that far. Please don't punish me...Sir."

Grant cupped my chin and leaned in close. Concern was written all over his face. "You didn't cross the line, baby girl. I love your sassy mouth. I'm not gonna give you a spanking for punishment."

"You're not?" I exhaled in relief. "Then, what are you..."

"Carrying you up here, I enjoyed swatting your sweet cheeks so much, I'm going to give you a pleasure spanking."

I had no idea what a pleasure spanking was, but it sounded a hell of a lot better than a punishment spanking. "So, it's not going to hurt?"

"Oh, it's gonna sting," he promised with an evil grin. "But in a good way."

I wasn't convinced. A *good sting* was an oxymoron in my mind.

"Do you trust me, Emma?"

He only called me by my given name in the bedroom or at the club when he was *checking in*...making sure I was still mentally, emotionally, and physically okay.

"Of course, I do," I softly nodded, peering at him over my shoulder. "You've saved my life...twice."

A tender smile, teeming with love and pride, glowed on his face. He cupped my wrist and drew my hand to his lips before pressing a soft kiss in my palm.

"Then put your hands behind your back, close your eyes and relax, and let me send you to the heavens, baby girl."

Jenna Jacob

I did as he instructed, then held my breath and waited for the first blow.

"I said, relax, little one," Grant softly chuckled.

Gathering both my wrists in his big hand, he lifted slightly, then hauled us both back to the center of the bed. I was still draped over his thighs, but my chest, shoulders, head, and legs were now supported by the mattress. It was way more comfortable than dangling toward the floor like a rag doll.

Still holding my wrists in place, Grant caressed my ass with his palm...gliding it over my skin in slow, gentle circles.

"So soft. So supple. So warm," he murmured. "So silky smooth and white...for now."

He lifted his hand, then, using his fingers and thumb, he massaged my backside. Repeating the same slow, circular motion, he pressed his digits deeper and deeper into my muscles until I was boneless and moaning in bliss.

"I can smell your sweet cunt, little one. You're making my mouth water. I know how wet and juicy it is for me. For my tongue. For my... fingers," he taunted before lifting his hand from my ass and driving two fingers deep inside my core.

Like a new log tossed onto a crackling bonfire, sparks sailed through my system in all directions. Crying out in pleasure, I lifted my hips off his lap and rocked against his busy hand. As quickly as he'd impaled me, Grant yanked his digits from my pussy.

As a disgruntled moan rolled off my lips, he landed a sharp spank across the entire lower, fleshy part of my butt cheeks.

"Ahh," I shouted in surprise as a heated sting melted into my skin.

"I didn't give you permission to fuck my fingers, little one," Grant chided, delivering a harder slap over the first.

While fiery waves rolled up my spine and down my thighs, I sucked in a hiss. My pussy clutched and my clit throbbed as I struggled to process the strange burn rippling through me. Yes, it stung, like he said it would, but the blistering pain I'd expected and anticipated wasn't searing me...at least, not yet.

His hard cock, pressing into my stomach, grew impossibly bigger.

224

The ache between my legs sharpened, and I could feel my slippery, hot juices spilling from my core.

Without warning, Grant landed a series of hard, harsh slaps to my ass, setting my flesh on fire. Pain ignited up my back and down my legs. I gulped in a shock of air, but before I could release the scream gathering in the back of my throat, his masterful fingers were deep inside me again, while his wide thumb strummed my clit.

Pain and pleasure collided before coiling together in a mind-bending whirlpool of pulsating bliss I'd never felt before.

"More. Please…more," I begged as the embers of orgasm flickered to flame, dulling the blades of pain.

"Oh, fuck, yes," Grant hissed, dragging his hand from my pussy before drawing it over my ass in another series of stinging smacks.

Over and over, he set fire to my flesh, then stirred the flames of ecstasy until I could no longer distinguish one from the other.

"That's it, you naughty, little girl. Suck my fingers with your slick cunt," Grant taunted, teasing my clit with his thumb and scraping my G-spot with his fingers.

"You want my cock buried balls deep inside you, don't you, my dirty, little slut?"

"Yes," I shrieked, bucking against his hand.

"Not yet," he growled, firing up my ass again.

Wailing and writhing, the vortex of pain pressed in all around me.

"Look at you, riding those waves crashing through you," Grant murmured, driving his fingers into my quivering pussy again and burnishing my screaming clit. "You're fucking stunning…fucking perfect, baby girl."

As the fangs of pain receded, the claws of orgasm tore me to ribbons. Keening and panting, I ground my pussy against his hand. Chasing the ecstasy I desperately craved, I mindlessly begged and pleaded for more.

"You're so fucking beautiful. You're hanging on by a thread, aren't you, sweet slut?" Grant murmured.

"Y-yes," I panted. "H-help me."

With a feral roar, he released my wrists, pulled from my pussy, and flipped me onto my back. Before I could process what was happening, he gripped my thighs, spread them wide, and hovered over me.

"Let go, baby girl. Let me pull you under," he growled, claiming my lips with a raw, urgent kiss.

Wedging his fat crest against my throbbing pussy, Grant thrust his glorious cock deep inside me. Stretching and filling my narrow tunnel, he swallowed my screams.

Releasing my lips, he drove in and out of my body, grinding my throbbing ass cheeks against the comforter. Lust and love etched his face while filthy words spilled from his tongue, driving me higher and higher. And when Grant wedged a hand between us and strummed my clit, my limbs grew numb.

As the whirlpool of pleasure and pain pulled me under, I clutched Grant's shoulders and shattered into a million sparks of ecstasy, screaming his name.

Pussy clutching, and body quaking, I was still screaming and coming when Grant roared and exploded inside me.

Long, panting, moaning, and quivering minutes later, I was still dazed and confused by the stupendous annihilating orgasm echoing through me. Grant dropped to his elbows and kissed my lips, before he raised his head and grinned.

"Looks like spankings have moved from your yellow column to the green one now?"

"Super green." I laughed.

He chuckled and nodded, then sobered. "I guess we'll need to move bondage to the red column for a while."

"Why?"

"Why?" he repeated, cupping my hand and tracing his fingertip over the light scar on my wrist.

"Not necessarily." I frowned.

"Still, I want to wait before we try any form of bondage. I don't want to have my fingers and tongue inside your juicy little cunt and you to have a flashback and freak out because I tied you up too soon."

I grinned and shook my head. "If you honestly think I'd freak out with your thick fingers and talented tongue in my *juicy little cunt,* you'd better think again…Sir."

"Good save, slut." Grant chuckled. Sliding his arm around my waist, he rolled to his side, taking me with him. He lifted my hand and stared at it for several seconds.

"What are you doing?"

"Deciding what size diamond needs to be on your pretty finger." My heart swelled and sputtered. "I was thinking a big four or five carat one. But since I've turned you from designer Emma to Wally World Emma, I'm thinking a one and a half carat is more your style."

I laughed and shook my head. "I don't need a diamond. Hell, I don't even need a ring. All I need is you, cowboy, err…Sir."

Grant hugged me tightly and brushed a feathery kiss across my lips. "You've already got me, baby girl. I'm yours…forever."

Epilogue

Grant
Saturday, September 9th

"The fridge and cabinets are stocked with food," I said, walking Mack through his new home situated between the rebuilt barn and main house. "If you don't like anything…the furniture, bedding, dishes, or the paintings and knickknacks Emma picked out—Lord, that woman loves to shop—we can exchange them for whatever you want."

"I don't mean to sound ungrateful, but why the hell did you build me a *house*?" Mack asked, gazing around the open living room and kitchen, totally shellshocked. "I would have been fine living in another bunk inside the barn."

"*You* might have been fine with it, but not me. And I didn't build it, it's a modular."

"I don't care what it is. It's fucking beautiful. You shouldn't have done all this, brother."

"Yeah, I should have. Ever since you came to visit…*and never left*," I chided with a grin, dragging a chuckle out of Mack. "And refused to take one of the guest rooms, I've wanted to get you out of that damn barn and into a place of your own."

"I don't know what to say...thank you, man." His voice was thick with emotion.

"You don't have to say anything, brother," I assured as we stepped out the front door and onto the long, wooden porch. "I'm just thankful you're still alive, and finally out of rehab."

"Aw, fuck. Me, too," he groaned. "I don't ever wanna go back to that place again."

"Hopefully, you'll never have to." I exhaled a deep breath and shook my head. "I'm sorry, I wasn't here when shit went down."

"I'm sorry I failed you."

"You didn't. You never have, and you never will."

Mack grimly nodded. "Hey, did you two get things straightened out at your bank?"

"Yeah." I nodded, remembering how nervous Emma had been yesterday as she handed the stack of fraudulent cashier's checks to a suit-clad federal agent from Dallas...who'd arranged to meet us at *my* bank this time.

After telling her father what she'd done with her inheritance, Rupert made some calls. A few days later, an FBI agent contacted her about the checks—still made out in my sister's name. Claiming his daughter had been under the same duress as Congressman Swanson, Rupert convinced the Feds not to press any charges against Emma, and to help her deposit the monies into an account under her own name.

"It's frightening how people with a ton of money magically make things happen."

"Lucky for both of you, her daddy's got a shit-ton." Mack chuckled.

"Amen, brother." I nodded.

The sound of crunching gravel had us both snapping our heads toward the driveway. As a shiny, silver Porsche 911 headed toward us. Thinking Dalton had splurged on a new sports car, I softly chuckled. But when I saw a woman with long black hair behind the wheel, I shook my head.

"Looks like somebody's lost." I glanced back at Mack, and did a doubletake.

His eyes were shining, his face glowing, and a crooked grin kicked up a corner of his mouth. Like a kid with a new puppy, his excitement and happiness were palpable.

"No, she's not," he said, stepping off the front porch and striding toward the sports car.

Gaping at him in shock, my curiosity spiked like a fever, and I followed him. "She who?"

"My angel," Mack replied like a love-sick schoolboy.

"Your *what*?"

"Oh, I ahh, I-I mean," he stammered, as if realizing he'd said his thoughts out loud. "That's Harper Wells. *Doctor* Harper Wells. She's... she's the surgeon who got me all fixed up."

"Looks like she's got you *all fixed up* in other ways as well." I chuckled.

"I sure fucking hope so," he murmured, eating up the distance between them as the doctor stepped from her car.

As her black hair whipped in the wind, the tall, pretty, willowy woman with bright green eyes flashed Mack a blinding smile.

"A little bird told me you were getting out of rehab today," she said coyly. "So, I thought I'd stop by to make sure you weren't over-doing it, or getting into any more trouble."

"I haven't been home long enough to over-do it or get into trouble," he assured before flashing a cocky smile. "But the day's still young."

You sly bastard. You've been holding out on me.

As Mack introduced us, I made a mental note to interrogate his balls off once the doctor left.

Using the excuse of needing to check on Emma—who, once I spilled the news about Mack's pretty new *friend*, would interrogate him ten times worse than me—I made my way back to my house, while Mack invited Harper to join him inside his.

After searching for Emma on the main floor, to no avail I bounded up the stairs.

231

Jenna Jacob

She was sitting in my office, staring at the photo of Aubrey and me...the last one ever taken before my sister died. Easing in beside my girl, I peered at the picture, too. As the familiar fingers of pain and regret squeezed my heart, I stroked my hand down Emma's arm.

"Whatcha doing, baby?" I whispered.

"Wishing I'd been able to tell Aubrey goodbye."

"You weren't at the funeral?"

I'd been so focused on hunting down the fucker who'd killed her; I barely remembered Aubrey's funeral. I knew the church had been packed, overflowing even. The only person...the only face I remembered seeing that day was my mom's. Her haunted expression, pale skin, and the unmitigated pain shimmering in her red, swollen, and tear-filled eyes was forever branded in my brain.

"No." Emma sniffed and swiped a tear from her cheek. "Before the news about Aubrey hit the airwaves or internet, my father called and asked if I knew her. When I'd stopped crying long enough to tell him she was my roommate, he sent the *police* to my dorm room. They wouldn't even let me pack my things, they just escorted me to their squad car and drove me back home."

Though I knew her mother and father were making a genuine effort to be the parents she'd always needed them to be, it didn't stop me from wanting to knock them both on their asses for everything they'd stolen from Emma.

"They wouldn't let me fly here to attend Aubrey's funeral. Hell, they wouldn't even let me go back to my dorm. I had to finish my courses and get my degree online."

Without a word, I gathered Emma into my arms and cradled her to my chest before easing into the chair. Tracing my finger over Aubrey's smiling face in the photo, I pressed a kiss to Emma's forehead.

"I know it's not the same, but if you'd like, I'll take you to the cemetery so you can tell Aubrey goodbye."

"Oh, Grant," she moaned and nodded. As another tear slid down her face, Emma threw her arms around my neck and hugged me tightly.

After she dried her eyes and slipped on her sandals, we strolled out the front door.

"Whose car is *that*?" Emma asked, eyes wide and pointing to the Porsche.

"Oh, hell, I almost forgot." I grinned, helping her into the truck. "I'll fill you in on the way."

After telling her about Mack's new doctor *friend*, Emma pelted me with questions—most I couldn't answer yet—from the ranch, to the florist shop, and all the way to the cemetery. When I pulled to a stop and parked near a massive shady oak, her excitement over Mack possibly finding love evaporated.

Clutching the flowers, Emma solemnly accepted my hand as I helped her from the truck. I slung my arm around her waist, and we silently walked to the row of headstones beneath the tree. After lifting two of the three bouquets of flowers from her hand, I left Emma standing at Aubrey's grave, staring at her headstone.

I placed a bundle of flowers on my mom and dad's headstones, then sat on the grass between them and did what I always did...talked to them.

"Her name is Emma. She was Aubrey's roommate back in Columbia. Yeah," I nodded. Feeling Emma's eyes on me, I kept right on going. "The rich one Aubrey always talked about. We're getting married next spring. No, I haven't gotten the ring yet, Dad...it's on my to-do list." I chuckled, knowing that would have been the first question out of his mouth. "And, no, Mom, I haven't knocked her up...yet."

Emma gasped. I turned and flashed her a grin as her cheeks grew pink.

"What?" I asked, trying not to laugh. "A lot's happened since I last came to visit them. I need to fill them in."

Emma chuckled and shook her head. When she plopped down to the grass beside Aubrey's grave and began talking to my sister, tears stung my eyes.

"I know you know I've met your brother. I'm pretty sure *you* had something to do with him rescuing me from that damn tornado. A tornado? Really, Bree...you couldn't have made it a hailstorm or a blizzard? You had to go all out and drop down a damn twister?" Emma chuckled, then somberly reached out and traced her fingers over the letters of Aubrey's name on the headstone. "Thank you, Bree. Thank you for sending him to me, or me to him, or however you made it happen. I've never been this happy in my whole life. Well...except that time you verbally emasculated Martin Monroe for shoving me against the wall and sticking his tongue down my throat at that stupid frat party." Emma giggled.

Watching her from the corner of my eye, I brushed the fallen leaves and grass clipping from my parent's headstones and smiled.

"I miss you so much, boo. You were the best friend I ever had."

A sob tore from Emma's throat. Instead of rushing to her side, to hold and comfort her, I remained sitting on the grass, and gave her the freedom to purge her grief.

"If I'd known the night you left our room was gonna be the last time I ever saw you, I would have gone to the library with you, or blocked the door, so you'd still b-be...h-ere now," Emma wailed, then curled in on herself and sobbed her heart out.

Though it ripped me to shreds, I let her cry until her tears ran dry. Then I helped her place the flowers on Aubrey's headstone before I scooped Emma into my arms and carried her back to the truck. She didn't say a word all the way home, simply held my hand and rested her head on my shoulder.

She was tapped out...emotionally, physically, and mentally depleted. But I knew how to fill her up again.

When we arrived at the ranch, the Porsche was still sitting by the barn.

We exchanged a knowing glance before I parked by the front porch and killed the engine.

Instead of offering her my hand, I lifted Emma from the seat and cradled her against my chest. Then I carried her into the house and straight upstairs to our bedroom. I pressed a soft kiss to her lips and eased her onto her feet.

"You've been through a hell of a lot these past few weeks, little one," I murmured, slowly lifting her shirt over her head. "I know you're drained and still trying to process everything you've been through."

"It's been a lot," she softly agreed, as I slowly eased her shorts off.

"It *has* been. It's been too much." Reaching behind her, I unfastened her bra and caressed my hand over her back. "That's why I'm gonna spend the rest of the day, and all night, pampering you. I'm going to fill the soaker tub you love so much with that sweet-smelling bath oil and gently bathe every inch of your soft skin. Then I'm going to wash your hair and massage your scalp before I pat your boneless body dry. I'm gonna dress you in your favorite pajamas, carry you to the couch, and turn on a chick flick for you to watch while I make dinner. Then I'm gonna—"

"Wait. I thought I was the one who's supposed to pamper you, *Sir*." She smiled softly.

"There's no Sir in here tonight, baby girl. It's just me, the man who loves you and is going to pamper you like you've never been pampered before. And you, the love of my life, who'll let me."

Emma's chin began to quiver, and unshed tears glistened in her eyes.

"What's wrong, little one?"

"Nothing's wrong," she whispered, cupping my cheek. "Everything's right...too right."

"Too right? How can it be too right, darlin'?" I asked, brushing a feather-soft kiss over her lips.

"Because every day I fall more in love with you."

"Aww, little one. I know the feeling," I murmured, cupping her cheeks. "I fall in love with you more each day, too."

Emma tossed her arms around my neck, and simply stared up at me.

As light and love flickered in her eyes again, I leaned down and hovered over her ripe mouth. Breathing in her warm, wet breath, I caressed her soft cheek. "Forever, Emma. Me and you forever."

"And a day," she whispered, melding her lips to mine.

~

235

T*hank you* for reading ***Forbidden Obsession***. I hope you enjoyed the combustible connection between Grant and Emma. If you did, I'd love for you to leave a review and recommend this book to *all* your friends.

And if you'd like to be the first to hear about my upcoming releases and read exclusive excerpts, please sign up for my **newsletter**. Oh, and if you want to let your hair down, get a little rowdy, and grab some freebies, join my private Facebook group **Jenna Jacob's Jezebels**. I'd love to see you there!

I can't wait for you to see what's happening next at Club Genesis.

FORBIDDEN INDULGENCE

Mack Boone, the rugged former sniper turned cattle rancher has nothing in common with Dr. Harper Wells, the gorgeous skilled surgeon who saved his life…or does he?

FORBIDDEN INDULGENCE
Club Genesis – Dallas, Book 2
Premiering October 3, 2024

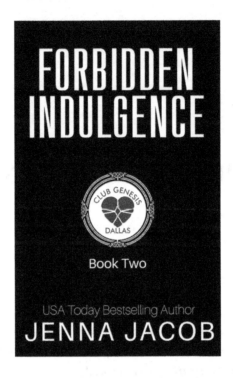

Check out the FREE series starter from Club Genesis-Chicago... where it all began.

A powerful, reluctant, Dom and a desperate, lost submissive collide with a forbidden, yet destined passion that burns up the pages.

AWAKEN ME

Club Genesis – Chicago, Book 1
FREE

He was more than a ghost haunting my dreams...he was real.

By day, I'm **Julianna Garrett**...a prim, proper accountant. By night, I'm tormented by dreams of an alpha, amber-eyed Adonis who makes me ache with forbidden desires. After swimming in a dating pool of lacking losers, I discover Club Genesis, a private oasis that caters to my unconventional cravings. But even immersing myself in this sensual, secretive world, I still can't find what I'm looking for.

Until I see…

Mika LaBrache, Club Genesis owner, loner, enigma. I know instantly my soul has found its one true desire, and a blistering night of passion proves that beyond any doubt. But Mika is no stranger to tragedy. The dark secrets ruling his world soon tear us apart. When danger creeps into the club and threatens me, he's my savior…but will Mika's emotional scars drive him to reject me, or will he open his heart to claim and…*Awaken Me?*

CLUB GENESIS - CHICAGO
Awaken Me
Consume Me
Seize Me
Arouse Me
Ignite Me
Entice Me
Expose Me
Bare Me
Unravel Me
Command Me
Tame Me
Tempt Me

ABOUT THE AUTHOR

USA Today Bestselling author **Jenna Jacob** paints a canvas of passion, romance, and humor as her alpha men and the feisty women who love them unravel their souls, heal their scars, and find a happy-ever-after kind of love. Heart-tugging, captivating, and steamy, her words will leave you breathless and craving more.

A mom of four grown children, Jenna, her husband Sean, and their furry babies reside in Kansas. Though she spent over thirty years in accounting, Jenna isn't your typical bean counter. She's brassy, sassy, and loves to laugh, but is humbly thrilled to be living her dream as a full-time author. When she's not slamming coffee while pounding out emotional stories, you can find her reading, listening to music, cooking, camping, or enjoying the open road on the back of a Harley.

CONNECT WITH JENNA
Website - E-Mail - Newsletter
Jezebels Facebook Party Page

ALSO BY JENNA JACOB

COWBOYS OF HAVEN

The Cowboy's Second Chance At Love

The Cowboy's Thirty-Day Fling

The Cowboy's Cougar

The Cowboy's Surprise Vegas Baby

BRIDES OF HAVEN

The Cowboy's Baby Bargain

The Cowboy's Virgin Baby Momma - Includes Baby Bargain

The Cowboy's Million Dollar Baby Bride

The Cowboy's Virgin Buckle Bunny

The Cowboy's Big Sexy Wedding

THE UNBROKEN SERIES - RAINE FALLING

The Broken

The Betrayal

The Break

The Brink

The Bond

THE UNBROKEN SERIES - HEAVENLY RISING

The Choice

The Chase

The Confession

The Commitment

STAND ALONES

Small Town Second Chance

Innocent Uncaged

Made in United States
North Haven, CT
04 December 2023

45069132R00143